The Virtual Debra wore black lace panties, just a flimsy triangle concealing the dark fur within. With knowing eyes on Jack, she unclasped her bra to reveal small pointy breasts with large red nipples that he wanted to take in his mouth at once.

'I've been a bad girl, remember?' she said, bending over the arm of a chair. 'Come on, Jack, punish me the way I deserve.'

Debra's naked buttocks, framed by a black throng around her hips and down her crack, were irresistible. His palm itched to make contact with all that plump smoothness.

'What are you waiting for?' she cried impatiently and Jack realised that whatever the real Debra might want, the Virtual Debra was dying for it ...

Touch Me, Feel Me

Rosanna Challis

HEADLINE
DELTA

First published in 1995
by HEADLINE BOOK PUBLISHING

A HEADLINE DELTA paperback

10 9 8 7 6 5 4 3 2 1

ISBN 0–7472–4802 8

Printed and bound in Great Britain by
Cox & Wyman Ltd, Reading, Berks

HEADLINE BOOK PUBLISHING
A division of Hodder Headline PLC
338 Euston Road
London NW1 3BH

Touch Me, Feel Me

Chapter One

Jack Bedford was sitting in a singles bar, being chatted up by the delectable Dorabella. She was leaning close to him, close enough for him to see right down the neck of her dress where her deep cleavage was exuding an odour of Passion. Her full red lips were smiling up at him. They were made for something far more exciting than conversation. But for the moment he had to be content with her small talk.

'It's a long time since I've seen anyone as good-looking as you in here.' She crossed her legs slowly, so the shiny silk of her stocking made a sleek rustling noise. 'I can tell you're my kind of guy. Where shall we go – your place or mine?'

Jack deliberated. His place was a bachelor penthouse apartment, hi-tech but comfortable. Her place would be either a French-style boudoir, all frilled drapes and satin cushions, or a rustic log cabin with a sheepskin rug in front of a roaring log fire, or a luxury hotel room with king-size bed, en suite bathroom with jacuzzi and champagne on tap. On the whole, he preferred the idea of screwing Dorabella on her home ground.

He could feel his cock becoming upwardly mobile as he followed her swaying butt out of the bar and into the sleek limousine. Once he was settled in his seat Dorabella bent over and kissed him, a foretaste of things to come. Her mouth tasted of peaches. As she drove the dream machine, very fast, through the almost deserted streets her tight skirt rode up giving him a glimpse of her stocking-top. The charcoal-grey welt was secured with a suspender on a ribbon of black lace and, when she really got going and shifted her arse into gear, he could just see the matching lace of her panties. His shaft tingled its way to half-mast.

'Nearly there, lover boy,' she told him, with a wink, as they entered the forecourt of the Lovenest Hotel. They went up to her top-floor suite, where the panoramic window could give the illusion – should he desire it – of making love under the stars.

'Champagne?' Dorabella asked, already taking a bottle from a minibar. She flicked off the wire cage with practised fingers and the foam spurted out, spewing down her cleavage and soaking the red satin of her dress so that her nipples stood out like decorative buttons.

'Oops!' she giggled, pouring the froth into two glasses. She handed one to Jack and he took a sip. The dry, grapey taste was there all right, but he couldn't quite feel the tingles on his palate.

'Think I'd better get out of this wet dress,' Dorabella purred, presenting her back to him. 'Would you help me, please?'

While Jack's fingers inched the zip down she smiled at him over her creamy-smooth shoulder, inducing a new urgency in his groin. He passed his palms over the naked flesh of her back. Hm, not bad! Her skin felt a lot softer and warmer than before, giving an impression of cushioned plumpness although there was no visible fat anywhere on her streamlined body.

Dorabella side-stepped out of the dress and stood there in black lace bra and panties, her bulging nipples and curly muff playing peek-a-boo behind the flocked netting of her underwear. Tiny bubble-beads were still clinging to the steep slopes of her breasts and trickling down her midriff to collect in a pool at her navel. Jack began salivating.

'I'm soaked right through,' she announced, giving him a coquettish look. 'And it seems a shame to waste all this lovely champagne on a towel!'

Dorabella was lifting her boobs towards him now, offering them to his eager tongue. He bent his head as she came close enough for him to drink in her scent. 'That's it, lover,' she murmured. 'Give them a good tonguing!'

Jack took a couple of experimental licks. The subtle blend of champagne, exotic perfume and female sweat delighted him. If they could bottle that they'd make a fortune! He must speak to Alistair about it later.

As he lapped his way round the nursery slopes of her generous tits, Dorabella reached behind her back and released them from the confines of her bra. Instinctively, Jack opened his palms to receive them. They weighed

3

good and heavy, like a couple of ripe cantaloupes.

Dorabella was moaning gently as he rubbed her turgid nipples with his thumbs, squeezing the surrounding mounds until the chasm between them was more than ample depth for his prick. Was that what he wanted, a tit-wank? Maybe. He mentally reviewed the menu on offer. Perhaps a blow-job? No, he needed to get into pussy-power again, to remind himself of the delights of a plunging into a juicyfruit quim. He had an urge to do without the preliminaries this time, to strike while his iron was hot.

'Wow! You've got me creaming myself already, naughty boy!' Dorabella murmured, as his fingers grappled with her suspenders. They opened with a satisfactory ping. Jack slid his hands over her thighs, feeling the slight ridge where her silk stocking ended and her silken skin began. 'Ooh! I can't wait to feel you inside me!' she gasped, as he pulled down the scrap of black lace to reveal her mons. Her pubic hair, framed by the dangling straps of her suspenders, was trimmed to a neat heart-shape.

Jack was ready to go now, his dick straining for release. Dorabella danced tantalisingly away from him and reached the satin plateau of the bed where she lay, in classic split-beaver pose with her panties around her knees, awaiting his pleasure. For a few moments Jack savoured the sight of her elegantly sprawled body, her thighs spread as far as the constraining lace would allow. The pink folds of her vulva were well displayed beneath the point of her pubic heart: soft and shining, slick with love-dew. He could hardly bear the suspense, even though it was self-inflicted. His savouring of the throbbing torture of anticipation was bordering on the masochistic as he felt his prick rear repeatedly, like a wild stallion, within its leather pouch.

Suddenly, with a knowing smile, Dorabella reached out towards the bedside table. Jack thought at first it was 'that condom moment'. Some men liked the feel of having a woman roll one on, even when it wasn't necessary, so it was an option they'd decided to retain. She'd probably select one of the novelty varieties. For him, though, it would be a waste of time.

Jack started to opt out but then, before his disbelieving eyes, she took a cigarette from a pack, lighting it quickly between her pursed red lips. Then she reached down between her thighs and, to Jack's alarm, placed it between her pursed pink lips. Rapidly working her vaginal muscles, she began to perform the notorious party-trick of smoking with her quim.

'Shit!' Jack exploded. 'She's not supposed to do that now!'

He tore off the visor and gauntlets then stalked across the room, followed by trailing wires, to the computer console. His lust subsided as he switched into programming mode, all thoughts of sexual satisfaction dismissed. His fingers flew over the keys to hack into the programme, the lines of commands rapidly scrolling down the screen until he got into the hotel room. Yes, there was the rogue routine. It must have somehow invaded from the Strip Club. Or maybe it was a sub-routine from the Circus scenario. Whichever, she definitely shouldn't be performing that particular trick in the Lovenest Hotel. No way!

It was odd that she hadn't been wearing a spangled skirt though, or a G-string. Jack frowned his way through line after line of code, trying to puzzle out the cause of the bug. He cut out the whole sequence and pasted it on the clip-board, then called up each of the alternative scenarios in turn. Eventually Jack had the stray performance back in its rightful place, in the night-club arena. He sat back in his swivel chair and wiped a hand across his brow. Time for coffee!

VR Gameplans UK, a subsidiary of Global VR Games Inc., was housed on the twelfth floor of a futuristic office block in London's Docklands. Far below, through the glass walls of the walkway, Jack could see toy trains worming about in their fluorescent livery, while across the river were the bright lights of the city. It was reassuring, after the hothouse fake reality of the Virtual World, to know that the Real World still existed out there, messy and haphazard. Jack strolled down the short corridor, his soft soles making no noise on the pink carpet spattered with VRG monograms. At the end was the restroom, where the employees could take a short break whenever they liked.

Jack poured himself a coffee from the dispenser and sank into one of the leather hammocks. He put on the headset and was treated to a few minutes of soothing sound – a cross between Bach and trickling water. Then the door to the restroom slid aside and he saw Debra Newcombe enter.

'Hi!' she mouthed, fixing him with her turquoise gaze for a few seconds while her frosted pink lips formed a semi-pout. Jack watched her take coffee from the machine, her arms sculpted with muscle (she worked out three times a week). Her dark cap of hair was bent to the cup and Jack noticed how, beneath the line of the scissor-cut, downy hairs skimmed her nape. As Debra turned he saw the outline of her small breasts, rock firm above her rib-cage, and felt a brief stirring in his dick. Not that she was really attractive to him. It was just that he was still horny from his frustrating encounter with Dorabella.

Jack decided to be sociable, and removed the headphones. 'How's it going, Debra?'

She pulled a face. 'So-so. I'm having trouble with the male characters. It's hard not to make them look like wimps when the Vixies are overpowering them all the time.'

Jack remembered that Debra was currently working on characters for a women's sex fantasy game. 'Maybe you're hampered by your own psychology?' he suggested, with a grin.

'What's that supposed to mean?'

'I mean if you regard all men as wimps then it's difficult for you to characterise them as anything else.'

Debra squatted beside him, thighs like lean planks, and sipped at her coffee. 'I don't find *all* men wimpish.' She was looking up at him, her cyan eyes gleaming in frank appraisal. 'Even some of the married ones still have balls.'

She was throwing him a challenge, daring him to prove

7

his own virility by asking her out. No chance! Jack had enough problems with one woman. Two would only compound them, especially if the second was as voracious as Debra appeared to be. She put one cool hand on his forearm. Calmly, Jack removed it.

'What is it?' she persisted, her mouth pursed with scorn. 'What role are you playing now, "Happily Married Man" or "Never Mix Business with Pleasure"?'

'I save my role-playing talent for the job,' he smiled, trying not to let the woman rile him. After swinging himself out of the hammock he made for the door with long strides, tossing the Styrofoam cup into the recycler as he went. It was no use being nice to Debra, she only took it as encouragement. Somehow all his conversations with her ended up more like confrontations, no matter how amicably they'd begun.

Back at his computer, Jack felt daunted by the task in hand. The whole hotel scenario would have to be re-checked for bugs, just in case there were any more rogue loops in the programme. He was growing a little tired of Dorabella's predictable charms: the inane small talk, designed to make even a mouse feel like a man; those suggestive wriggles and pouts, calculated to by-pass any man's rational mind and make a full frontal assault on his genitals; the limited range of her love-play. There was nothing Jack could do about it, because he was only responsible for the scenarios. Dorabella was the brainchild of some emotionally retarded dork from Silicon Valley USA. The best that Jack could do was to make sure she strutted her infantile stuff in as many interesting locations as possible.

As Jack scrolled through the endless variations on the theme of Boy Fucks Girl, his mind wandered back to Debra. It wasn't the first time she'd made advances towards him. There was the embarrassing memory of the office party, when she had tried to remove his trousers in front of everyone – and almost succeeded. She fancied him something rotten, there was no doubt about that. Probably just because he seemed unobtainable. Jack gave a sardonic laugh.

Even so, he allowed his mind to wander around the subject of her bedworthiness. That lithe, well-tuned body would certainly have stamina. He imagined her as aggressively demanding, frigging herself while she straddled him, wanting him to lick her pussy before, during and after. She seemed the type to know exactly what she wanted and how to get it. Still, you could never tell. Women often surprised you between the sheets. Take Suzanne, for instance . . .

For once screening a mental video of his wife was enjoyable – perhaps by contrast with Debra. Jack was remembering Suzanne not as she was now, but as she'd been when he'd first met her. She'd been so grateful to him for introducing her to the delights of sex that she'd been sweet and compliant, prepared to do anything for him. And he'd known, from the way she moaned and sighed, wriggled and creamed, that her pleasure had equalled his own. That was in the good old days when she'd enjoyed sucking him off almost as much as screwing. Just lately, though, on the rare occasions when they made love he suspected that she might be faking her orgasms.

Sighing, Jack replaced his helmet and gloves. He would go back to the Lovenest Hotel, to where his coitus had been so rudely interrupted, and fuck the hell out of that simulated whore!

He threw the switch that took him straight back into Fantasyland . . .

'Take me, big boy, I'm all yours!'

Dorabella was completely naked on the bed, her hands cupping her generous globes and her thighs spread wide. Jack's libido returned as he approached the bed, his cock pulsating with hot new energy. 'Kiss my clit!' the image whispered. 'Lick my love-button! Taste my trickle! Prepare me for your probing prick!'

Inside the Feelie-Pouch (© Global VR Games Inc.) Jack's boner had returned in full. He touched her wet pussy and felt its smooth slickness on his fingertips. He raised his hand to his nose and smelt the aroma of cunt juice, perfectly reproduced. Alistair was a bloody genius! He could synthesise any smell known to man and, like an expert wine blender, could mix and match a variety of scents to provide a subtle bouquet that brilliantly mimicked reality. Here, the smell of Dorabella's sex was almost imperceptibly tinged with her sweat and her perfume. Jack's dick throbbed eagerly. He decided to take the plunge.

Entering Dorabella was like being in a wet dream. Ripples of sensation teased Jack's rigid shaft as his glans dipped in and out of what felt like a warm pool of melted butter. Except that butter wouldn't melt in Dorabella's cunt, of course! It was all in the electronic mind. Every small detail simulated then transmitted, partly through the tactile electrodes of the Feelietron, and partly through the ultrasonic signals which issued from the headset and targeted specific areas of his brain. It was amazing what brilliant illusions the Perception boys had achieved once they'd identified which bits of the brain did what.

'Brush my buttocks!' Dorabella invited him, keen as a conscientious whore that he should get the most out of this screw. 'Munch my melons! Nibble my nipples!'

Jack dutifully tested all her erogenous zones. The nipples were particularly good, with their exciting rubbery texture and faint, nostalgic flavour of milk. That could put some men off, of course. He flicked his right forefinger and the taste disappeared.

Now the walls of the fake vagina were gripping his tool more tightly, urging him on to his climax. Dorabella continued to whisper dirty messages into his ear. 'My cunt loves your pounding prick, big boy!' Jack had the sensation of a finger in his crack now, jiggling him senseless as the build-up to orgasm intensified. His sphincter relaxed and the phantom finger pushed further in, exciting the virgin membranes of his arse. At last he came, in a series of violent explosions that sprayed the disposable lining of the Feelie-pouch with thick cream and rendered him almost deaf to the last, lingering compliments of the indefatigable Dorabella.

'Oh God, I feel like a million stars are exploding inside me! What an incredibly satisfying technique you have, darling! You're the most fantastic lover in the universe!'

The Docklands train was crowded as usual when Jack slipped through the doors at the last minute and grabbed the nearest strap. Uncomfortable as his journey home invariably was, it was quicker than trying to drive through the city in the rush hour. And there was a bonus. After spending his days contemplating the ersatz charms of Dorabella and her kind, it was pleasant to look at a few flesh-and-blood females for a change. Weary after their day's work, few travellers bothered to make eye contact on those crowded trains, so Jack felt free to cast his gaze over ankles and breasts, lips and eyes without risking discovery.

Tonight there was a particularly attractive Chinese girl, with lustrous black hair and a small pert bosom. She looked as if she regarded sex as a healthy and natural outlet. Beside her, engrossed in *Vogue*, was a snooty-looking type who might have been a model. Presumably girls became models because, like actresses, they enjoyed dressing-up and trying out various personae, which was always sexually promising. A flash of dark thigh caught his attention but its owner, a young black girl, caught him looking and frowned. Jack couldn't make out whether the lowering of her thick-fringed eyelids and the sultry pout of her mouth was a come-on or not. Sighing, Jack decided not to risk another look and directed his eyes towards the adverts.

After the hectic changeover onto the District line, Jack

was lucky enough to get a seat for the long ride to Ealing. He arrived at his suburban semi to find Suzanne in a frisky mood.

'I've put some champagne in the fridge,' she greeted him, her kiss softly persuasive.

'What's the occasion?'

'None. I just felt like it, that's all.'

He noticed that she'd made up her eyes to look tarty, was wearing black stockings and a slinky red velvet dress, and reeked of Obsession. His heart sagged a little. Obviously he was in for a seduction scene. There had been a time when he would have been delighted, but now it was just more pressure. Still, he would play along as usual.

'That's nice.'

'And how was the delightful Dorabella today?' Suzanne asked, as she poured the champagne with a lot more care than the creature in question. Jack's wife got perverse enjoyment out of pretending to regard the fantasy figure as her rival.

'Had a bit of trouble with the action. A bit from another scenario slipped in by mistake and she started doing things she wasn't supposed to do.'

Suzanne wore an expression of mock horror as she said, 'Dear, dear! You mean she turned irrational and unpredictable, like a real woman? Can't have that now, can we?'

Jack slipped off his shoes, sank into the nearest armchair and took a sip of his champagne. He wasn't in the mood for his wife's sarcasm. 'Our scenarios have to be internally consistent,' he explained. 'Of course there must be a degree of unpredictability as far as the punters are concerned. But we don't want our programmes going haywire. We have to remain in control.'

'That's why you like the work so much, isn't it? Because you can control her every move.'

'It's one attraction, I suppose.'

'When are you going to try her out on the unsuspecting public, then?'

'We're hoping for a test run before Christmas.'

'Can I be one of the testers?'

Unaccountably, Jack felt shocked. 'Oh no! It's for men.'

'That's a very sexist attitude, Jack Bedford!'

'I only meant that I didn't think women would find it arousing. Unless they're lesbian, of course. But Debra's game would be more appropriate for that market.'

Suzanne perched herself on the arm of Jack's chair, her generous bum squidging over the edge. Absently, Jack reached out to stroke her velvet-clad thigh. She leaned over, her breasts pushing against his arm, and whispered, 'Want to come to bed?'

Jack suspected that the idea of his work turned Suzanne on. That didn't help. He already felt guilty about the fact that he found it easier to get his rocks off with Dorabella than with his wife. There had been a few unprecedented failures in the marital bed lately. Pressure of work, he'd told himself, since Alistair had come up with the November deadline. But now he felt pressured at home too, and that was even worse.

'Do you mind if we wait till later?' he asked. 'It takes me a while to unwind.'

'How about a nice shower, then? Only I've been feeling randy all day.'

The champagne was blurring the edges of his mind, making it easier to say yes than no. Jack followed his wife upstairs and let her undress him then lead him into the shower. Suzanne stood with her green eyes closed and her face uplifted to the stream, her hair flowing like black water down her back.

Her eyes opened. 'Come here, let me soap you.' She took the pink shower gel and squirted some into her palm, then rubbed his arms and chest to a lather. Jack stood passively, even when she took the slippery fish of his penis between her palms and cleaned it with loving efficiency. As she reached under him to soap his balls, his arse, her breasts were pressed against his chest and the nipples felt slick and puckered, like half-sucked wine gums. He bent to take one in his mouth: it tasted of the strawberry shower gel. Suzanne gave a groan, clutching his thigh, and threw back her head exposing her long, pale neck. Once Jack would have found the gesture provocatively erotic, but now it seemed a touch too theatrical.

'Where's the towel?' he grunted, reaching through the shower curtain.

Suzanne stepped outside and, while Jack turned off the flow, found two large fluffy towels. They went through to the bedroom, where the champagne was waiting in its insulated collar on the bedside table. 'More bubbly?' she smiled, already pouring.

After taking a few sips, Jack lay down on his back with

15

a sigh and Suzanne, recognising her cue, anointed her palms with scented oil and began to massage him. Slowly Jack felt the tensions ooze out of his body but he felt more inclined to doze than make love, even when she succeeded in rousing him to a semi-erection. She told him to turn over and kneaded his buttocks, letting her fingers slip tantalisingly into his crack from time to time then smoothing down his hairy thighs. Gently she rolled his balls between her fingers and thumbs, making his dick stir as it pressed into the duvet. Then, when she turned him over onto his back again he was almost ready for her.

Smiling, Suzanne put the tip of his glans into her mouth and licked it round and round. Her fingertip still played with his balls, moving them about in their tightening sac while she pressed her tits against his knees. She must be getting horny by now, Jack thought. Soon she would want her payoff.

Sure enough, a few seconds later she manoeuvred her body so that he could lick her while she sucked him. Her quim tasted of strawberry shower gel. Jack would have preferred it to taste of cream – Suzanne's cream. Nevertheless he allowed his tongue to suck all the alien juice out of her crevices, trying his best to ignore the faint soapiness, until the fake strawberry flavour vanished and the familiar salty flavour of his wife's secretions returned.

'Oh, that's so good!' she moaned, as his tongue-tip flicked over her clit with practised ease. Jack could feel her pleasure-knob emerging from its hood, like a snail from its shell, and he tasted it like an exquisite delicacy. She was caressing his shaft now and his erection was

16

solidifying. If only she would be content with this mutual pleasuring he could relax, but he knew that, as far as Suzanne was concerned, this was only foreplay. He licked down the grooves between her engorged lips, then slipped his tongue into her hole. She gasped, thrusting her pubic bone against his upper lip in her eagerness to let him in. Jack flicked his tongue in and out like a snake, slurping her juices, until she stopped stroking him and shifted her thighs, preparing to lower herself onto his tumid organ.

Almost as soon as his wife straddled him Jack could feel his erection weaken, but she managed to get it in and began squeezing him vigorously with her cunt muscles. Her fingers were frigging away at her clit while she rode him, eyes closed, her face intense with concentration. Jack felt his squirt arriving and was powerless to stop it. He came weakly, without pleasure, his penis spilling its seed in slow motion, like water oozing from a leaky pipe. Suzanne stopped riding him and simply held him tight within her vaginal walls while she rubbed herself to climax. He felt the fleshy tube undulating uselessly around his flaccid member until he dribbled out of her and collapsed by her side, his head on the pillow, his arm across her midriff.

'That was nice,' she murmured, cosily, snuggling into the crook of his arm.

Jack felt angry denial take hold of him. He said nothing, being in a state of emotional as well as physical exhaustion, while she pretended they'd had great sex.

'I like it earlier in the evening,' she cooed. 'Before we get too tired.'

He knew she was rejuvenated, exhilarated by her self-pleasuring. For him, though, the experience had been empty, less satisfying than even the artificial pleasures that Dorabella had to offer. It didn't seem to bother Suzanne, but it bothered him. What was going wrong with their marriage? Should they talk things over, try to get to the root of it? As long as his wife refused to admit that they had a problem discussion was impossible.

'I'll cook supper now,' she announced, after about five minutes. 'You just lie there, darling, have some more champagne. Do you want the news on?'

'No!' Jack's tone was more harsh than he'd intended. It had been Suzanne's idea to put the TV in the bedroom. 'I'm ... er ... too tired. I'll doze for a bit.'

As soon as he closed his eyes, however, Jack found himself thinking about work. More specifically, about Dorabella. It disturbed him that he found it easier to get a stiffy with that fantasy doll than with his own wife. And his orgasms were more intense with the Feelietron too. Had they actually succeeded in making computerised sex more satisfying than the real thing, or was it just some quirk of Jack's own psychology? They would know more after the November trials, of course. Recalling Suzanne's earlier suggestion that she would like to be one of the testers Jack felt nervously excited, much as he imagined a man would feel if his wife suggested that she should meet his mistress. There was a certain attraction in the idea, he had to admit. Yet he was afraid that if Suzanne poured scorn on the fruits of his labours it would kill his enthusiasm for the work, and he couldn't afford to let that happen.

Once he'd got the bugs out of the Dorabella programme Jack could begin work on his own brainchild,
Around the World in Eighty Lays. He'd told no-one
about that yet, but he was confident that Alistair would
buy the idea. His boss wanted to develop more in-house
games, to cut down on the bench-testing that their parent
company insisted on, and start to build a reputation as a
small but ultra-creative powerhouse in the expanding
world of VR games.

Idly, Jack let his mind wander through some of the
scenarios he'd already invented, from South Sea Paradise
through Amsterdam Sex-Market to London Swings
Again! Instead of having just one constant bed mate, as
in the Dorabella game, the lucky punter would be able
to choose from a variety of dream women, each one
ethnically suited to their context. Jack felt new stirrings
in his groin: the idea excited him every time he thought
about it. His prong stiffened and, automatically, his hand
drifted towards it. He imagined a dark-skinned girl on a
palm-fringed beach, and his erection received an instant
boost as his glans thrust into the hole he had made with
his finger and thumb. Her knockers would be peeking
out from the garland of white flowers that hung round
her neck. They would be smooth and brown as the inside
shell of a coconut, tipped with milk-choc buttons. At
the thought of plunging in through that grass skirt to the
secret cave beyond Jack's hand grasped his shaft and
began to rub vigorously, sending firm signals to every
part of his body that he was definitely into climaxing
good and proper this time. It didn't take him long. The
image of the hula-hula girl lifting her skirt to display her

pink, wet labia finally carried him over the edge and had him spraying the duvet cover with white flecks.

Jack heard his wife's footsteps and hurriedly turned over onto his stomach, closing his eyes. 'Are you asleep?' she called softly. 'Only I'm about to dish up.'

Jack turned his head with a feigned yawn. 'I'll be down in a minute.'

But as he dressed his heart weighed heavy in his chest. Why couldn't he get as much, if not more, pleasure from Suzanne as he did from those fantasy girls? She was still attractive, still made an effort. She just didn't turn him on like she had before he began working for Global. It was as if a chip had been implanted in his brain, making him only respond to certain programmes. Still, maybe it was just a phase he was going through, a side-effect of working in the VR world. He might mention it to his colleagues sometime, to see if they'd noticed similar symptoms.

Still glowing from the satisfying orgasm he'd just enjoyed, Jack climbed back into his clothes and went to join his wife.

Chapter Two

Debra waylaid Jack next morning as he swept through the swing doors. She had that determined look on her face, almost provocative, that he knew meant business. Her blood-red lips were smiling with secret pleasure, suggesting she had some surprise in store for him.

'Hi, Jack!' she called across the foyer. 'Would you drop by some time this morning? I've something to show you.'

'What is it?' His tone was suspicious.

'A new programme. I thought you ought to see it.'

'I'm really very busy with my own . . .'

'It won't take long. Alistair thinks you should see it too.'

She knew she had him then. Jack couldn't afford to ignore his boss's wishes. 'Okay, then. Better make it around eleven.'

Debra gave him a triumphant smile verging on the smug. Pushing out her small breasts beneath the lace-trimmed propriety of her beige silk blouse, she entered the lift. Jack cringed inwardly and pretended to be busy reading the bulletin board on the VDU at reception.

Inside, though, his guts were churning. What wouldn't he like to do to that woman! He had a sudden vision of those pert buttocks stripped naked and his hand giving them a thorough slapping. Better yet he would have her gagged and bound, so she couldn't nag at him with that snotty voice of hers, or wriggle free. The idea of her squirming under his punishment, her bum cheeks the same humiliating hue as her face, made him even more excited. Feeling somewhat disturbed, Jack bounded up the stairs two at a time, hurried into his own room and switched on the computer.

Soon Dorabella's pouting face was on the screen. He made her wink, turn her pink lips into a plump kiss, take a few sashaying steps. In a few seconds he'd transformed her image into a screen-saver. In future, whenever he wasn't using the keyboard four Dorabellas would appear – one at each corner – winking, kissing and pouting their way across the screen in an infinite loop.

As Jack worked away at his programming he was still puzzling over Debra's invitation to view her own efforts. Just what was that bitch playing at? For one horrible moment he wondered if she could have stolen his Round the World in Eighty Lays idea, but he knew he hadn't spoken of that to anyone. And they hadn't yet invented a mind-reading machine, had they?

Well, there was only one way to find out what she was up to. Promptly at eleven, Jack went to the rest room for a coffee, then presented himself at Debra's studio. It was bigger than his, much to his chagrin. She had been taken onto the staff before him, and Alistair had given her the pick of the two rooms. Now she opened the door to him as if he were entering her boudoir, for purposes far removed from the mundane job of computer programming.

'Welcome to my humble abode, Jack,' she grinned, rubbing it in. He noticed that she'd feminised the place, with superfluous potted plants and a holographic image of some kid on the wall. Probably her own love-child. Jack knew nothing about Debra's private life, and he intended to keep it that way.

She leaned back against her desk with that infuriating grin on lips that were a few shades paler now – after coffee? – and Jack could see her nipples clearly outlined beneath the stretched fabric of her blouse. Was that the idea? Well, if the silly cow thought she was staging a seduction scene she had another think coming!

'I expect you're wondering why I called you in here,' she smiled.

'Some new programme?'

'Yes. Shall we?'

She handed him a headset and some wired gauntlets. Reluctantly he took them and saw her pick up another set for herself. 'We're both going to view at once?'

'That's the idea.' Her blue eyes were sparkling with an excitement that Jack recognised as sexual. The bitch was on heat, damn it! The feeling that he was somehow going to be taken advantage of grew as he covered his eyes with the visor and strapped on the belt with its sensor-laden crotch pouch. He reminded himself that it was all an illusion and if, at any time, he grew uneasy he had only to disengage his senses from the Feelietron.

'Ready?' Debra's voice came, cool and slightly amused, in his ear. He nodded. At once a familiar scenario appeared. It was the rest room that he had visited only minutes ago. There was the drinks dispenser, the wall-hung screen, the easy chairs. And there – Oh God! – lying seductively in the hammock was Debra herself!

'Hell, what are you doing in your own scenario, Debra?' he mumbled. It was a very good likeness. She was wearing the same get-up that she'd worn at the office party: an off-the-shoulder black dress with a diamond clip accentuating her cleavage. She even smelt of the same damn perfume, Amerige. Remembering her attempt at de-bagging him, Jack felt a hot flush of embarrassment in the area of his groin. At least, that was how it started out. But as she leaned forward out of the hammock, her small tits nearly falling out of her neckline, Jack realised that the heat in his groin was by now purely erotic. He could feel his tool thrusting uselessly against the soft plastic sac.

'I think you and I have some unfinished business don't we, Jack?' she cooed. 'Remember that Christmas party? I can understand you being embarrassed in front of all the other staff, but now you and I are entirely alone, so there's nothing to worry about. Just come here, and let me untie that necktie of yours. It's so hot in here, don't you find?'

Jack felt paralysed. He knew he ought to get the hell out of there, but it was all too fascinating. To see a scene from his life replayed – well, almost – before his very eyes. To be able to take up in fantasy from where he'd left off in reality ... that was truly fantastic!

He felt himself being drawn towards the hammock. Debra reached up and the soft touch of her fingers on his neck sent warm signals down his spine. There was a loosening sensation in his clothes, her eyes came close to his and soon his lips were feeling the gentle pressure of hers. They tasted of vanilla.

'Come on,' he heard her murmur. 'Help me out of this dress.'

He fumbled with the zip but the garment slid easily down over her hips, falling in a heap on the floor. The virtualised Debra wore a strapless bra of black lace and matching panties, just a triangle of lace over the dark fur within. She took a few steps back from him and, with knowing eyes, unclasped her bra to reveal small, pointy breasts with disproportionately large red nipples that Jack wanted to take in his mouth at once. He moved towards her, but she shook her head.

'No, Jack, I've been a bad girl, remember? I embarrassed you in front of your colleagues at the party. And I've never been properly punished for it, have I?'

The blood was pounding in Jack's brain as she casually bent over the arm of a nearby chair, smiling up at him all the while. 'Go on, Jack, give me the thrashing I deserve. I know you want to.'

Again the thought crossed his mind that somehow they'd made a technological breakthrough and could read his thoughts. But the sight of Debra's naked behind, with just a black thong around her hips and down her crack, was irresistible. Her bum had been honed to perfection in the gym. It was round and firm and pink, and his palm itched to make contact with that plump smoothness.

'Come on, what are you waiting for?' she urged him, impatiently. Jack realised that whatever the real Debra might or might not be into, the Virtual Debra was dying for it. He raised his right arm and his rod reared in sympathy. When he brought the flat of his hand down on her rump there was a wonderful slapping sound, and he could feel the springy resistance of firm flesh beneath her warm skin.

'Again!' she sighed. 'Slap me again, Jack. I've been so-o-o naughty!'

Jack soon got into a satisfying rhythm of whacking. The harder he hit her, the more she seemed to like it. Soon she was rubbing her mons against the chair arm, pulling at her nipples until they peaked huge and hard, moaning gently all the while. Jack wanted to explore the rest of her body, but every time he tried to put his hands elsewhere she cried in protest, 'Not yet! I've not been punished enough yet!'

Eventually his hand felt tired. When he complained, she suggested he use his other hand. But the pressure in his penis was becoming unbearable. He wanted to slip inside her from behind, to feel those reddened arse-cheeks cushioned against his stomach as he pounded her. He seized her roughly by the waist, and this time she didn't protest but spread her legs wide to give him access. Jack thrust between her lean thighs and felt no resistance as his dick plunged up to the hilt in warm lubrication.

'Oh, yes!' came the groaning response. 'Give it to me good and hard!'

Jack obliged, wresting her hands away from her breasts as he did so. They flattened under his palms, but he pinched the nobbly teats between finger and thumb and heard her cry out, her pleasure bordering on pain. She was bucking and thrusting against his groin now, fingering her own clit as he rode her frantically from behind. The hot waves were spreading up to his stomach and chest and down to his knees. Jack drove his ramrod home, feeling the slick walls of her cunt convulse as she came over and over again. It was enough to trigger him. He felt the inevitable tide sweep him away in spasms of release, the shock of sensation weakening his legs so that he dropped, helplessly, to his knees.

'Fucking hell!' he groaned, as his system began to stabilise after the onslaught.

Debra, her inner thighs streaming, smiled at him over her shoulder. 'Are you sure you don't mean "Fucking heaven"?'

The quality of the sound made him realise that it was the real, not the simulated, Debra who had spoken. He tore off the goggles and saw her sitting open-legged on her swivel chair, grinning at him, her own headset dangling loose from her fingers.

'Did you see all that?' he gasped. She nodded, serenely. 'Fucking hell!'

'I can understand your amazement,' she said coolly. 'It's a real breakthrough. Couples will be able to experience Feelietron sex simultaneously, without fear of disease or distaste. They can explore sides of themselves they would never find the courage to explore in real life. Think of the implications for sex therapy!'

Jack frowned. 'If this catches on, will people bother to have real-life relationships at all?'

Debra shrugged. 'Who knows? Probably some will, some won't. Personally, I don't think we'll ever be able to beat the real thing.'

She was looking at him in that predatory way again. Jack wanted to get out of his sticky pouch and into the shower, but he was driven by curiosity too.

'How long have you been working on this?'

'Oh, a few months. With Alistair, of course. He wants to network eventually, to get a whole crowd of people experiencing the same thing at the same time.'

'You mean, a Feelietron orgy?'

She smiled. 'Yes, but with options. Imagine walking round a room with lots of people offering various sexual favours. You could pick and choose. The possibilities are exciting, aren't they?'

'Maybe.'

'You sound unconvinced.'

'It's just that it gets to a point where it's technology for the sake of it. I mean, Feelie sex is just a wank when all's said and done.'

Debra smiled, coming towards him with her headset still in her hands. 'You want a replay, from my angle?'

Jack didn't think he could have heard it right. 'What?'

'A replay of the little adventure we both had just now, but from my point of view.'

28

'You can do that? Really?'

Her smile was infuriatingly smug. 'Really!'

'But how? I mean . . .'

'You mean you don't have a vagina, right? Okay, but we're working on it. Put this on and see how far we've come already . . .'

Jack felt apprehensive, almost fearful, but he did as he was told. Immediately he was back in the rest room, but this time he was the one lying in the hammock. Looking down he was amazed to see that he was wearing a little black dress and had long, smooth legs, one of which was hanging provocatively over the side.

The door opened, and Jack was stunned to see a passable image of himself enter the room. They hadn't got the eyes or the hair quite right, but the mouth was good and the overall physique. He was wearing one of his favourite ties.

'I think you and I have some unfinished business don't we, Jack?' he heard himself coo. 'Remember that Christmas party! I can understand you being embarrassed in front of all the other staff, but now you and I are entirely alone, so there's nothing to worry about. Just come here, and let me untie that necktie of yours. It's so hot in here, don't you find?'

To Jack's amazement he had the knot of his own tie beneath his fingers, felt it loosen. As the scene proceeded he experienced the weird sensation of being stripped to his underwear – women's underwear! – and then found himself bending over the arm of a leather chair. He knew that, in reality, he was still standing. Yet the image of himself staring at the studded cushion, and the way his blood rushed to his head, was so persuasive that it effectively blotted out his awareness of being upright.

'. . . I've been a bad girl, remember?' he heard Debra's voice say. Except that the sound came from inside his own head, as if he'd uttered the words himself. 'I embarrassed you in front of your colleagues at the party. And I've never been properly punished for it, have I?'

When the spanking began, Jack felt humiliated at first. It was like being a small boy again, being made to look stupid in front of his mates. He felt his fleshy buttocks vibrate with the slapping and, after a few times, start to sting like mad. It wasn't long, though, before they felt numb and then a pleasing warmth followed. His tadger began to tingle in anticipation of each smack, growing a bit stiffer each time, and he enjoyed hearing the clean, sharp sound of contact between her palm and his behind.

'My hand's getting tired,' Jack heard his own voice say. 'I want to stop now.'

'Not yet!' came Debra's reply. 'I've not been punished enough yet!'

But Jack knew that the flagellation would stop, eventually. It was the action to follow that preoccupied him now. As each stinging stroke brought that moment of penetration closer, Jack felt his erection strengthen and his desire grow. At last he had the sensation of his legs being set wide apart and, his prong bursting with anticipation, felt his arms brace themselves against the leather upholstery. Unable to resist taking a peek at his own simulated parts, he saw that he'd been somewhat overendowed. Yet the resemblance to his own member was still uncanny as far as its shape and colour was concerned. Uneasily he tried to recall whether Debra could possibly have taken a look at his tackle at any time. Or had Alistair been taking mental notes in the Gents?

There followed the most extraordinary experience of his life. Somewhere between his arse and his cock, in the region known as the perineum, he had the sensation of being given an internal massage. At the same time he was experiencing a realistic blow job, while hard flesh seemed to be banging against his bum in a fast, insistent rhythm.

'Oh, yes!' came the groaning female response. 'Give it to me good and hard!'

Fingers were tweaking his nipples, making his eyes water. He felt impelled to wriggle his hips, thrusting his backside against the wall of flesh, as the sensations of tingling warmth filled the whole of his genital area. Inside he was a molten pool, as if he were flooding with come-juice before his climax, but through it all he could feel the ramming percussion of something hard and unrelenting, pushing him on and on towards their mutual goal.

Then, in a change of pace, he felt the ultimate pleasure pulse slowly through him. It was unlike any other orgasm he'd experienced. Jack felt he was yielding up the inner core of his being to soft fingers that were gently caressing surfaces that had never been touched before. His internal organs felt as if they were being kissed by infinitely tender lips. At some deeper level, where sensation and psychology merge, his very soul seemed to be turning inside out.

When the exquisite feelings died away Jack was left

with a sense of loss, and of wonder. Had he really experienced what a woman feels? Of course, his rational mind told him, there was no way of knowing if it were truly so.

He heard Debra's voice coming from outside the headset. 'Okay, Jack? I'm going to switch off now.'

She helped Jack remove his gear – he needed a helping hand. Staggering into the nearest chair, he put his hands over his eyes, finding reality too much to bear after his virtual experience.

'I know how you feel,' she assured him. 'When I first had sex as a man through the Feelietron it was like being broken down and re-assembled.'

'You've done it too?' He stared at her, bemused, as if they were two initiates in a strange cult.

She nodded. 'With Alistair. He and I . . .' she paused just long enough for Jack to realise that they'd shared sex outside the Feelietron too. 'We perfected it together. I'm sorry you had to be left out, Jack, but someone had to continue with the routine work.'

'So you weren't working on that Vixies scenario after all?'

The edge to Jack's voice had Debra on the defensive. She moved over to the rack and began hanging up the gear, throwing the disposable lining from Jack's pouch into the bin without batting an eyelid. 'We had to keep it a secret, even from the other employees. That's because we didn't know if it would work out. But it has, and now Alistair has authorised me to let you in on it. He wants you to make us some new scenarios.'

'Oh, does he?' Jack felt piqued, betrayed.

'Don't take it badly, Jack. Think of it as a wonderful new opportunity, which it is. We're thinking of calling it Mutual Reality. When it takes off, you'll be in on the ground floor. You could become a rich man, Jack.'

She was talking sense, and he knew it. Nevertheless he hated being manipulated by a woman. 'It's not wealth I want, it's job satisfaction.'

He knew he shouldn't have said it. Debra's mocking lips curved into a smile. 'I think we've just proved that you can have that till the cows come home, haven't we? Wasn't it incredible, Jack? Almost as good as the real thing, wouldn't you say?'

For a fleeting moment Jack remembered his unsatisfactory encounter with Suzanne. He could never admit that today's little adventure had been more exciting than last night's. 'We're on the way,' was all he could think of in reply.

Debra came close, uncomfortably close. He could smell her Amerige for real and, out of habit, mentally compared it with the simulated version. But she was there in the unmistakable flesh now, her blue eyes looking down at him with an expression he found not at all hard to fathom.

'How about it then, Jack?' she asked, softly, and he knew she wasn't referring to the latest developments at work.

Jack gulped and got up out of his chair. 'I'll ... er ... have a word with Alistair about it. You two are to be congratulated, you really are.'

'That's not what I meant and you know it.' She was

33

reaching out for him now, wearing the smile of a confident woman. She thought she had him in the palm of her hand.

After all he'd experienced that morning it would have been easy for Jack to respond. The Feelietron tended to blur the lines of demarcation between fantasy and reality. In fantasy he'd already explored that well-tuned body of hers, slapped her taut buttocks with his palm, felt her firm little boobs, penetrated the damp tightness of her quim. And he was curious – yes, he had to admit it – curious to know whether the real Debra matched the computer model.

'You want to know how it would be for real, don't you Jack?' her voice insisted, quiet, insidious. 'You want to know how close we've come in our simulation. It would be in the interest of scientific investigation for you to find out, now wouldn't it?' She flung her arms around him, her small breasts pressed against him, her breath hot against his neck. Jack wavered. 'Come on, Jack, give it a try. I want you to, really I do. We might even get a research grant for our little experiments!'

Debra giggled and that did it. He couldn't stand her giggling. It reminded him of that awful party, when they'd both drunk more than was good for their image. Impatiently he thrust her away from him.

'I have to get back to my own desk, Debra. I told you I was busy. But thank you for showing me what you've been getting up to with Alistair.'

His tone made his words pointedly ambiguous. Striding from the room, Jack suspected he was making a big mistake in rebuffing Debra, but he didn't care. He was only prepared to go so far for the sake of his career.

Jack went straight to the showers and symbolically cleansed himself of the whole business. Then, refreshed and invigorated, he went back for what he hoped would be the last bench test on the Dorabella scenarios.

In the middle of the afternoon, Alistair put his head round the door. 'Jack, can I have a word?' he called.

When the two men were seated, face to face, Alistair asked what he thought of the latest project. Jack tried to choose his words carefully, aware of the serious scrutiny that Alistair's brown eyes were giving him.

'I think it has enormous potential. Almost frightening. The idea that you can switch roles – switch bodies and minds, almost – is revolutionary.'

Alistair held up a small chip, embedded in transparent plastic. 'This is the MR chip, Jack. Amazing, isn't it? Just one chip to link two people's bodies. One day, who knows? Maybe we'll be able to join people's souls.'

Jack took it into the palm of his hand, peered at the tiny, insect-like object as if he knew what it signified, but his knowledge of hardware was minimal. 'This chip could be worth millions!'

'Take it, Jack. Keep it in your spares box in case the other chip fails.'

Jack felt flattered that Alistair trusted him. But as he pocketed the plastic case he was more concerned with the implications of the new technology. 'Surely this could have uses beyond VR games?'

'That's what we believe. Debra envisages all kinds of

usage, from medical diagnosis to marriage guidance. But
for the moment we're thinking exclusively games, and a
Feelietron game is only as good as its characterisation
and scenarios, Jack. That's why we need you. We need
your creativity. What you've done with that airhead Dorabella is truly stunning. If you can make a cardboard cut-
out like that come alive with imaginative scripts and
settings, just think what you could do with our new
technology.'

'You don't have to convince *me*,' Jack grinned.

Alistair smiled back. 'I know that you're the right man
for the job. Don't let me down now, will you?'

Jack rose to go, but then paused. He knew he had to
tell his boss about his idea. He had to get even with that
Debra bitch, who had probably been gaining an unfair
advantage by screwing Alistair, and he couldn't let her
get all the Brownie points. She was just the type of
woman whose sexuality was at the service of her
ambition.

Thanking his lucky stars that he hadn't let her seduce
him, Jack said, 'Just a minute, Alistair. I've something on
the drawing-board that I think you might find interesting.'

Much to Jack's relief, Alistair found his Round the
World in Forty Lays idea very interesting indeed. It was
always a pleasure to talk to a man with such a quick
intelligence, who not only saw what you saw but took it
several stages further. Jack had conceived of his scenarios
using the old technology but, adapted to the new Mutual
Reality, they took on an exciting new dimension.

'As far as we can see, MR has no-holds-barred potential,' Alistair explained. 'There's no reason why a woman shouldn't know what it feels like to be a gay man, or a man shouldn't experience lesbian sex. As for locations, well the sky isn't even the limit. We have computer simulations of planetary conditions. We can literally fly people to the moon, and beyond.'

Alistair's zeal was almost religious. Jack had heard him talk like this before, of course, but always theoretically. Now, he thought wryly, it was virtually reality!

'Look, why don't you take the rest of the afternoon off,' Alistair suggested. 'You look tired. Probably the result of all this mind-blowing you've been through. I know what it's like. Who was it said, "human beings cannot bear very much reality"? Some poet, probably. Anyway, I suggest you go home, have a lie down and think about it in a calm and creative way. See what the old subconscious comes up with by tomorrow.'

Jack managed to avoid Debra as he left the building. He was glad. The way he felt about her it would have been impossible not to say something damaging. The idea of her sucking up to the boss – literally! – behind his back then using his own virtual image in her pathetic flagellation fantasy made him mad. He hated the way he'd been sucked into it all, drawn into her twisted game. That harlot knew he'd come in his pouch, damn it! She'd probably been gloating over the fact ever since. If she couldn't have him in the flesh, then she'd have him in the Feelietron. In many ways he would have preferred a straightforward affair to that sordid masturbatory exercise. At least he'd have been more in control.

Once he was on the train, though, Jack tried to think of pleasanter things. Alistair had managed to awaken a new enthusiasm for his project, which now seemed to offer almost limitless possibilities. He looked up and saw the face of the Chinese girl he'd seen several times before. This time she gave a faint smile before lowering her eyes to her book, and Jack felt a surge of confidence. He would definitely include a visit to Hong Kong in his world tour.

Walking across the green at Ealing Broadway, Jack was lost in pleasant thought. He followed his habitual route until he came to his road, still in a dream. It was only when he was about ten yards from his gate that he was suddenly jolted out of his reverie by the sight of a small green sports car parked outside the house. His eyes travelled upwards to the front bedroom window. The curtains were roughly drawn, but there was a gap in the middle through which the mellow glow of a bedside lamp could be seen.

Instinctively, Jack knew that someone was up there with his wife.

Chapter Three

Jack entered quietly, pausing in the hall to listen. He thought he could hear sounds from upstairs so he slowly began to climb, half afraid of what he might find. The door to the master bedroom was ajar and now he was sure that he could hear Suzanne gasping, the way she did when she was wanking to a climax. Feeling strangely detached, Jack tiptoed to the door and pushed it open a bit more.

He could see her clearly now. His naked wife was kneeling on the bed on all fours, her back arched to thrust her pale bottom further into the air. Behind her, on his knees, was a muscle-bound youth with blond hair and an all-over tan. Between the two of them stretched a condom-clad prick the size of a cucumber, its swollen purple head just inching into Suzanne's wet hole. The guy was teasing her with it, letting his glans slurp about in her entrance while her cunt lips licked his shaft. She was going delirious with pleasure, wriggling her hips and clenching her arse to milk every last thrill from the contact between that giant prong-head and her sensitised clitoris.

Jack felt a sick anger in his stomach, but he was transfixed. The idea of his wife with a toy boy was ludicrous on one level, frightening on another. Yet he had to watch. The cucumber was covered with slick dressing now. He could see it gleam with her juices as it began to go further in. Suzanne moaned, 'More, more!' and the guy murmured, 'Easy does it!' as he slid in and out with slow control. Each time the guy pulled back Suzanne's arsehole was clearly visible, the pink puckering stretched and taut. Jack saw her lover put his finger in his mouth and gently rim her, evoking a squeal of ecstasy. Fuck the bastard! And fuck her, too!

Now he was almost all into her and she was giving low, guttural groans. The pace was quickening. Suzanne was half collapsed on the bed and he was ramming it home still, apparently, in full control of himself. Jack could hear the squelching as the thick rod wallowed in his wife's copious fluid, cranking away like a well-oiled machine. She was making incoherent sounds, her breath coming in quick gasps, and it wasn't long before she gave the long, low moan that signalled the arrival of her orgasm. Jack stood with gritted teeth, heart hammering in his chest, as the moaning went on and on. When it finally ended in a sigh, Suzanne lay face down on the bed, utterly spent. Her lover withdrew his dripping dong, which looked as if it had been dipped in pearlescent liquid soap. Jack panicked: what the hell was he supposed to do now? He had a weird feeling of being utterly out of his depth.

While he hesitated, Suzanne and her lover changed places. Now it was his turn to lie down, lean torso stretched out languidly, while Suzanne knelt between his legs. Jack could hardly believe it when she bent her head to the huge erection. She began by licking her own cream off the condom, with as much relish as a kid eating ice-cream, then she unpeeled it and her lips closed over the naked glans. The man gave a grunt of pleasure and Jack tasted envy in the poisonous cocktail of emotions that was festering in him. She'd not done that for him since those early nights of marriage. He'd asked her to, a few times, but she'd said she hated the taste of his spunk. Bloody hell, it wasn't fair. It just wasn't fair!

But it was enough to goad him into action. Flinging wide the door, Jack strode into the room bellowing, 'You two-timing bitch! What the hell do you think you're doing with this bastard? And in *our* bed, too!'

The man sat up in alarm, fear in his blue eyes. Suzanne sprang back off the bed, obviously shocked but prepared to defend herself. Jack grabbed a handful of her shoulder-length hair and barked at the intruder, 'Get the hell out of here!'

The lover grabbed his clothes and fled. Seconds later the front door was opened then slammed. Jack pushed Suzanne face down on the bed and flung himself on top of her, still holding her hair. 'You unfaithful cow!' he snarled into her ear. 'How bloody dare you!'

'Ouch! You're hurting me! Can't we talk sensibly about this?'

'*Sensibly?* Who are you kidding? There's only one language you understand, bitch!'

Jack found he was enjoying this. It was real, raw.

Unlike their recent half-hearted attempts at love-making he was now fuelled with passion. He kept thinking of that bastard shafting his wife doggy-fashion, and of her loving it, and he wanted some of that action too. With a gasp he got to his knees.

'I'm going to punish you, whore!'

The first stinging slap on her backside made her cry out in protest, but Jack was in no mood to show mercy. He continued to smack her, relishing the feel of the plump, shuddering flesh beneath his hand and the warm tingle in his palm. Suzanne's bum cheeks turned from pink to red, and she was gasping – but no longer in protest. Jack had the distinct impression that his wife was beginning to get off on it just as much as he was. His tool was up and ready, making him feel strong and masterful, like he'd felt at the beginning of their marriage before his desire for exercising his conjugal rights had waned. He knew he could screw her every bit as thoroughly as the brainless prick he'd just ejected from their bed.

Suzanne moaned as he heaved her hindquarters into the air and spread her thighs. A brief manual examination of her vulva showed that she was still wet, her hole gaping and her clit hard as a bead. Jack felt the adrenaline surge through him as he slipped his turgid penis between her labia, letting the glans just nudge at her entrance. Although he felt an almost irresistible urge to strike home Jack managed to keep it there on the brink, savouring the anticipation, teasing her just as lover-boy had done.

He leaned forward and grasped her dangling breasts, his fingers and thumbs seeking her small nipples. Recently he'd been ignoring her tits, being more concerned with getting and keeping his erection, but Suzanne used to like him to give them a good kneading. The soft flesh squidged between his fingers and she gave a moan of encouragement. He could feel her boobs becoming taut and firm, the nipples peaking with urgent abandon, and he let his shaft nose a bit further into her soft, wet hole.

Jack wanted her now, with a steaming lust that brought back memories of happier times. He gave one sudden plunge, making her gasp, and then withdrew very slowly to tease her lips with his glans again. Suzanne was using her muscles on him now, trying to suck him further in and fill her up, but he was not to be seduced into playing her game. She wanted him right in there, the bitch, but he wasn't going to give her the satisfaction. Not until she was screaming for it. And he'd make her scream for it, the cow!

Jack's hands left her breasts momentarily to squeeze her pink buttocks, while he leant back to survey her arse. Making his forefinger slick with her juice, he poked into the tight little hole and felt the sphincter muscle contract tightly. Undeterred, he pushed further in and wiggled it about, loosening the flesh and making her groan with guttural sensuality. He managed to synchronise his finger and prick so that he was dancing around in both holes with a satisfying rhythm, and her hips were beginning to roll in response. Through it all Jack felt elated but still distanced, as if he were performing a professional operation extremely well and perfectly in control.

'More!' Suzanne begged, as he half plunged then quickly withdrew. Jack smiled at the echo of her previous pleading. The action replay was going even better than he'd hoped, but now it was time for a variation. He lowered his face between her buttocks to give her a good tonguing from behind. Her juices were copious, sweet and fresh, convincing Jack that he was turning her on himself and she was not merely still wet from before. He slid his tongue into her gaping slit, lapping her like a dog. With his fingertips he tickled at her exposed clitoris, wanting her to come. It didn't take long. There was a sudden gush of liquid as she wriggled in his face, crying 'Oh God!' and her vaginal muscles contracted over the tip of his tongue. He licked and jiggled fiercely to prolong her climax, his cock thrusting futilely into the duvet between her legs.

Suzanne collapsed at last, but he wouldn't let her rest. Roughly he turned her over, staring down into her sweaty face and glazed eyes. 'Okay, bitch, now it's my turn!'

Jack straddled her at chest level and thrust his stiffy into her mouth. Suzanne gave a cry of protest but he pinned her shoulders against the pillow and squeezed her sides between his knees. 'Do it, and do it good!' he snarled. 'Or I swear I'll ram it down your throat!'

Still in control, he began sliding slowly in and out of her mouth. 'Lick me as I move,' he told her. 'Suck your own juice off me! You're going to swallow mine in a minute, so you might as well get used to the idea!'

Suzanne groaned, and he smiled down at her. Reaching behind him he found he could easily finger her vulva. The clitoris had retreated behind its hood, but the juicy lips were still plump and engorged. He dabbled away until she began to wet herself again. His rod was hard as steel, working in and out of her mouth like a piston. Jack felt like a sex machine as he simultaneously fingered one set of lips and plunged into the other.

His wife was loving it now, wriggling her butt against the bed and reaching for her boobs to intensify her arousal. Jack could never remember them having it so good! The memory of her betrayal had faded and all he cared about was screwing the maximum satisfaction out of every moment. By leaning back he could get three fingers into her cunt, and he could feel the knobbly projection of her clit against his wrist. He twisted his hand to give it a circular massage and she gave a grunt of renewed pleasure.

Jack was almost sliding over the edge himself, relishing the wet kiss of her lips as he filled her mouth with his throbbing dick. He wanted her to squeeze his balls gently, but he didn't trust her. There was still a wild look in her eye. He took his hands off her shoulders and played with her tits instead, pushing them up so that they made a soft cushion for his scrotum. He could feel his balls tighten in the sac then the first rush came, like fizz from a shaken bottle, propelling him out of his senses and onto a mindless roller-coaster of thrills and spills. He was vaguely aware of his wife's choking and spluttering as the hot milk shot down her throat, then he slowly withdrew his limp prick and fell back onto the bed.

A sudden thump in the solar plexus brought Jack abruptly out of his post-coital trance.

'Bloody bastard!'

He opened his eyes to see pure hatred staring down at him.

'Fuck you, Jack Bedford!' screamed Suzanne as she got up and reached for her clothes. Dazed, and with his stomach churning, Jack mumbled, 'What the hell . . .?'

'If you thought that was some kind of sick revenge . . .'

'What, are you fuckin' crazy, woman? Just who's supposed to be in the wrong here?'

'It's not a matter of right or wrong. Anyway, I can't stay here.'

'Why not? You're the one who wanted to talk.'

'That was before you forced your disgusting penis down my throat.'

'Don't kid yourself, Suzanne. You loved every second of it, and you know it!'

She gave him a scornful look and left the room. Jack lay back, utterly drained, and after a few minutes heard the front door slam again. He was glad, he needed to be alone. On the other hand, he was scared. What was she up to? Alongside his anger, curiosity was aroused when he thought of that blond bastard. How long had he been shagging her in the afternoons? Where had they met? Just what was going on?

He thought of how Suzanne had been the day before, hot as hell for it, and his anger was rekindled. Had she been making it with lover-boy yesterday afternoon as well, before his return from work? Or had she been unable to wait until today? Either way, it was pretty obvious now that her lust hadn't been for him. No doubt as she'd brought herself off she'd been thinking of donkey dong. Afterwards she'd come over all lovey-dovey out of guilt. The thought sickened him.

Jack rolled over and, exhausted, gave himself up to sleep. The sound of the bedside phone wakened him. It was Suzanne.

'I'm staying with Rupert tonight. I need to think things over, Jack. I don't know when I'll see you, but I'll keep in touch. 'Bye.'

She left no room for him to reply, but put the phone down at once. Jack gave a disgusted snort. 'Rupert!' It suited the bugger all right. What a wanker! Well, Suzanne would soon discover her mistake and come crawling home. After the session they'd had she would realise that he could be as good a stud as the next man when the mood took him. And he had a feeling that the mood would take him rather more often in future. Okay, so things had been getting a bit stale between them lately. Maybe a spot of rivalry was just what he'd needed to kick-start him into action again. And what action! Say what she liked, it was obvious that Suzanne had relished his overpowering of her. Their love life was entering a new and more exciting phase, no doubt about that. Once she realised which side her bread was buttered, she would beg him to forgive and forget. He might give her a bit of a tough time at first – she'd probably enjoy that, too! – but eventually their marriage would become far stronger than before. They'd both end up being grateful to 'Rupert' for teaching them to appreciate each other more, which would bloody well serve the tosser right!

Buoyed up by these and other pleasant thoughts, Jack got up and went into the shower. It was only when he went to bed that the doubts returned, but sleep soon replaced them with a delightful dream in which he indulged in a sensual threesome with Suzanne and Dorabella.

Now that Alistair had given Jack the go-ahead to develop his Round the World game, finishing off the Dorabella scenarios became a chore to be finished as soon as possible. Next morning Jack checked the programming assiduously for bugs before embarking on the last exhaustive (and exhausting) run through of all the scenarios and their various options. By lunch time he was finished, and went to his boss's office to report the successful conclusion of the project.

Jack buzzed but was given the red light. He went into the rest room, had a coffee and a chicken tikka roll, then tried again. Just as his hand reached for the buzzer the door opened and Debra emerged, with puffy eyes and wet cheeks, her hairstyle mussed out of its usual geometrical neatness. For a second, Jack was filled with the hope that she'd been sacked. His working life would be so much easier without her around.

'Oh, it's you, Jack,' she said, blinking hard and obviously trying to sound normal. 'Alistair's free to see you now. And perhaps you'd pop into my office later, would you?'

Jack's already cool smile froze on his lips. She wouldn't talk like that if she'd just been fired. Whatever had just gone on between her and Alistair must have been personal. But how dare she adopt that supercilious tone, as if she were his boss and not just a colleague?

Alistair, at least, appeared unruffled. His manner was courteous and enthusiastic. 'You've finished well ahead of target Jack, excellent!' he grinned. 'We've got the trials booked for three weeks' time but we might try to bring them forward. Meanwhile, you're free to start work on that project you told me about yesterday. Nothing like striking while the idea's hot, I always say!'

'What do you want, initially?'

'A game plan, a few outline scenarios, maybe a script or two. Whatever you think it needs to give me a flavour of the thing. Oh, and work fairly closely with Debra on this one, will you?'

Jack was nonplussed. 'Er . . . what exactly do you mean by that?'

Alistair gave him a keen-eyed look. 'I outlined your idea to her and she thinks she can provide some input. She's a talented girl, Jack. And she knows what the new technology's capable of. Together I'm sure you'll make a great team.'

Jack left the room feeling decidedly down. He regarded the Eighty Lays theme as his own brainchild. He preferred working on his own in any case, but the idea of having that bitch Debra breathing down his neck every minute, and probably taking more credit than was her due, really pissed him off. But maybe, just maybe, he could palm her off with working out the technicalities, leaving the creative side to him.

It was a faint hope, though. As Jack sat at his desk working on the game plan his heart was only half into it. The project didn't seem like his baby any more. Curse the woman! Then he thought of Suzanne. Curse all women!

By three, though, he had some ideas on the screen. The player of Round the World in Eighty Days would start with an open plane ticket and a fistful of travellers cheques, which would have to last him through the game. His object was to screw his way round the world without catching any social diseases, getting ripped off or losing his potency. He could gain points by satisfying his various partners, trying as many sexual variations as he could and spending as little money as possible. Jack made a list of eighty countries and programmed the computer to plot a course between them, which gave him the basis of a journey which began in London and ended in New York. However, realising that this would probably take forever, he also planned a shorter version involving only twenty countries.

Suddenly a window appeared on the screen stating: I LIKE IT! WHY NOT COME OVER AND WE CAN DISCUSS THIS FURTHER. DEB.

'Shit!'

Jack realised that Alistair must have given her permission to invade his computer privacy. All in the name of teamwork, of course! But there was nothing he could do about it. To refuse to work with the woman would seem churlish. He had to play this one very carefully indeed. Jack sent back a message to the effect that he would join her shortly and, ten minutes later, he was in her room.

'Why don't we just communicate through the screen?' he suggested sarcastically as he entered.

Debra had obviously repaired her hair, make-up and self-esteem. She gave a flirty grin. 'Oh, that wouldn't be half as fun, would it? Technology is all very well, but sometimes you want to smell the sweat of honest toil, don't you find?'

'Remind me to change my deodorant.'

'Hallelujah, he has a sense of humour after all! Seriously though, Jack, you want to lighten up a little. After all, we are supposed to be in the entertainment business.'

How could he tell her that *she* was the pain in his ass? Jack gritted his teeth and pressed a couple of keys to bring up his game plan on Debra's screen. 'Here's one I prepared earlier . . .'

Jack did try to 'lighten up a little' but it was difficult when Debra insisted on putting her oar in at every turn. She wanted the number of lays reduced to eighteen for a start, which he promised to think about. In many ways it made sense, and kept the title near enough to the original quote to raise a smile. But they couldn't agree on which countries to leave in the list. Debra was of the opinion that one African and one South American country were enough whereas Jack, who had travelled quite widely in both continents, insisted that this would be unrepresentative.

'Tell you what,' she suggested, brightly. 'I'll make my

list and you make yours, then we'll see how much of an overlap we've got.'

She was doing her best, he had to give her that. But Jack felt increasingly uncomfortable as the afternoon wore on and she became more and more flirtatious. She seemed to be drunk on his nearness, laughing too much and too loud, wriggling on her seat, even removing her embroidered waistcoat when she became too hot and revealing a blouse in a thin fabric through which her large, red nipples clearly showed. Was she looking for a new lover, after being jilted by Alistair? The thought horrified him.

Soon after five, Jack glanced at his watch. 'I think it's time to call it a day,' he announced.

'I don't mind continuing for a bit. It seems a shame to stop the flow.'

'Best to stop while you're still fresh,' he frowned. 'Anyway, there's nothing to prevent you giving it more thought if you want to.'

Debra swivelled a little on her stool, looking up at him with wide, voracious eyes. 'I've enjoyed working this closely with you, Jack. It's a great idea and I think that, together, we can really make something of it.'

'Thank you,' he said, wryly. Jack had to admit it hadn't been quite as bad as he'd feared. In fact, some of her contributions had been helpful. If only she would stop all this intrusive flirtation.

'Of course, I won't be able to give your game absolute priority,' she went on, making music for his ears. 'I've still got the Mutual Reality work that I'm doing with

Alistair. But I think it's important for me to keep up to date on this project as well, so that when we've perfected the mutual technology the two can come together.'

She injected an innuendo into her last two words that made Jack raise his guard again. 'Of course,' he said, stiffly. 'Excuse me now, Debra, I must be going.'

'Er . . . I was wondering if we might continue our discussion informally, over a meal,' she suggested, laying a restraining hand on his arm. 'Then we could carry on brainstorming for a bit. There's that new Italian place over the road . . .'

Didn't the silly cow ever give up, Jake wondered, irritably. She was laying it on thick with body language too, showing a lot of dark-stockinged thigh beneath her hitched-up skirt, her nipples stiffening provocatively beneath the semi-transparent blouse.

'No, sorry,' Jack tried to sound decisive. 'I must get off home.'

'I see. Back to little wifey, is that it? You know your trouble, Jack? You won't take risks. Not at work or play. But you've got it in you to be more adventurous, I know you have. You're wasted at Global, Jack. Your talents deserve more recognition. At least I can recognise genius when I see it, even if others can't.'

Debra got to her feet, assailing him with her perfume and a seductive smile. For a few seconds Jack began to weaken. It would be so easy to transport her back to his house, to shag her senseless on the very bed where his wife had betrayed him. There was no denying that would give him enormous satisfaction.

Flashbacks of her rest-room scenario caught him off guard: Debra with her pink bum cheeks smarting under his hand; Debra's tight, wet little pussy inviting him in; Debra wriggling her bum against his groin as he plunged into her ... But then he thought of how it would be afterwards, having to work with her every day. No, whatever suicidal game the girl was playing she wasn't going to drag him down with her and that was that.

'Sorry, Debra, no chance. I've got to hurry now, or I'll miss my train.'

He left quickly, his loins still throbbing from the unwanted vision that had plagued him. On the Docklands train he tried to avoid looking at the Chinese girl, who kept staring at him with interested eyes and an inscrutable smile. He remembered Debra's words about him being wasted at Global. It was a thought that had occurred to him, but it was disturbing to hear it echoed by someone else, even someone as obviously on the make as Debra.

As he toiled through the side streets of Ealing, Jack was dreading the prospect of finding the house empty. He tried to persuade himself that Suzanne would be back, dinner in the oven as usual, tearful apologies followed by passionate love scene, burnt dinner – but what the hell, it was worth it! – followed by a take-away which they would eat in bed as a preliminary to further love-play. The warmth of his vision carried him through the cold streets, but when he approached his house and found it dark and uninviting his dread returned.

There was no message on the Ansaphone. Miserably,

Jack took a prepared meal out of the freezer and stuck it in the microwave but he had no appetite for it. Instead he raided the drinks cupboard. Now he was really scared, with a gut-churning fear. The once unthinkable idea of a life without Suzanne was becoming a hideous possibility. He tried not to dwell on it and turned on the TV, but the images danced before blind eyes and the words fell on deaf ears.

Just as the nine o'clock news reader was delivering the daily dose of fear and loathing, the phone rang. Jack leapt from his seat and grabbed the receiver, almost knocking the apparatus off the shelf in the process.

'Jack? It's Suzanne,' came his wife's matter-of-fact tone. 'No, please don't say anything, let me speak first. I'm afraid I won't be coming back to the house. At least, not to stay. Rupert has asked me to move in with him and I've agreed. Of course I'll need to collect my things, but I'd rather do that while you're out at work. Most of what I need can be transported by car. There's one or two bits of furniture I wouldn't mind having, but there's no urgency about that. Eventually, I'll want half the value of the house but I'm not forcing you to sell straight away . . .'

'Good of you!' Jack spat into the phone. He had never felt so angry in his life.

'I know you're feeling bad, but it won't last Jack, honestly. You'll come to realise that we couldn't go on like before. Our sex life was a farce and it's so important to me. When Rupert came into my life I realised just what I'd been missing . . .'

'Lying bitch! I gave it to you as good as he did!'

'You forced yourself on me, Jack. Rupert would never do that. He's kind and sensitive. And he lives in the real world, not some masturbatory fantasy . . .'

'Fuck you, Suzanne!'

'I'm sorry, Jack.' She hung up.

Jack paced the room, unable to find a suitable vent for his anger. He yanked open drawers and cupboards, but found nothing incriminating. The thought of his wife with that wimp made him want to puke. He wanted to beat seven shades of shit out of him, but he had no idea where the bastard lived. As for Suzanne, her duplicity confounded him. How long had she been deceiving him with that pumped-up toyboy? Their relationship could never last. Not like their marriage had. Jack tried to comfort himself with the thought that he had all that time on his side. All those cosy little routines and understandings they'd developed over their eight years of marriage couldn't be shrugged off in a single, impulsive gesture. No, she'd soon come to realise exactly what she'd lost and come begging him to take her back. When she grew tired of cucumber-cock and his pea brain.

Mentally Jack rehearsed the scenario. After all, he was good at that.

SUZANNE: I'm sorry, Jack. I've made a terrible mistake. Can you ever forgive me?

JACK: You've hurt me, Suzanne. More than I can ever say.

SUZANNE: I know, Jack, and I'm truly sorry. But I'm willing to make amends, if you'll

	only give me a second chance.
JACK:	Will you be my sex slave and do anything I say?
SUZANNE:	Oh yes, Jack. Anything!
JACK:	Strip and get down on all fours, then. You're going to lick my prick until I come in your mouth and you're going to love it, do you hear? And you're going to beg me every single night to let you do it again. Do you understand?
SUZANNE:	Yes, Jack. Of course I will.
JACK:	Okay, start now and do it exactly as I tell you. Give the shaft a good licking first, to get me well lubricated. Then put the glans in your mouth and roll your tongue around it. Now suck it gently – I said gently! Do it too hard and I'll give you a good spanking!

Jack had a stonker. He went up to the shower so he could have a hygienic wank. It was about as satisfying as sneezing. At last, after drinking most of a bottle of whisky, Jack collapsed on the bed in merciful oblivion.

Chapter Four

For a while Jack lived in daily expectation that Suzanne would return, but as time went on it seemed increasingly unlikely. She had crept in one day and removed most of her clothes and portable possessions, which Jack had found very depressing. Their wedding anniversary came and went without so much as an acknowledgement, and he was forced to the conclusion that she had meant what she said: their marriage was over.

Work turned out to be Jack's salvation over the next few weeks. Round the World was shaping up nicely. A merciful distraction, it occupied most of his waking thoughts. Debra proved to be not so much of a problem as he'd feared, since she was spending a lot of time working with Alistair on the technicalities. But she did have an annoying habit of breaking into his programming without warning, to offer hints of her own. Some of these were useful, so he told himself he shouldn't complain. And at least he didn't have to put up with her embarrassingly flirtatious presence more than once or twice a week.

Once Alistair had approved the game plan, Jack was

free to let his imagination roam through all the highways and byways of erotic experience. The player's sexual odyssey began in Soho, where he had the opportunity of taking part in a live sex show with Marilyn and Camilla, being disciplined by Miss Terry Martinet, or enjoying the buxom delights of Page Three Girl, Fiona Fulsome.

'Be careful to pace yourself,' Debra warned him. 'You've got a threesome, spanking and tit-wanking in London. You want to leave plenty of options for the other cities.'

'Don't worry,' Jack grinned. 'I've plenty more ideas where they came from.'

She laughed. 'I'm sure you have. I'm prepared to believe you have a most fertile imagination where sex is concerned.'

He ignored the subtext as usual, but it still annoyed him that Debra couldn't resist making those sly digs. It wasn't as if he really fancied her. But he had to be careful. Three weeks without a shag and he was in danger of screwing anything!

Instead, Jack relied wholly on his fantasy world for satisfaction. Writing out the scenarios was a real turn-on, even before they'd been virtualised. If the player, let loose in London's Soho, chose the sex show he was ushered into a sleazy club with a small stage, where he sat in the front row. The performance began with Marilyn's striptease and then Camilla came on, allowing Marilyn to undress her so they could indulge in some lesbian foreplay. After a few titillating minutes of mutual caressing Camilla would turn to the audience and say, 'But what we really need is a man to play with. Any volunteers?' Of course, the punter in the front row would be chosen and then he would enter into the action, enjoying an orgy of programmed sensuality with the two women.

Alternatively, if the player chose Miss Martinet he would be taken down into her cellar, where she had an impressive display of canes, birches, whips and straps. Dressed in leather, with fishnet tights, high-heeled shoes and lips red as blood, she had a voice like a fairground barker.

'You are a wicked boy, and must be punished!' she would inform him. 'Bend over my whipping stool, worm, and let me see if I can't beat the devil out of you!'

To show what a reformed character he was after his chastisement, the player would be invited to perform whatever duties the ferocious Martinet required to her complete satisfaction.

An altogether more cushy time was offered by Miss Fiona Fulsome, who boasted a forty-six inch chest. The player would be encouraged to bury his face in her fleshy mounds, to suck his fill on her large nipples and then, if he so desired, to allow his dick to be kneaded and pounded between her ample boobs until he shot his load. Then, after licking her tits clean of his juices, he would be invited to lower his head to a part of her anatomy where she could really appreciate his tongue-tickling expertise.

'We'll get these four characters up and running while you work on the scenarios,' Alistair had told him. Jack was happy to work overtime on the project. Home was a comfortless and empty place now, so he left it early and returned late. It was so often past midnight by the time he left the office that he wondered if he should keep a makeshift bed there.

Meanwhile, the test runs for Dorabella had begun. Although the volunteer testers were all given a questionnaire to complete at the end of their game their reactions were monitored electronically, since Global VR Games insisted on scientifically accurate results. Every slight increase of a pulse rate was recorded, every minute widening of a pupil, every small twitch of a penis as the testers interacted with Dorabella in her various guises and locations. When the first batch of results was run through the computer they confirmed what Jack had expected, that the most arousing – and therefore the most popular – scenarios were the more unusual ones. The testers loved the snowballing/log cabin scene, the scuba diving, the parachuting. Less popular were the penthouse and bathtub sequences.

'We should learn from this,' Alistair informed Jack and Debra at a de-briefing in his office. 'In a fantasy game, men want fantasy action. They don't want to repeat all the boring activities they can do in their own homes with their own wives and girlfriends.'

'That should have been obvious!' Debra scoffed.

'Nothing is certain until you have the data to prove it. Well, now we have. So I want the pair of you to make Round the World as whacky as possible. Do some brainstorming, see what you come up with.'

So Jack found himself in Debra's room, each of them

throwing out ideas which she typed onto the screen. 'Okay, what do we associate with Paris,' she began. 'The Moulin Rouge?'

'Too obvious. How about all that phallic French bread?'

She giggled, typing 'fucking a French loaf'. Then she suggested, 'Snails and frogs' legs?'

'Hm. The mind boggles. What about the Eiffel Tower? They sell candy versions as souvenirs . . .'

'And there's always the obelisk in the Place de la Concorde!'

'Okay, let's move on to Amsterdam. Canals? Windmills?'

'How about window shopping – in the red light district.'

'Again, obvious, but one can hardly make a trip to Amsterdam without going there. There's clogs, of course. And tulips. And Edam cheeses . . .'

The session was a success. By the end of the day they had several original ideas for scenarios, and Jack went so far as to thank Debra for her help.

That was a mistake. Immediately she sidled up to him, saying, 'How about taking me out for a meal then, to show your gratitude?'

'I'm sorry, Debra, I just can't.'

'Another night, maybe?'

He shook his head. 'Sorry, Debra.'

'I don't get you, Jack,' she pouted. 'Doesn't this stuff turn you on at all? Talking about sex, thinking about it all day long really gets me going. Don't you fancy me?'

Jack felt it was time for some straight talk. 'Look, Deb,

it's not a question of that. You're a very attractive girl. I simply don't want the complications, that's all.'

'Well, all I can say is your wife must be quite something! I don't know anyone married as long as you who doesn't play around.'

Jack gave a stoical smile and said nothing. It suited him to let Debra think he was still happily married. That way she might cross him off her wanted list, eventually. Her manner with Alistair was decidedly cool these days, and she was obviously looking for a replacement lover, but why him? Was the girl a nympho, or were there some devious office politics at work here? Either way, it made him decidedly uneasy.

When he returned home that night he was amazed to find a message from Suzanne on the Ansaphone. It was the first time she'd contacted him in over a month. Her voice sounded detached and distant.

'Hullo Jack, this is Suzanne. I mentioned that I'd like to pick up some furniture sometime. Would it be convenient if I turned up this Saturday afternoon? I don't want much, but I will take the desk that Aunt Mary left me. And the hall table and the pink velvet armchair. Oh, and the rug in the bedroom and the two paintings that are mine. You can leave a message on 081–667–3366. It's not Rupert's number, it's an answering service we use. 'Bye for now.'

Jack flicked back the switch and, stiff with rage, listened to the whole thing again. It was hard to believe that she could be so sickeningly civilised about it all. The bitch had cut him out of her life as efficiently as a surgeon excising a tumour, and left him to deal with the pain alone. She was enjoying rubbing it in, too, with that 'service *we* use' crap. Making sure he still couldn't find out where she was. Letting him know that she and Rupert were definitely 'an item'. He had a good mind to ignore her message altogether. Maybe he could change the lock on the front door, that would show her!

But then he had a better idea.

Saturday afternoon found Jack sitting in a state of heady elation beside a bottle of Scotch. He couldn't wait for his ex-wife to arrive, couldn't wait to see her face when she noticed the pile of firewood that had been Aunt Mary's bloody Queen Anne desk! He wouldn't have to say anything, just smile at her.

Around four the doorbell rang. At least Suzanne had the decency not to use her key and march in. For a split second Jack almost regretted what he'd done, but when he opened the front door and saw that she'd brought lover boy with her, his righteous anger returned.

'Hullo, Jack,' she smiled, uncertainly. 'We've hired a van, so it won't take long.'

He gave a smirk and led the way into the sitting room. All the things she wanted were in there: the two paintings resting on the seat of the pink chair, the rug rolled up on the hall table.

And the neatly bundled pile of wood. The four bandy legs were tied up separately. The top, with its elegant marquetry pattern, had been sawn into four sections. The drawers had each been pulled apart and split into thick sticks. The writing desk was a total write-off.

The sight of Suzanne's face when she first realised what he'd done was the most rewarding experience Jack had had since she left him. Her large eyes were blazing neon green and her mouth was contorted with rage.

'You bastard! How could you?'

'Funny, that's exactly how I feel about you, Suzanne!'

Rupert strode up to the wooden wreck, nostrils flaring. He looked – and spoke – like an actor in an old B-movie. 'Did he do this? This is your desk, isn't it, darling? That valuable antique desk your aunt left you?'

She nodded, too choked to speak.

Rupert started at Jack with controlled fury. 'This was Suzanne's property. We'll sue you for criminal damage.'

Jack shrugged, started to pour himself another whisky. But Suzanne knocked both glass and bottle out of his hand, sending yellow liquid flying everywhere. Her fist caught him on the point of his jaw and he staggered back.

'Leave him to me, babe,' he heard Rupert say. His arms were suddenly pinioned behind his back, while Suzanne spat in his face. 'Get something to tie him with, darling.'

She returned from the kitchen with a spare length of plastic washing-line. Rupert quickly tied Jack's hands together and pulled tight.

'Okay,' he grunted. 'He can't do much harm now.'

Suzanne was kneeling to examine the dismembered desk. She was crying. 'I can't see how it can possibly be restored,' she moaned.

'It might be possible, we'll take it to an expert. The important question right now is what are we going to do with this bloody vandal?' Jack squirmed in his bonds. He hadn't counted on Rupert being there too and a knot of fear was forming in the pit of his stomach.

'Smash up something of his,' Suzanne suggested. 'I know! There's his precious computer games. They're in the bedroom.'

Jack felt sick as he was frog-marched up the stairs. Suzanne knew exactly how important his collection of early computer games was to him. They dated from the period of the very first home computers, when you needed a cassette recorder to play them. Stored in boxes decorated with lurid sci-fi pictures, they were early examples of computer art and now worth a small fortune. He kept them in a case in the wardrobe.

As soon as they entered the bedroom Jack was reminded of the last sex scene that he'd played with his wife, and his sense of betrayal returned.

'This is all your bloody doing!' he snarled at her, as Rupert threw him onto the duvet and proceeded to tie his wrists to the brass posts of the bedhead and his ankles to the footposts.

Suzanne soon found the case. She turned it upside down and all the small boxes spilled out. Picking up a tape (*Bardic Lore* – one of his favourite adventure games) she let it unravel before Jack's horrified eyes.

'What shall we do with these?'

Rupert grinned. 'Make a bonfire? Decorate the house? No, I know!' His eyes glittered with devilish light. 'Let's wrap him up in them. Like a mummy!'

Jack groaned. 'No, for God's sake Suzanne!'

But she tossed the end of the brown magnetic tape to Rupert, gleefully. 'Great idea!'

They set to work with perverse efficiency. Starting at his feet and working up, they bound Jack tightly in the stretchy tape. Every time they opened a new box he sobbed at the demise of another old and valued friend. It wasn't the money he cared about. It was all the pioneering work that those primitive games represented, work that he was proud to be carrying on today. Those tapes symbolised the start of a new technology, and to those who cared about human progress they were worth far more than their auction price.

Still the iconoclasm went on. Now his legs were entirely encased in shiny brown bands. Jack felt hot and itchy, wanted to scratch. This was going to be hell on more than one level. Suzanne was binding his crotch now, going round and under his thighs, giggling as she had her revenge. Soon he was encased up to his waist and there were still more cassettes to go. Rupert bound his arms while Suzanne did his chest. Occasionally one of the thin bands snapped, but there were always plenty more.

'What about his head?' Suzanne asked, at last.

'I think it would be good to cover it, don't you?' Rupert grinned. 'I suppose we'd better leave a few airholes, though.'

When they had finished Jack felt utterly weird, as if his whole body were turned into some alien substance. He felt constricted all over, hot and plasticised, and the holes they'd left for his nose and mouth were only just adequate so that he had to breathe in gasping pants. He could still see them, though, gloating over their victory.

'I wish I'd thought of this before,' Suzanne quipped. 'I might even have been able to bear being married to him if he'd been parcelled up like a mummy.'

'No sex, though. You'd have had to take a lover.'

Suzanne giggled. 'You'd have been my lover, wouldn't you, Rupert? We could have made love whenever we felt like it, not just in the afternoons.'

'I feel like it now. How about you?'

'What do you think!'

Jack writhed in torment at the thought of having to watch them once again, yet there was nothing he could do about it. Helplessly he stared through the mask of tape, fascinated and repelled at once. First he saw Suzanne draw her top over her head with casual ease, revealing her full, naked breasts. At once Rupert took them in his hands, fondling the white globes while he nibbled gently at her burgeoning nipples.

'Mm, you have such beautiful breasts!' he murmured. 'I could kiss and caress them for hours and hours!'

'Last night I came when you were kissing them,' she smiled. 'You didn't have to do anything more. Just your licking and sucking them like that turns me on a treat!'

Jack was well aware of the implied reproof in his wife's words. She'd always said he didn't pay enough attention to her boobs. Now Rupert was unzipping her jeans and pulling them down over her slim thighs. She had red silk panties on, trimmed with black lace. They were probably new, bought specially for Rupert. Or had he given them to her? Jack's breath came out in a harsh sigh. The pressure on his chest was becoming unbearable.

'Oh, I can smell your musky quim, darling!' Rupert exclaimed, kneeling at her feet. Jack was forced to watch him part her dark minge and kiss the pink lips within.

'That's so good!' she murmured. 'But get undressed yourself, sweetheart, so I can feel your gorgeous prick at the same time!'

Jack felt an unwanted stirring in the area of his groin. It felt horribly ticklish. He was getting all hot and sweaty down there, too. Then, when Rupert's great prong sprang out of his pants, it was like being kicked in the balls.

'Let me taste your beautiful penis,' Suzanne enthused. Positioning herself so that Jack couldn't help but see, she softly enclosed the bulbous end of her lover's member in her pouting mouth. She appeared to be enjoying every second of it as she slid her lips slowly up and down the glans to the ridge where the shaft began.

'You're so good at giving head, Su,' Rupert sighed.

'That's because your penis is so clean and beautiful. I hated sucking Jack off because his spunk tasted foul, but your cream is sweet and delicious. I can't get enough of it. Shall I milk you now?'

'Only if you let me lick your clitty afterwards!'

'It's a deal!'

She knelt before him, taking more of the swollen cock into her mouth and moaning with pleasure. Jack couldn't believe it: beneath the packaging, he was getting a hard-on! The tight constriction of his genitalia, painful though it was, wasn't enough to prevent his arousal.

Suzanne was tossing her dark head back and forth now,

relishing the smooth movement of the meaty prick in and out of her mouth. Every so often she would stop to run her tongue appreciatively round the groove below the helmet. Her fingers were playing with his dangling balls while he did similar service to her jutting tits, softly caressing her taut flesh and twiddling the pert nipples. Jack felt his cock grow, pressing urgently against the tight bonds, and he groaned aloud. Suzanne looked round for a moment, giving a triumphant smile.

It was obvious that Jack's wife had learnt a lot about fellatio since being with her new lover. She was putting on a virtuoso performance and that blond beast was loving every second of it. He was swaying on his feet now, groans of sensual pleasure emerging from his lips as she took his obscenely enlarged member well into her mouth. Jack watched in envy as Rupert began slowly moving his hips, fucking Suzanne in the mouth. His own tackle was straining to enjoy similar pleasures, but there was no chance. Instead, Jack's torment grew, the tight constraint making the bulge in his groin ever more uncomfortable.

At last Rupert came, with a violent shuddering and weakening of his knees that made his whole body sag. 'God, that was fantastic!' he breathed, as Suzanne swallowed hard then rose into his embrace. He pulled up the brocade-covered armchair and sat her on it, sinking onto the carpet in front. 'Just give me a minute to recover,' he grinned. 'Then it's your turn.'

'Mm, I can't wait!' Suzanne smiled.

She hooked her knees over the arms of the chair,

exposing her cunt to full view. Jack groaned. He remembered just how snug that wet pussy had felt last time they'd made love, and he was aching to plunge in there ag. n. Instead, he must endure the torture of seeing that smug bastard take his place. He stared forlornly at the gaping pink flesh beneath the darkly curled hair, feeling his tool rear in desperation against its confining bands.

Rupert got to his knees and lovingly parted Suzanne's labia, giving Jack a good view of her already engorged clitoris. His tongue tried a few experimental licks and, uttering a deep sigh of contentment, she shifted her bum to allow him easier access. Rupert continued to suck and lick her with enthusiasm while his roving hands played with her heavy breasts and round belly, increasing her arousal to fever pitch. She was moaning loudly now, her hips undulating in rhythm with his touch as the fingers of one hand tenderly probed her inner lips. Jack watched her wriggle excitedly as the questing fingers disappeared into her eager cunt and heard her cry, 'Oh, yes!' His balls felt on the point of bursting, and his dick was stewing in its own juice, held in cruel suspension on the verge of orgasm. The longed-for release wouldn't come, not even when Suzanne arched her back and made the fierce noises that signalled the approach of her own climax, which had usually triggered him in the past. Rupert's mouth went down to suck her steaming sex and drink her abundant juice, but still Jack was locked in his private hell, unable to ease his own painful frustration.

Now he had more than just his genitals to think about. The prolonged immobility of his arms and legs, stretched to their limit, was wracking his muscles in sheer torture. He was unable to stand it any more.

'Okay, you've made your point, you two!' he snarled, the words forced out from the small airhole they'd left round his mouth. 'Now untie me, for God's sake! I'm hurting all over.'

Suzanne stared at him with bleary eyes, still in the warm throes of her afterglow. 'You ruined my valuable desk. Now you must suffer.'

'Bitch!'

Rupert turned round with a superior smile. 'Anyway, we've not finished yet. You might think that a ten-minute screw is good enough for your wife, but I know otherwise. Sometimes we make love literally all night, don't we, darling?'

'We certainly do,' she sighed, contentedly. 'And when you're ready, lover, I want you to fill my hole with your wonderful big penis. You know, those people who say size doesn't matter are fools. Of course it matters. No woman who has experienced a well-plugged cunt would want to bother with half-measures again.'

Rupert rose to his feet, and Jack saw that his huge pole was sticking up in readiness once again. They changed places, Rupert sitting in the chair while Suzanne prepared to lower herself onto his rearing member. She did this with slow relish, supporting herself with the arms of the chair, until the length was fully inside her and she relaxed with a sigh.

'This is wonderful, darling!' she murmured as his lips sought one nipple and his fingers the other. 'Make me come again, Rupert. I love it when you're inside me, filling me completely.'

Jack felt himself twitch in sympathy as Suzanne raised and lowered herself over Rupert's tumid member. His balls ached, crammed to bursting with unshed sperm. He could see his wife clenching her bum cheeks, squeezing her internal muscles to heighten the sensations for her lover and herself. His desire was utterly tormenting him, keeping him in a state of suspended tumescence that he had no way of escaping from. If only he could spill his seed and ease the tension, but the bandage-like restriction made it impossible. It might help if he closed his eyes. He tried for a few seconds, but the squelching sounds of fucking and sucking made it impossible to blot out the scene altogether and, in some ways, what he was imagining was worse. Besides, he was filled with insatiable curiosity.

They were going at it like the clappers now, Suzanne clinging to the back of the chair as she slammed her hips in and out. She was gasping like a steam train and, in a few seconds, her second climax had her making deep-throated noises accompanied by Rupert's ecstatic groans. When their mutual orgasm subsided, the pair of them tumbled out of the chair onto the thick-pile carpet where they lay in each others' arms, apparently oblivious of their unwilling voyeur.

'God, that was the best ever!' Jack heard his wife say as she covered Rupert's face with kisses. 'I love you, darling. And this time, it's going to be forever.'

'I love you too,' Rupert murmured, raising himself on one elbow.

It was all too much for Jack, his pecker still rampant beneath the swaddling tape. Angrily he called out, 'Fuck the pair of you! Aren't you going to set me free?'

Rupert clambered to his feet, an amused smile on his face. 'Oh yes, I nearly forgot. What are we going to do with your pig of a husband, Suzanne?'

She came towards the bedhead then pulled a tissue from the box on the bedside table, wiping herself between her thighs. 'Did you enjoy that little show?' she sneered. 'Better than your stupid fake games, wasn't it? More convincing.'

'Too bloody convincing!'

She laughed. 'I do believe you're jealous! Well, you've every right to be. You see, Rupert and I are in love and we plan to stay together. We might even marry, as soon as I get a divorce. Which I will, of course, just as soon as the law allows.'

'As if I care what you do now!'

Rupert came to put an arm round her shoulder. 'Shall I release him?'

She gave a casual nod. 'Okay.'

Soon Jack was freed from his tethering to the bed, although still mummified. 'Now get me out of this crap!' he snarled.

Rupert gave Suzanne a quizzical smile. 'Shall we?'

She shook her head as she pulled on her jeans. 'I think not. The bugger's arms and legs are free, let him fight his own way out. We ought to be going.'

They left swiftly and, as Jack was wondering how the hell he was going to escape his bonds, he heard them carry the furniture out to the van. Then the front door slammed and he knew he was alone in the house. He managed to roll off the bed and lever himself to his feet, but his fingers, encased in tight brown mittens, seemed unusable. Somehow he had to get the tape off, but he didn't know where to begin.

The kitchen seemed as likely a place as any, so Jack stumbled his way downstairs. His cock was still stiff and rubbed against the tight binding as he walked, reducing his movements to a hobble. He felt near to bursting: did he need a leak? No way of knowing, with that stuff taping down his parts into a hot and clammy hell, like wearing too-small plastic pants over a too-tight nappy. The sooner he got out of that damn mess the better!

If only he could get his hands free, he could undo the rest. Jack cast desperate eyes round the kitchen. It was no good trying to use a sharp knife or he'd risk doing himself an injury. Then his eye lighted on the wall can opener, fixed at the end of a unit. He hobbled over and tried to catch some of the tape in it. After several goes he succeeded in snagging it a little, so he slashed away and soon had enough of a loose end to take it between his teeth and tug. The shiny stuff began to unravel, and soon there was a long streamer dangling to the floor. Sighing with relief, Jack freed his fingers and was then able to take a knife to his other hand. He was soon unwinding the tape at top speed, leaving great festoons everywhere. His head was freed, then his chest and arms, then his waist and hips, and then – oh joy! – he was able to unzip his trousers and pull his erect penis out of his pants.

Almost as soon as he touched the rigid shaft a hot fountain shot right across the kitchen, spraying the front of a cupboard. The relief, after such prolonged tension, was incredible and gave him such a buzz that he trembled from head to foot and had to sink to the floor. After a while he unbound his legs and feet, then gathered the debris into a bin bag and shoved it outside the back door. Every fibre in his body was tingling as the blood rushed back into the small capillaries, and his head felt as if it were splitting in two. Thank God it was Saturday and he had a day to recover! He didn't want to think about the wreckage of his precious computer games. Still less did he want to contemplate the wreckage of his marriage. Eventually, taking the whisky bottle to bed with him, he decided that the best thing he could do was to drink himself into a state of unconsciousness.

Chapter Five

Jack decided it was time to explore the fleshpots of Amsterdam. It was the third scenario to be up and running, and the first two – London and Paris – had been very successful. It was amazing what you could find to do with French loaves besides eating them. Like male sex organs they came in many sizes but always the same basic shape. Jack felt he could never again look a woman in the eye if she was carrying one in her shopping basket.

After putting on the elaborate gear needed for the Mutual Reality game Jack pressed the starter button. At once he was transported into a cobbled alley lined with gabled houses, most of which had their large ground floor windows lit up. As he strolled along he could see the ladies of the night displaying themselves in various outrageous ways, each trying to outdo their neighbour in order to attract more custom.

There was a petite blonde wearing nothing but a cut-off T-shirt bearing the name *Dolly*. The garment just skimmed the bottom of her enormous knockers making it obvious what her greatest asset was. She even had a recording rigged up, to whisper softly at the passing trade and whet their appetites. 'Come and feast your eyes on my beautiful big boobs,' Jack was urged. 'Feel them, taste them and then, if you so desire, let them satisfy you completely.'

As he moved on, he heard her change her tune. 'Or, if you prefer, I could be the Dutch au pair, come to look after you and give you a nice bath . . .'

The next window showed a stern-faced, leather-clad Madame with two of her lovely young whores beside her. She, too, had a sound system but this time it was two-way. 'Hey, you!' she called, as Jack came into view.

'Who, me?' he grinned.

'Yes. You want to try out my gorgeous girls?'

'Maybe.'

'Well, I like to look after my girls, so you can only play with them if I'm there too. And if I don't like what you're doing, I'll give you a good thrashing. Understand?'

'I understand completely.'

But Jack had to walk the length of the alley to make sure that all the options he'd programmed were available. Next door he found an Indonesian girl, who offered to be his sex slave. She sat, demure and submissive, with her eyes lowered and her small perfectly formed body half exposed beneath a pink negligée. After her was a black transvestite and then the one Jack was most interested in, the Neo-Hippy. She sat on a colourful cushion smoking dope, her embroidered waistcoat hanging open to reveal her cleavage, the dark shadow of her pubic hair visible at the crotch of her semi-transparent Indian loon pants.

Jack had put a lot of work into her. He hurried down to the end of the alley just to make sure the canal was where it should be, then he returned to Fantasia's door. Once inside, the smell of patchouli incense assailed his nostrils, taking him straight back to the free festivals of his youth.

Fantasia approached him, her brown eyes unfocused and sensual, and he could smell her sultry perfume. She handed him the spliff. He took a drag and felt the familiar mellow fuzziness fill his head. Once again it occurred to him that Alistair was a genius.

'Hi!' she smiled, lazily. 'So glad you chose to share sex with me. Shall we go next door?'

She led the way into a dark den lit only by a few candles. There was dreamy music and the sound of trickling water. The walls were swathed in curtains and the whole floor was covered with cushions. 'Take off your shoes,' she whispered, at the entrance. 'You are about to enter the Temple of Love.'

Jack felt the softness of the cushions beneath his toes as he crossed the room to where a small feast was laid out. 'I am a practitioner of the Tantric Art,' she told him. 'We cultivate the full celebration of the senses, for we believe that it is only in fully satisfying the body that we can become one with God.'

She took off her waistcoat, revealing smallish breasts that were high, round and firm. 'As you take off your garments, imagine that you are stripping yourself of all inhibitions and restrictions, freeing your spirit to explore the world of the senses to the utmost.'

Jack tried to follow her advice while he had the

impression of undressing. He was soon feasting his eyes on the girl's trim lower quarters as she slipped out of her baggy trousers. He could feel his penis rearing at the sight of Fantasia's dark triangle, nestling beneath a smooth stomach and between slim thighs.

'I see you are ready and eager,' she smiled. 'But we believe in savouring every moment. We must not be impatient for the delights to come, but prefer to enjoy the present experience to the full. Come, join me in tasting some of these delicious *sattvic* foods I have prepared.'

There was yoghurt sweetened with honey, syrupy dried fruits and plump nuts, washed down with a delicious white wine. As Jack drank and nibbled he could taste each flavour, perfectly reproduced. A warm fire was burning and its flame seemed to be entering his body, filling his veins with primal energy. He took another toke and entered further into the dream world that Fantasia seemed to be constructing for him, forgetting completely that he was the author of it all.

'Lie down,' she murmured. 'Let me give you a soothing Thai massage.'

She took a bowl of warmed oil and anointed her body with it. Jack longed to feel those slick curves himself, but soon she was lying on top of him, transferring some of the scented oil to his own skin. It was pleasant to feel no resistance between their two bodies as she gently wriggled against him. Her thighs, stomach and chest were all involved in her circular motions, caressing him with subtle force. Her feet caressed his calves, her elbows

stroked his sides, while her forehead and chin worked on
his facial muscles, stimulating every part of him with her
hard and soft flesh. When he tried to grasp her buttocks
she restrained him saying, 'Not yet. Just lie still and let
me do all the work.'

Looking up, Jack saw that there was a strategically
placed mirror on the ceiling, and his delight was increased
by the sight of her plump bum cheeks wiggling away.
Even though it was a case of 'look, don't touch' he could
still imagine how they would feel cushioned up against
his stomach as he took her from behind.

Fantasia turned him over and applied the same treatment to the back of his body which, if anything, was even
more erotic. He could feel her breasts rubbing against
his shoulder blades, and her pubic hair brushing his crack,
as she wriggled and rolled all over him. Then he became
aware of her kissing various parts of him, all the way up
from his toes to the top of his head.

'What are you doing?' he whispered.

'We call it "closing the gates of the city". It gives
psychic protection and makes sure there's no leak of
sexual energy.'

Jack frowned. He couldn't remember putting that bit
in. Still, it was all very pleasant.

She turned him over again and they embraced kneeling
face to face. Jack felt almost disembodied, he was so
floaty and relaxed. They kissed deeply, and he took her
breasts in his hands and gently squeezed, feeling the
nipples harden as he did so. 'Suck my berries,' she smiled.
'Their milky essence is sweet and nurturing.'

Jack took one of the pink nipples in his mouth while he cupped her breasts. Fantasia put her legs around his waist and crossed her ankles behind his back, so her already damp vulva was pressed against his stomach. She moved her hips slowly, rubbing her sex against him, and his tool brushed her buttocks which he found most arousing. 'Oh-um!' she moaned as her spreading lips exposed her clitoris to the friction.

Soon she turned around so they could get into the sixty-nine position with her on top. 'Part my pleasure lips so you can lick my golden bud,' she urged him. 'And then, when you wish to drink deeper of my honey, put your tongue inside my purple chamber and lap it up like a cat tasting cream.'

Jack willingly complied, while his own jade sceptre was given a most expert blow-job. She used her tongue and lips to create infinite variety, now with butterfly-light kisses on his glans, now with strong sucking on his shaft, now with delicate licking of his frenum. She seemed to sense when he was becoming too aroused for comfort, and always managed to delay his climax without deflating him.

When they were both ready for the moment of penetration they remained seated on the cushions at first, with Fantasia raising her knees to her chest and crossing her legs behind his back, to ensure a snug fit. While Jack plunged slowly into her ripe juiciness she was humming softly. She continued to hum while they proceeded to swing back and forth in a gentle rhythm which Jack felt he could keep up indefinitely. In a while, though, she lay back and placed her legs on his shoulders, allowing him to plunge into her more deeply. He could feel her drawing his penis up towards her womb, as if to absorb him and, at first, he resisted. But once he had let go and allowed himself to nudge her cervix he felt as if he were swimming in a warm bath of bliss. His body seemed to have no boundaries as the effortless stimulation continued.

'Ah – hum!' she moaned, seeming to open up to him like a flower. He felt her yoni softly undulate and knew she was having an orgasm, but it was slow and languid, caressing both shaft and glans in one long gentle squeeze.

Fantasia put her legs down and they lay side by side for a while, not moving or speaking, just letting the warm energy flood their being along with the soft music and sweet scents. Then they kissed and her mouth tasted fruity. She raised herself up to kneel on his thighs, still maintaining contact at the groin. Jack lay back, happy to let her do the work, and she drew her cunt up until she was just holding onto his glans with her swollen vulva. The sensations were exquisite as she used her lower lips on him like a bee sucking honey, letting the head of his penis stimulate her bud. Jack found he had lost the urge to plunge into her and was content to stay in that dreamlike state of arousal without wishing to increase it.

He gave himself up entirely to her, spreading his arms and legs wide and feeling the delicious warmth feed his extremities. Then he became aware of something extraordinary. His big toes and his fingertips had begun to tingle, and he was sure he could feel something warm and wet making contact with them. He opened his eyes and saw, to his utter amazement, that he was making love not to one woman, but to five! They were identical to Fantasia and he was pleasuring them all, either by inserting his toe into their well-lubricated quims and wiggling it to their obvious satisfaction, or by fingering their pussies until their clits were bulging and their thighs were wet with juices.

Suddenly all five women climaxed at the same time, sending electric shock waves throughout his body and pushing him over the edge into pulsating oblivion. It was an orgasmic orgy such as he had never before experienced, but it was also unreal, like a wet dream. His own sexual energy seemed to have spawned the women then sustained them for just as long as his arousal lasted. They began to fade away as the throes of his climax waned. Then, when the last tremors had died away, there was only Fantasia left, offering him a drink of wine with a smile.

'You have just experienced the Sacred Union of the Five Senses,' she informed him. 'That's worth a thousand dollars of anyone's money but, because I like you, I'll settle for five hundred.'

He laughed and, looking down, saw himself taking a traveller's cheque out of his wallet. 'That'll do nicely, sir,' she smiled. 'And would you like to rub my tits, as well?'

I don't recall putting that quip in, Jack frowned. His virtual persona got dressed and left the Hippy Haven. He could have gone on to more adventures but he'd had enough for one day. The Amsterdam encounter had worked superbly, far better than he'd hoped, and he was anxious to write a report on it for Alistair.

Unplugging the headset, Jack slithered out of the harness and removed the disposable lining to his pouch. He'd certainly filled the bag that time! Probably because he'd not had a wank for a few days. He walked over to the screen and saw a message from Debra that stopped him in his tracks: I ENJOYED MY AMSTERDAM TRIP ENORMOUSLY. HOW WAS IT FOR YOU?

'Sod the woman!' Jack exploded. Alistair must have let her link up for the game itself, as well as at the planning stage. She might have told him!

The door buzzed and Jack knew it was her. He was tempted to put off the encounter but he knew he'd have to face her eventually so he let her come in. She had the smuggest of smiles on her face, and there was still a hint of a flush in her cheeks. God, had she really shared all of what he'd just been through?

'It works a treat, doesn't it?' she stated simply, flopping into the spare chair. 'Sorry I couldn't let you know I was in on it, but Alistair wanted it to be a kind of blind test of Mutuality mode. We've got to compare notes now.'

'What?' The last thing he wanted was to go through it all again with Debra slavering over every quivering moment. But on second thoughts he realised it would be scientifically useful.

'We'll put in a joint report,' she suggested. 'Head it *Amsterdam Scenario – Evaluation.*'

'Okay.' Resignedly, Jack swivelled on his chair and typed the heading. 'Tell me what you remember first.'

'I saw you coming down the alley . . .'

'Did you, indeed?'

'You paused in front of the Dolly bird, then passed the dominatrix, the Indonesian submissive and the black transvestite. You gave Fantasia the once-over, walked to the end of the alley then returned.'

'Hundred per cent, so far.'

'Right. You came into the Hippy house and took your shoes off at the door. Then . . . No, wrong order. You took a toke of her joint first, *then* you took your shoes off and undressed. By then you had quite a hard-on.'

'Correct,' Jack said coolly, hoping to hide his embarrassment.

Debra went on to detail all the preliminaries, but when it came to the actual sex she played the mean trick of getting him to describe the proceedings. At first he protested, but she said, 'I've done all the work so far. Now it's your turn. We have to make sure we both recollect equally.'

Jack tried to sound as impartial and scientific as possible as he ran through all the variations of the sexual act that he remembered performing in simulation. When he mentioned the procedure described as 'closing the gates of the city,' Debra giggled.

'Did you like that?' I added it to the program myself. I read about it in some Tantric manual.'

'I see.' Jack knew it was irrational to be angry with her. Alistair had already made it clear that he should welcome her input. Yet he disliked the sneaky way she'd gone about it.

'The Secret Dalliance was my idea too,' she smiled,

going on to explain. 'Where you made love to five women at once. It was kind of my present to you. I hope you liked it. Judging by the reading on your orgone monitor, you certainly did!'

Jack felt a humiliating flush colour his cheeks, verging on anger. Was there to be no end to this woman's attempts to seduce him? She had evidently decided that if she couldn't have real-life sex with him she would have the simulated version as often, and in as much variety, as she could.

'You look quite put out, Jack,' she told him, teasingly. With her legs crossed and her skirt hitched halfway up her thighs she was giving him a heavy come-on. 'But you don't have to worry, your secret is safe with me. I don't even have to tell Alistair about that last part if you don't want me to.'

It was tempting to beg her to keep quiet, yet Jack knew he would then be in Debra's debt. And it was a debt she would have no hesitation in calling in when it suited her.

He shrugged. 'Tell him what you like.'

'I'll tell him you enjoyed our little orgy then, shall I?'

She was being deliberately provocative now. Jack snapped, 'Look, can we get this de-briefing over with? I want to get on.'

'All right. But you have to admit, we make a brilliant team! Sometimes I think working for Global is putting the brakes on you, Jack. Think what you could do if you had total creative freedom, without those American bozos calling the shots!'

She had touched a raw nerve. Jack had often thought

the same, but he wasn't going to admit it to Debra.

'I like working here,' he replied lamely.

'Ever been head-hunted, Jack?' He shook his head. Debra gave him a long, thoughtful look. Then she returned to the job in hand. 'So what was it like, having sex with five women at once?'

'Different.'

'How different?'

'Sort of . . . like being plugged into the mains.'

She threw back her head to laugh, exposing her white throat. Jack decided he would write a Dracula scenario sometime, so he could go for her jugular.

'Oh, that's great! I like that!'

'And how was it for you, *darling*?' he sneered.

'Sublime. I felt eaten up, consumed by your great thrusting penis . . .'

'Not *my* penis, exactly,' he reminded her.

'It felt like yours to me. I was thinking of you all the time you see, Jack. Only of you.' She rose from her chair and moved over to him, making his pulse beat a warning tattoo. 'Now I've no way of knowing how your prick would really feel inside me, but the power of the imagination is amazing, don't you find? The very idea of you screwing me was such a turn-on that I had this multiple orgasm. It went on and one, Jack, taking me higher and higher. I've never known anything like it.'

'Hurray for the Feelietron,' he said, uneasily, shifting his chair back a fraction.

She put out her hand and touched his cheek. Her crotch was level with his eyes and he could see the bulge of her mons beneath the thin dress material. He swallowed hard. 'Look, Debra, I really think . . .'

'And I really think we should get together, Jack.' She dropped down on her haunches. 'I don't think I've ever wanted anyone as much as I want you.'

Before he could stop her she had taken his face in her hands and was kissing him with hungry passion, forcing her tongue between his lips and moaning as if in pain. Jack pushed her away forcefully and she fell back onto her bum. 'For God's sake, Debra!'

She stared at him wildly, still lost in her dream. 'Jack, it was so beautiful, what we had together . . .'

For the first time he questioned her sanity. 'It wasn't us!' he snapped. 'It was a simulation, okay? It might have seemed real, but it was all happening through the computer and the Feelietron. It was nothing to do with us as people, okay?'

She shook her head. 'I fantasise about you when I'm masturbating, but it was nothing like that. That was real. Why can't you acknowledge it?'

'Look, Deb, you'd better get your head sorted on this or you'll end up with serious problems.'

'It's you who has the problem, Jack. Why don't you admit you want me? We could make love right here and now.'

To his horror she began to strip off her dress. 'No, don't! Debra!'

But she was offering him her small naked tits, cupping her hands beneath the stiffening nipples, smiling at him in a disturbingly erotic way that played on his nerves.

'We've made love in fantasy so many times. Why not in reality? You've got me so wet, Jack. I'm halfway there already. Just kiss my tits and I'll suck you off. It'll be even better than before . . .'

'No!' Jack got up and began to stride for the door, but she clung to his ankles.

'Don't go! It's only sex, Jack. The same as we do through the Feelietron only more real . . .'

Now Jack knew she'd really flipped. He didn't know how to handle it, but eventually managed to kick her off and flee through the door, his instinct driving him towards the men's cloakroom. There he sat in fearful contemplation for several minutes, wondering what the hell to do next. Surely Alistair ought to know, but he was on tricky ground there if they'd been lovers. And he was ninety-nine per cent sure they had. What to make of that bitch's psychology was another question, and one which he couldn't begin to answer. To be honest, he didn't care. All he cared about right then was saving his own skin.

Perhaps it would be best to keep a low profile for the rest of the day until the whole thing blew over. Cautiously he opened the door of the men's room. The corridor was empty, so he headed for the lift. If anyone challenged him he could say he was suffering from AILS (Artificial Insulation from Light Sickness – the latest fashionable condition amongst office workers) and needed his fix of daylight. Only when he emerged into the stench and bustle of the street outside could he breathe easy.

After wandering round for a while, unable to make up his mind whether to tell Alistair or act as if nothing had happened, Jack returned to the office. It seemed unnaturally quiet. He went into his room and found it empty so he resumed his work at the computer, resolving to put the Debra episode out of his mind. Hopefully she had finally got the message that he wasn't interested and would trouble him no further.

A smile spread over Jack's face as he remembered the success of his scenario. Amsterdam – or, more specifically, Fantasia – would he a hard act to follow. He must move on to Venice now, where he had some original ideas about what a gondolier might do with his pole . . .

Around four, a message from Alistair came up on his screen: PLEASE SEE ME BEFORE YOU LEAVE TODAY. Jack felt uneasy. Perhaps it would be best to get this interview over with straight away. He saved his work and went down the corridor to Alistair's office.

'Ah, Jack. Good of you to see me so promptly. Take a seat.' He sounded friendly enough. Jack relaxed. 'How's it going?'

'The Amsterdam sequence is superb. You did a brilliant job on Fantasia.'

'Good. I must find time to try it myself. And how are things going generally – at home, for instance?'

Jack frowned. Alistair didn't normally concern himself with his employees' personal lives. But perhaps it would do him good to get it off his chest.

He cleared his throat. 'My wife's left me, actually.'

Alistair's dark eyes widened. 'Really? I'm sorry to hear that. But not entirely surprised. I guessed you must have been under a strain of some sort.'

Jack felt a touch of panic. 'Why? Is my work not up to scratch?'

'On the contrary, your work has been excellent.' Alistair got up abruptly and walked to the window. He had his back to Jack as he asked, 'How have you been getting on with Debra?'

So it was about that incident, after all. Debra must have said something. And it was not likely to have been the truth. Aware that he could be in a sticky position, Jack said cautiously, 'To be honest, things have been a little difficult.'

'Oh?' Alistair turned, his leonine head silhouetted against the Docklands skyline. 'How do you mean, exactly?'

'She . . .' Jack looked away from those solemn eyes. 'She seems to fancy me. I can't imagine why. It's been going on a while, but this afternoon . . .'

'Yes?'

'She came on a bit strong.'

'I see.'

'Has she . . . did she say anything to you?'

Alistair put his thumbs in his trouser pockets. 'I'm afraid so. To put it bluntly, Jack, she's accused you of sexual harassment.'

'*What?*'

'Naturally I had to take it seriously, although it puts me in a very awkward position. I didn't want this going into the public domain, but Debra and I have just ended a two-year relationship. I suspect you've been caught in the flak.'

Jack couldn't have invented a more nightmarish scenario for himself. He just sat and gaped.

Alistair went on, smoothly, 'Now, I make no judgement about what might have happened between you two. I know how easily one can become confused in our business. I gather you'd just emerged from the Feelietron. Debra comes into your room, you're still in fantasy world, you make a pass at her. All perfectly understandable.'

'No! It wasn't like that. She was the one who made a pass at me!'

Alistair raised his brows a fraction. 'Look, Jack, you're making this very difficult for me – and for yourself. I'm trying to be objective about this, and I don't want to make any more of it than is strictly necessary, but we are governed by the law here and the law takes a dim view of such goings-on.'

'She wants to *sue* me?'

'I don't think so. At the moment she's shocked and upset, so I told her to take a taxi home. If you're prepared to offer her an apology...'

Jack leapt from his chair. '*Apologise?* When she's in the wrong?'

Alistair tried a different tack. 'It's possible that she misinterpreted your behaviour, Jack. But we have to be so careful in this business. We're dealing with risqué material all day long. If we turned the working day into a sexual free-for-all none of us would get any work done and our firm's reputation would suffer.'

'But I didn't do anything, honestly! Look, I admit I'd just come out of the Feelietron, but when she came in I was back to normal. I was about to start work at the computer. But she told me she'd been through the Amsterdam scenario at the same time as me, and said we should compare notes. Then she started going on, as she often had before, about how much she fancied me and stuff. And then she kissed me, and started taking her clothes off.'

'She says that you forcibly kissed *her*, and started ripping her clothes off.'

'Well, I'm sorry, Alistair, but she's lying. And I'd swear it in any court of law.' Jack's tone grew desperate. 'But I suppose it's just my word against hers.'

'Unfortunately, that's the way it looks. Like I said, this is all extremely awkward for me. But I'm pretty sure that if you'd just apologise we could let the whole thing blow over. You know the sort of thing, "Don't know what came over me . . . terribly sorry . . . won't happen again." There's no real harm done, after all.'

Jack fell silent, appalled at the prospect of crawling to that dreadful woman. Yet he could see how bad it looked for him. If only he had proof of some kind that she'd been harassing him. Suddenly he remembered the experimental Mutual Reality program she'd devised. It was a long shot, but it was worth it if it cleared his name.

'Alistair, are you aware that Debra made a program especially for me, with herself in the starring role?'

He frowned. 'No? When was this?'

'A few weeks ago. She called me into her room and said she wanted me to try out her new game. It turned out to be the first Mutual Reality scenario.'

'I remember. There was some spanking involved, wasn't there?'

'There certainly was. Only it was Debra who was taking the punishment. Afterwards she confessed that she'd experienced it too, and she let me do a re-run from her viewpoint. I felt embarrassed, to tell you the truth. Especially when she went on about how useful it would be to compare that with the real-life version.'

'I can't believe Debra said that.'

'Would you believe it if you saw the scenario?'

Alistair squirmed. 'I don't know.'

'Will you at least let me show you. It's all I have to offer in my defence.'

Jack knew his boss was a fair-minded man. He even felt sorry for him in his dilemma. If Alistair ignored Debra's complaint it would look like he was trying to oust her from her job now they were no longer lovers, which would reflect badly on him if it went to a tribunal. But he felt sorrier for himself. He'd been Debra's fall guy, for whatever reason, and she wasn't going to get away with it if he could possibly help it.

They went into Debra's room and Jack switched on her computer. He searched her directories until he came to the one marked *Mutual 1*. That ought to be it. He linked it up to the Feelietron, handed Alistair one of the headsets and put the other on himself.

Jack recognised the scenario at once: the rest room at Global. But as he entered through the door the woman awaiting the player was not Debra but a totally different character! Horrified, he stared at her red curly hair and buxom form as she lounged provocatively in the leather hammock.

'She must have changed it!' he gasped, tearing off the headset and motioning Alistair to do the same. He went back to the keyboard and began searching again, more frantically, but he knew it was futile. Debra must have put herself into the scenario for him alone. Once he'd taken part in her simulated sex game she had deleted herself and substituted the red-head. The more he thought about it, the more her behaviour seemed like a carefully planned campaign. But why, for God's sake, why?

'Look, this is a waste of time,' Alistair said, finally. 'Honestly, Jack, I recommend that you apologise to Debra and have done with it. Even if you believe you did nothing wrong, it would save time and a lot of anguish if you humoured her.'

'*Humoured* her?' Jack stared at his boss in disbelief.

Alistair looked at his watch. 'It's a quarter to five. Why don't you go home and think it over? Sleep on it. Things may look very different in the morning.'

There seemed nothing more to say. Jack left the building feeling shattered, but his resolve was still firm. He would never apologise to that bitch Debra for something he hadn't done, even if his job depended on it.

Chapter Six

The estate agent's board outside his house brought it home to Jack what deep shit he was in. His marriage was on the rocks, his job on the line and soon he'd have nowhere to live. To rub it in, there was a message on his Ansaphone telling him that an offer had been made on the house. 'There's no chain,' the woman's voice said, chirpily. 'So they'd like to complete by Christmas, if possible.'

Great, Jack thought, I'm in for a wonderful Christmas!

The more urgent question of what to do about his job preoccupied him for the rest of the day. He half persuaded himself to swallow his pride and give in. After all, he and Debra knew the truth of the matter, knew what a bloody liar she was. She'd have to live with that on her conscience – if she had one.

But then he imagined how it would be if he kept his job and had to go on encountering that woman daily. There was no chance of him being moved to a different department or working with another colleague. The work that he, Debra and Alistair did was very specialised. If he stayed, how would Debra behave in future? Would she be cold towards him? Bossy? Smug?

There was no accounting for the behaviour of women Jack decided, as he lay in bed that night. The old adage of 'Feed 'em, Fuck 'em and Forget 'em' seemed the only rational way to deal with the creatures. He thought of Suzanne. It was easy for him to find excuses for her when he remembered how all-absorbing his work had been for the past year or so, and how uninspired he'd been in the sack. It was her choice of partner that seemed strange. Jack had calculated that Rupert was at least ten years younger than her. When the kissing had to stop, as it had to sometime, what on earth did they find to talk about?

If Suzanne's behaviour seemed strange, Debra's was positively bizarre. What real-life scenario had she been working on? He remembered the hints she'd been dropping lately about how his talents were wasted at Global. Had she been attempting some covert head-hunting herself, but found him unreceptive? He wouldn't put it past her to take her revenge on Alistair by moving to a rival firm. Had the harassment charge been a ploy to get rid of him too, leaving the MR program without its lifeblood? Or was it some even more obscure game of sexual office politics?

The more he thought about it, the less he wanted to remain in the company – or rather, in *her* company. Jack had a strong suspicion that an apology wouldn't satisfy Debra. If she went for a tribunal hearing she'd probably win and he'd end up not only losing his job but having to pay her compensation, which would be even worse.

All in all, his best option seemed to be to look around for another post. He would tell Alistair tomorrow and at least make sure he got the promise of a decent reference. Surely the man owed him that.

Next morning Jack woke feeling as if a lead weight were on his chest. He washed and shaved as usual, dressed smartly and set off for the station, but it felt unreal. At the news stall he bought a copy of *Computer Jobsearch* and flicked his eyes through the hundreds of posts on offer as he rode to Docklands on the tube. He marked half a dozen, but without enthusiasm. Now that the reality of it was sinking in, Jack feared he'd never find another job as stimulating, both mentally and physically, as his work at Global had been. With a shock he realised he was already thinking of it in the past tense.

Alistair was in the rest room getting a coffee when he arrived. 'Want to come into my office, Jack?' he said. 'Grab a drink.'

'I've thought it over very carefully,' Jack began, sitting in what he'd come to think of as the hot seat. 'And, believe me, I've not come to my decision lightly. But I really don't think I can go on working with Debra after what's happened.'

'Then you know what this means.'

'I'm very sorry it's come to this, Alistair. I've enjoyed working here tremendously.'

Alistair's manner changed. His tone became conciliatory. 'Look, Jack, I don't want to lose you. There are very few guys in the business who have your imagination and expertise. Can't we find some way round this?'

'You could try talking to Debra . . .'

'I've given her the rest of the week off. She's in no fit state to work. And she sticks by her story. There's no shifting her.'

'I see. Well then, I've no option but to resign.'

Alistair sighed, pacing towards the window. 'Will you stay till the end of the week, at least? I'll have to put the MR work on the back burner until I can find the right team to continue it, but we're under pressure to complete the other stuff to a deadline.'

'Sure. I'd like to see it through'.

'Good. We'll advertise and hope to fill your post soon. I'm sure there'll be no lack of applications, although I might have to create two new posts to cover all aspects of what you did. And I can guarantee to give you a good reference, Jack. Whatever the truth of the matter between you and Debra, I'll give you the benefit of the doubt. It's the least I can do.'

'Thanks. I appreciate that.'

Later Jack felt sour at the thought that his job would be split into two. Maybe Debra was right and he had been exploited after all. He tried to get back his enthusiasm for fine-tuning the Dorabella game but his heart wasn't in it any more and, by the end of the week, he was glad to be going. Alistair invited him for a drink, tried to act man-to-man, but it was all rather forced. Jack wondered whether, if his boss hadn't been Debra's lover, it would have been any different.

The weekend threw Jack into a strange limbo. He'd applied for all six jobs but not yet heard from any of them, and the prospect of a blank Monday morning was unnerving. So far, Suzanne hadn't made any moves towards a divorce but the formalities seemed irrelevant now. The house sale was going ahead, and Suzanne said she and Rupert would be buying a place together once the money came through. Jack knew that would put their relationship onto a more permanent footing, and it made him feel worse. As for his own arrangements, Jack decided he would rent for a bit rather than rush into buying. After all, he didn't know where he'd end up having to work.

Despite Jack's fears of unemployment, he managed to keep himself busy. There was the updating of his CV for a start, and the hunt for flats and jobs took up quite a bit of time, as did his dealings with the estate agent and solicitor. He also began throwing out the debris of eight years of marriage, which had a certain therapeutic value.

It was at night that his negative feelings came to the fore. Not only did he have to deal with a sense of hopelessness about his own life, but he also had to cope with an impotent mysogynist rage. Then there was the sexual frustration. It didn't take Jack long to realise that he was suffering from Feelietron withdrawal symptoms. He was so used to having his sexual needs catered for by the fantasy games that to be suddenly deprived of them left his libido craving.

To try and fill the gap, he joined a video library and went through all their 'adult' films in a few weeks. Although he wanked away at the sight of various bodies doing various things to each other, that extra dimension of satisfaction was always lacking. He tried the sex phone-lines and, for a while, the novelty of having an anony-mous female voice talk dirty at him was enough to make him come. But soon their tired scripts and faked orgasms began to pall too.

In his lonely bed at night, Jack tried to conjure up his own fantasies. His favourite was one where Debra and Suzanne became his sex-slaves. He would have them make lesbian love to each other while he watched. They would be forced to play with outsize dildoes, the bigger and rougher the better. Sometimes one woman would be required to tie the other up and spank her. Occasionally he would give them a good thrashing himself. If all that imagined activity failed to bring him off he would picture one of them giving him head while the other sat on his face. That usually did the trick.

Even so, nothing could compare with the intensity of his Feelietron experience. If only it were coming onto the market soon. But Jack knew that it would take at least another six months before the Dorabella game appeared in the sex shops and mail order catalogues, and he wanted satisfaction now.

Remembering his new-found interest in discipline, Jack decided to ring 'Sexy Sadie, DD' who advertised in one of the sex mags. When he dialled her number she replied, in a deepish voice, 'Sadie here. How can I help you?'

'Er . . . I'm answering your ad in *Eroticon*. I was won-dering what the special services mentioned are.'

Jack felt embarrassed, but when she answered her tone was perfectly matter-of-fact.

'Here's what I do, then. Camp Commandant with uni-
form and whip. Schoolteacher with cane. Nanny with
slipper. Restraint is optional for all of those. Topless is
extra, so is hand job or tit wank. I don't do blow-jobs or
penetration or anything else. Okay?'

'You've got it all worked out, haven't you?'

'It's my job,' she replied, firmly. 'Now then, have you
decided or are you going to waste any more of my valuable time?'

'Er ... sorry, yes. I'll have the Schoolteacher, please.
Oh, and topless.'

She named her fee, Jack agreed and gave her his
address. She promised to be round in ten minutes. As
soon as he put the phone down he raced to the cash
machine at the end of the street and took the money out
of his account.

Sadie took twelve minutes arriving, but Jack wasn't
complaining. While he waited Jack remembered Miss
Evans, a teacher at his junior school that he, in his naive
way, had really fancied. She'd had huge knockers and
when she'd leaned over his desk the side of her tit used
to brush his cheek. Once he'd had some childish upset
and she'd taken him on her knee at break. He could still
recall the way she'd pressed his small head to her ample
bosom. He could also remember one occasion when she'd
been really cross with him and reduced him to tears.
After that he'd longed to be taken on her knee again
and comforted, but it hadn't happened.

When Sadie appeared she really looked the part, with
hair scraped back severely into a bun and round-rimmed

spectacles. She wore a drab buttoned-up cardigan over her huge bust and a tweed skirt, with thick lisle stocking and sensible lace-up shoes.

Her first words were, 'Where's your dinner money?'

Jack handed over the agreed sum and she put it in her large bag, then marched into the sitting-room barking, 'Wait outside my door, boy!'

He could hear her moving furniture around inside. At last she called, 'Come in!' and he entered to see Sadie sitting behind his coffee table as if it were a desk.

'Now then, boy, I've been having terrible reports from your teachers about your behaviour. Listen to this ...' she pretended to read from a note. 'Homework handed in late, or not at all. Disruptive in class. Cheeky to teachers. What have you to say to this?'

'Nothing, miss.'

'Nothing?'

Sadie rose, drawing herself up to her full, formidable height and bulk. 'Then there's only one thing I can do, and that is to punish you severely. I see that you have already had several detentions. You know what I have to do now, to teach you a lesson, don't you?'

Jack nodded. She barked, 'Well, what?'

'The cane, miss,' he muttered.

'Speak up, boy!'

'You've got to give me the cane, miss.'

She gave a small smile. 'That's right. Have you had the cane before, boy?'

Jack shook his head.

'I'll explain what you have to do, then. First you

remove your disgusting trousers and then your revolting underwear, so that your backside is completely bare. Do you understand me?'

'Yes, miss.'

'Then you must lean over my desk so that your obscene behind is sticking up, ready for me to give it a taste of the cane. Do you follow me?'

'Yes, miss.'

'Do you think you will like it, boy?'

'No, miss, I shouldn't think so, miss.'

She gave another, rather horrible, smile. 'Well that's where you're wrong, boy. You will like it, very much indeed. In fact, I shall go on giving it to you until I'm quite sure you *are* enjoying it. And do you know how I shall tell?' Jack shook his head. 'I'll see your miserable little dicky get all stiff, that's how I'll know. And when that happens, I'll be pleased with you and know you've learnt your lesson. But not until then. Now get out of your stinking clothes and let's begin the punishment.'

While Jack stripped his lower half and bent over the table, Sadie pulled a cane from her bag. It was in two sections that screwed together to make a long, flexible switch. Once Jack was in position she came round the desk and stood to one side, feet apart.

He heard the swish as the cane sliced through the air and felt the first sting on his buttocks, so keen it made him flinch.

'Stay still!' she commanded.

The second swipe was even more painful, but Jack braced himself and managed not to move a muscle. He didn't know how many such strokes he could stand, and hoped he would get an erection soon. He thought about Miss Evans, imagining that it was her who was administering this punishment with her large jugs wobbling away beneath her chiffon blouse, and the first faint stirrings began in his groin.

'Three! Four!' His tormentor was counting out his agony. Jack thought of nestling against Miss Evans' bountiful mammaries and his penis stiffened a little more.

After six strokes his buttocks were really sore, and he imagined that Sadie might even have drawn blood. She stopped for a merciful moment and told him to straighten up.

'Let's have a look at you. Are you beginning to enjoy it?'

He glanced down at his semi-flaccid prong. Sadie took it momentarily in her hand and gave it a brief tug, which resulted in more hardening.

'Coming on, but could do better. Bend over again, boy!'

Reluctantly, Jack resumed his position. His bum was stinging horribly now. He couldn't remember feeling this raw and tender since he'd gone horse-riding bareback when he was a lad. Yet still the torture continued and he tried, more desperately now, to fantasise himself into a full erection.

Six more strokes and she paused again for a progress report. This time it was more encouraging.

'Hm,' she murmured as she inspected his quite respectable hard-on. 'I can see a big improvement, but we're not quite there are we? Just a few more strokes, I think.'

Jack whimpered and pleaded to be spared the rod, but she was adamant.

'You must learn that to please me you have to be really hard,' was all she would say.

Several strokes later, she looked at Jack's throbbing prick and nodded.

'I think that will do now. You seem to have learned your lesson good and proper.'

'Oh, yes miss!' Jack said, eagerly.

'Trouble is, I seem to have made quite a mess of your backside, boy. You were so stubborn I had to give you more of a thrashing than usual. Just wait there while I see if I've got some cream in my First Aid kit.'

Jack stood in delicious suspense, relieved that his punishment would soon be followed by a delightful reward. He could see Sadie on the other side of the table, with a pot of cold cream in her hand.

'Here we are, this should do the trick. Oh, I'd better take off my woolly, though. This cream makes a mess if it gets on your clothes.'

With his elbows resting on the table, Jack watched as Sadie undid her buttons and slipped out of the cardigan. She was naked underneath, and the sight of her huge knockers sent a rush of excitement through Jack's tense body. Veined with blue, they hung down almost to her waist and had correspondingly large nipples of a tawny brown, a good few inches across. They lay flat on her mounds like outsize chocolate buttons, but Jack could imagine them in an aroused state and longed to lick and suck them into their inch-long glory. Instead he had to wait while she gouged out a generous dollop of cream then came to stand behind him.

'This will be cold at first, but nice and soothing afterwards.'

He flinched as the icy cream made contact with his inflamed rear. With delicate fingers she smoothed it all over his buttocks and soon he was enjoying the feeling. Every so often she would slip into his crack or down behind his balls, and soon he was the biggest he could get. His cock was rearing up so high it was knocking against the underside of the coffee table.

'That's much better,' she crooned. 'Big boys like you have to be taught how to behave themselves, don't they? Now come and sit over on the sofa, and we'll have a little chat.'

When Jack found himself sitting next to the bare-breasted Sadie with his pole sticking up at right angles, he could hardly contain himself. Her nipples were puckered and huge now, like great brown nuts ripe for chewing. His bottom still stung, so that even the rough material of the sofa was uncomfortable, but the urgent throbbing in his groin made him forget his discomfort.

'Now then,' Sadie smiled, patting his knee. 'You've been a good boy and responded well to your punishment, so I'm going to give you a little treat. Never let it be said that I don't use the carrot as well as the stick!'

'Yes, miss.'

'We're going to play a little game, boy. It's called, "Follow Miss" and this is what you do. Everything I do

110

to your nice hard willy, you have to do to my nice hard nipples. For instance, if I give your willy a little lick, you do the same. If I give your willy a good strong suck, or a tug with my fingers, you do just the same. Got it?'

Speechlessly, Jack nodded.

'But if you get it wrong and suck when I tweak, or lick when I stroke, then you lose a point. Three points and you're out of the game. All right?'

'Yes, miss,' he croaked.

'Ready, steady, go!'

She put her hand onto his dick and gave the shaft a long stroke. Jack imitated her by stroking one of her giant breasts, finishing off by tweaking her nipple in the same way that she softly tweaked his glans.

'Very good! You've got the idea.'

She bent her head and enclosed his bulbous tip with her lips. Jack just about managed to seize her breast and stuff the huge teat into his mouth, where he licked and sucked at it as enthusiastically as she did to his prick. He could feel the hot rush of energy taking him up to another level of arousal and his excitement grew. God, this woman knew her job!

Sadie sat up again and rubbed his stalk with her fingers, avoiding the sensitive tip. Jack rubbed away at her tit but accidentally brushed her nipple making her cry out.

'No, you touched me in the wrong place! You've lost a point, boy!'

She grinned and squeezed his glans gently between finger and thumb. He did the same to her nipple. Then she rubbed his shaft between her palms, so he took two hands to the sides of her breast and imitated her movements. It was extraordinarily stimulating to his penis, and Jack was sure he must climax at any moment. Sadie began to vary the pace, now rolling or stroking his dick with one or both hands, now paying attention to the swollen knob at the end. Every so often she would dart her head down and give him a little lick, so that Jack found it quite difficult to keep up with her and, all the time, his tension was increasing.

'Ha! Caught you out!' she laughed in triumph, as she licked where he stroked. 'Two penalty points. One more, and the game's over!'

The thought that this entertainment might come to an abrupt halt before he'd reached his climax enabled Jack to concentrate his mind wonderfully. Soon he could feel the first onset of his orgasm as he kneaded Sadie's enormous tit in time to her massaging his erection. At last he came in an explosive release that had him pumping and spraying all over the sofa. Fortunately, Sadie had had the foresight to put a newspaper down on the cushions beside them.

'There's a good boy!' she cooed, throwing some tissues into his lap as she rose to her feet. Dimly Jack was aware of her buttoning up the cardigan, unscrewing the cane and replacing it in her bag.

'You see,' she smiled down at him, as she began to leave. 'Corporal punishment really does work in even the most stubborn cases. Especially when it's administered with a little understanding. Goodbye, boy!'

Jack was called for two interviews out of the six he'd

applied for which, in the current economic climate, didn't seem at all bad. Just a week before Christmas he was offered the post of reviewer for a computer games magazine. It was quite a few steps down from creating the scenarios himself, of course, but he couldn't afford to be choosy. At least he could do quite a lot of the work at home and avoid the rush-hour traffic.

The only trouble was he didn't have a home and the solicitors were about to complete the sale of his house. Jack made the impulsive decision to put some of his furniture up for auction, put the rest in store and book into a hotel over the Christmas season. Then he could start flat-hunting in the New Year. He had a portfolio of shares in computer companies that had done rather well so he wasn't strapped for cash, even though half the proceeds from the house had to go to Suzanne.

As Christmas approached, Jack still felt bitter about his broken marriage. His own parents were divorced, his mother living in Canada and his father in Scotland, and Jack felt alienated from both of them, but they used to visit Suzanne's parents every year around this time. Soon she'd no doubt be introducing them to her new man. The thought pissed him off. He'd quite liked his in-laws.

Jack checked into a modest Bayswater hotel on Christmas Eve. A professionally jovial Santa offered him a sherry and mince pie in the foyer, but he declined and went up to his room. He was half inclined to stay there for the next two days, pigging out and watching cable TV, but then he reasoned that he might at least try whatever the hotel had to offer in the way of feasting and entertainment. If it wasn't to his liking he could retreat at any time.

The bar was busy when Jack entered, but he got his hands on a large Scotch as soon as he could and retreated to a corner table. A dark-haired girl was sitting there looking as if she was waiting for her man. She gave him a shy smile and he raised his glass to her, feeling he might as well appear sociable. 'Cheers! Merry Christmas!'

'Yes, Merry Christmas.' She leaned forward, emboldened a little, and he scented the heady smell of a perfume his mother used to wear. It seemed as good an opener as any.

'Mm. Rive Gauche, isn't it?' he smiled.

She looked pleased. 'Yes, it's my favourite. But I'm surprised you recognised it. You're not in the perfume or fashion business, are you?'

Jack laughed. 'Not at all! But I used to have a job where smells were important. I've just landed a new job, reviewing computer games.'

'That must be fun.'

'I'll let you know in six months' time!'

Her brown eyes were twinkling at him and he realised that she was an attractive girl in a low-key kind of way. She was wearing a red jersey dress that clung to her rather appealing contours, and Jack began to think that if she was on her own he might be in with a chance.

'My name's Jack,' he smiled, offering her his hand.

She took it readily. Her own hand felt warm and comforting. 'I'm Melissa. And that woman just coming out of the Ladies is my aunt. We're spending Christmas here, in the hotel.'

'Really?' Jack's interest was growing.

'Yes. Poor Aunty Clare has just lost her cat and I've split up with my boyfriend, so we decided to drown our troubles together!'

'Aunty Clare' had an impressive bosom and a ready smile. 'I see you've found yourself a nice young man already, Melissa,' she grinned, as she squeezed into an empty seat. 'Aren't you going to introduce me?'

'This is Jack. He plays computer games for a living.'

'Dear me! You couldn't pay me to play with those things! Look, darling, I must give your mother a call to let her know we've arrived safely. But you stay here. You can ring her tomorrow and wish her a Merry Christmas.'

'Mum lives in Canada,' Melissa explained. After that handy coincidence, conversation flowed like cheap wine. The Aunt was considerate enough not to reappear for at least half an hour, by which time they were all ready to eat.

'Do join us at our table,' Aunt Clare insisted.

Jack was starting to be filled with Christmas cheer.

The two women were pleasant company but Jack soon had the extraordinary feeling that they were vying for his attention. Despite her mature years, Clare was quite a sexy lady in an up front kind of way, while Melissa had the kind of subtle appeal that made Jack want to know more. It was absurdly ego-boosting to have the company of two such ladies at once.

'Well, that was a very nice meal. What shall we do

now?' Clare wondered aloud, her grey eyes flashing. 'I believe there's a disco going on in the cellar bar. Shall we take a look?'

Soon Jack was dancing between the two women, each of them showing off their curves with abandon. Clare had taken off her cardigan and her chief assets were well displayed in a pink angora top with a lowish neckline. Jack was surprised to find he had the hots for her.

His lust for the intriguing Melissa was equally strong, though not so surprising. She seemed to fancy him, too, from the way she latched on to him as soon as a slow number was playing. He held her close with his arm round her slim waist, enjoying her warm muskiness, but his eyes were on the swaying butt of her aunt as she danced by herself. Crazy dreams of enjoying them both began to spin in his head, but he thought he'd probably end up with neither.

His hopes rose, however, when the lights dimmed during the last slow number and Melissa whispered, 'I . . . er . . . wouldn't mind seeing you on my own later. Aunty and I have separate rooms because she snores. Mine is number twenty-five.'

Jack smiled, squeezing her hand. 'Right. I'll see you later, then.'

When they joined up with Clare again she gave Jack a rueful smile. 'I was quite envious of Melissa, getting all those nice slow dances. I'm not too old to enjoy a smooch too, you know.'

'Of course not! No woman is ever too old for romance,' Jack said, gallantly.

'In that case, how about giving me a nice goodnight kiss? Then I'll be off to bed and leave you two young things to dance till dawn, if you like.'

Jack went to kiss her cheek but she drew him forcefully into her arms and gave him a rather tasty kiss on the lips. After she'd gone, Melissa turned to Jack with a wink.

'Isn't she a sport? She knows I fancy you, so she's leaving the field clear. Mind you, I wouldn't be surprised if she didn't fancy you herself. She's quite a woman, is my Aunty Clare!'

'Would you like a drink?' Jack offered, as they climbed the stairs back to the foyer.

They sat in the bar for a while, but it was obvious that all Melissa wanted was to get him alone. Jack could hardly believe his luck. After bracing himself for a celibate Christmas he'd scored on the first night!

Melissa led the way into her room and switched on the bedside light. Then she turned coquettishly, taking the slides from her dark hair and letting it cascade down her shoulders.

'When I first saw you, in the bar, I could have sworn you were waiting for a man,' Jack grinned.

'Yes I was. You!' She came up to him, her eyes gleaming in the mellow light. 'Kiss me, Jack. I want to forget yesterday. And the day before.'

'Me too,' he murmured, feeling like he was trapped in a bad movie script as he bent his mouth towards her ripe, red lips. Melissa parted them instantly, giving the tip of his tongue access to the moist interior. As they kissed, Jack manoeuvred her onto the bed, where he began to inch the zipper of her dress down her back. He was achingly aware of the stiffness of his tool, the culmination of an evening's desire, pressing against her thigh.

Soon his hands were on the warm, smooth skin of her back and she was nibbling at his ear, making the hairs on his neck stand on end. Eagerly he pulled the jersey fabric off her shoulders and eased down the black straps of her bra. 'Wait!' Melissa whispered, shrugging the dress down to her waist. She stood up to step out of it along with her slip, allowing Jack to take in the trim curves of her bust beneath the black lace, the flat midriff leading down to the black silk French knickers that concealed her pubic mound. He put his arms round her waist and pulled her to him, burying his face in her perfumed belly and making animal noises while she stroked his hair.

'Come on,' she murmured. 'Let's get you out of your clothes too.'

He didn't need much encouragement. Swiftly he stripped off his shirt and trousers until he stood in his striped boxer shorts.

'Let's stay like this,' she suggested. 'It's more sexy to leave something on.'

Jack would have disagreed, but it didn't seem worth arguing over. Besides, he'd have those knickers off her in no time. He began to kiss her throat, pulling her back onto the bed. Melissa caressed his chest, pinching his nipples gently between her fingers. His penis reared between them, nosing into the silk of her panties through the cotton of his shorts, but she seemed in no hurry to

118

explore his body. Instead she let him lick his way into her cleavage, his tongue delving down the firm slopes of her breasts and nuzzling beneath the lace to find her swollen nipple.

'Oh, yes!' she sighed. 'I love having my boobs licked!'

'Let me take your bra off, then, so I can do it better.'

'No!' Melissa's voice sounded quite sharp. 'I prefer it like this.'

So Jack continued to suck on her nipple with the lace of her bra brushing his nose. He could feel her fingers travelling tentatively down towards his stomach and his cock grew optimistic. His own hands were caressing her firm buttocks. Beneath the cool silk they felt fantastic.

'Melissa, are we going to get between the sheets?' he asked, but she shook her head.

Jack had the uneasy feeling of being a teenager again, allowed to go so far but no further. Well, it was his job to make her want to go further. He slid his fingers round the tight top of the knickers searching for the fastening, but when he found it his hand was given a sharp tap.

'Leave it, please Jack!'

'Okay,' he murmured, but his fingers slipped down to the loose-fitting legs instead. Tentatively he felt the warm groove of her groin and the first brush of her pubic hair. She didn't try to stop him but gave a sigh of contentment. Jack put his fingers in, to tangle with her bush, and she wriggled a little to give him further access. He moved to her other nipple and she moaned with pleasure as it received the attention of his lips.

'Oh, that's so good!' she smiled up at him, her eyes

bright with arousal. Jack put both hands inside her knickers, reaching as far as he could, and felt the first damp hairiness of her quim. The gusset of her pants was tight in her slit, so he couldn't touch more than her bulging outer lips.

'I really think it would be better if you took these off,' he suggested.

'No! I like it like this. It's not so good if you make it too easy.'

Jack's cock disagreed quite strongly with that. It was straining at the leash for things to be made just a little easier. Then, quite unexpectedly, Melissa's hand was thrust into the fly of his shorts. Jack gasped as she took firm hold of his shaft and gave it an experimental rub. Did she know what she was doing to him? A few more tricks like that and he'd come in his pants, which would be a terrible waste.

Melissa was taking it roughly out, now, pulling it towards her. What the hell was she up to? Jack held his breath and moved his hands round to stroke her silky smooth bum cheeks. She pushed his knob end through the leg of her panties and began moving her mound against it in a slow circular motion. The rough hairiness against his glans was an irritation, and the frustration of being unable to get inside her pussy was acute.

'Look sweetheart, this is not very comfortable for me. Can't we get you out of these so we can be more . . . free?'

Melissa looked up at him, smiling coyly. 'I never take my knickers off on a first date, Jack. But we can still have fun.'

Resignedly, he pulled out his prick. 'Okay, but not like that, please. Why don't you let me lick you.'

'That would be nice.'

Melissa lay back with her thighs apart and pulled her gusset aside. At last her vulva lay exposed, pink and moist. Jack inveigled his tongue into as much of her slit as he could reach. While he licked her fat lips and poked his tongue into her hole she rubbed the swollen nub of her clitoris with her finger. Soon she was convulsing, making little gasping noises and bucking her hips. Jack sucked on the small trickle that came from her cunt. but it did nothing to ease the burning tension in his rod.

She pulled him up to lie beside her. 'Oh, Jack, that was great! You're a smashing licker.'

His prick was still straining in his shorts but she seemed to have forgotten it. Jack thought he had better remind her. 'What about me then, Melissa?'

She stared at him in surprise. 'What *about* you?'

'Well I've still got a stiffy, you know. Can't you do something about it?'

She frowned. 'Can't *you* do something about it?'

This really was turning into a bad dream of adolescence. Jack tried to stay cool. 'Well I could, of course. But I'd far rather you did it.'

'Did what?'

He didn't want to push his luck. 'Just . . . er . . . helped me to climax.'

'You mean, you didn't come when I did?'

'Actually, no.'

'I'm sorry. But I'm not really in the mood any more. I always lose interest afterwards, don't you?'

This was unbelievable. Jack had put his misogyny on hold for the evening, believing he'd found himself an easy lay. But now he catapulted himself off the bed in his haste to get out of there before he said – or did – something he'd very much regret later.

'What are you doing, Jack?'

He was pulling on his trousers. 'Like you said, I've lost interest.'

'Oh, I didn't mean ... Give me a few minutes, and I might get back into it.'

Jack was buttoning his shirt. 'Sorry, Melissa, I'm afraid you've blown it. I can feel my cock losing interest too.'

He put on his socks and shoes, thrust his tie in his pocket, hung his jacket over one shoulder, and fled.

Chapter Seven

Jack left Melissa's room feeling like a burglar who hadn't managed to get the loot. He began to walk down the dimly-lit corridor, trying to look as if he should be there, when the door to the next room opened a crack and Aunt Clare's face peered out.

'Jack? Is that you?'

It seemed pointless to pretend to be someone else. He tried to sound surprised.

'Yes, I think I got out of the lift on the wrong floor . . .'

She smiled, opening the door wider. Her full figure was resplendent in a black nylon negligee with pink ribbons. 'You don't have to pretend,' she whispered. 'Why not come in and share a night-cap with me? After all, it is Christmas!'

Jack hesitated. Did she suspect that he'd just given her niece a thorough rogering? If so, she'd be wrong, but he'd have a tricky job persuading her. On the whole, discretion seemed the wiser course.

'Er . . . thanks very much, but I think I'd better find my room.'

Clare grabbed his arm, half pulling him through the door. 'Nonsense! Your room won't run away! Just a little drinkie, to make a mature lady very happy.'

Jack grinned. 'Since you put it like that, I can hardly refuse.'

She had two glasses already set out, and a bottle of champagne on ice. 'Why not? It's a long time since I've spent the early hours of Christmas with such a nice young man!'

When they'd drunk some of the bubbly, Clare patted the bed beside her and Jack dutifully sat down. 'Now then, I know exactly what's been going on next door,' she said bluntly, her grey eyes sparkling with amusement. 'Well, not *exactly*, perhaps, but I've a pretty good idea. She's a little prick tease, my niece, isn't she?'

Jack was nonplussed. Clare patted his hand. 'It's all right, you don't have to say anything disloyal. I'm sure she let you get halfway there, at least. But I know Melissa. She won't let a man get inside her until she's practically engaged to him. I blame her Catholic upbringing. Fortunately, I'm more liberal-minded myself. More champagne?'

'Thanks. But I really don't think . . .'

'Good? It doesn't do people any good to think too much. So why don't you just lie back and relax, while I give that splendid equipment of yours what it so richly deserves.'

Jack couldn't believe his ears. Here was this seemingly proper mature lady talking dirty and, better yet, prepared to follow through with some equally naughty behaviour! The prospect was irresistible.

'You don't mind if I make myself more comfortable, do you?' she smiled, undoing the pink bow of her negligee. 'They always overheat these hotel rooms, don't you find?'

Beneath the black nylon garment was a pink nylon nightie, through which her large melons and dark vee were clearly visible. Jack felt his prick straining at the leash and was relieved when Clare gently eased down his zip and pulled off his trousers.

'What jolly shorts!' she smiled. 'Did Melissa get inside them?' He nodded speechless. 'Bet she didn't know what to do with Mr. Dicky though, did she?'

'Er . . . not really,' he admitted. 'But I don't mind betting you'd know exactly what to do with it.'

'Where to put it, you mean!' She smiled, easing out his tumid organ. 'Just for starters, how about putting him between my boobs and giving him a nice big squeeze? I think he'd like that, wouldn't he?'

'Mm!' Jack murmured, dumbly.

She lifted her nightie right up to her chin. Although there was rather too much flesh on her belly and thighs, they were still firm. And her tits appeared rock hard, jutting out proudly with their large brown nipples already standing to attention. Jack reached out and stroked them, amazed at how youthful they seemed.

'Gorgeous, aren't they?' Clare beamed. 'They cost me three thousand dollars each!'

'What?'

She giggled, girlishly. 'I'd always wanted a bust like Dolly Parton's, so I decided to have them done in the States. And I've never regretted it.'

'You mean they're . . . silicone?'

'Don't worry about the technicalities, Jack, just enjoy! My only regret is that my dear husband Tom never lived to feel them. But it was his money that made it possible, God rest his soul.'

Although it was rather like handling two over-pumped rugby balls, Jack stroked and squeezed the fake jugs, licked the (presumably) genuine nipples and then, at Clare's invitation, positioned his prong between them and let her massage him to even greater firmness. She seemed to be enjoying it, letting her tongue flick over his glans when it came within reach of her mouth, and clasping one of his thighs between hers so she could stimulate herself below.

At last she told him, in a hoarse voice, 'While I'm slipping a Johnny on your beautiful big one, you can do something for me. On the bedside table you'll find a pot of cream. Rub it into my pussy, there's a dear man. Then I'll be all oiled and ready for you, and horny as hell!'

Bleary-eyed, Jack leant over and found the pot. The label said, *Kumkwick Kreem.* He'd never seen such stuff advertised before, but perhaps she'd picked it up in America. He could feel Clare enveloping his dick with a condom as he unscrewed the lid and smeared some of the goo on his fingers. It smelt enticingly musky. Then he reached down and parted the loose flaps to get the cream well into her grooves.

She shuddered at his touch. 'Oh, that's so wonderful! It takes me by surprise every time, it works so well. Come into me quickly now, Dave, before the effect wears off.'

Although she'd called him by the wrong name, it seemed no time to be nit-picking. Jack slid straight into her, down the oil-slick he'd just created. Her insides were a bit dry and tight at first but soon loosened as he rocked too and fro, deeply relieved to be penetrating a warm cunt at last.

'Don't forget my beautiful boobs!' Clare growled. 'Be my demanding little boy and suck as hard as you want. You can fuck me harder, too. I like it a bit rough.'

Tired as he was, Jack summoned the energy to quicken the pace. She slapped and pinched at his buttocks as he rode her. 'Harder, you're not ramming me hard enough!' she moaned, digging her nails into the cheeks of his bum to spur him on. Jack began to suspect that he'd bitten off more than he could chew!

'Now take me from behind,' Clare demanded, when he'd almost shot his load.

She presented her large, pink posterior to him and he felt obliged to keep going although he was shattered. He slipped his cock back in and she placed his hand on her swollen clitoris. 'Rub me there while you screw me, and I'll soon come.'

The prospect of the end being imminent gave him heart. Once she'd got off perhaps she'd let him rest. Now she was wriggling her butt against his thighs as he slammed into her, his finger making a frenzied assault on her joy-button.

'Oh God, that's fantastic!' he heard her cry. 'I'm almost there, just a bit faster ... yes, yes! That's nearly it! Rub me, rub me! Thrust your enormous dick right into me, faster, faster!'

Jack was sweating like a marathon runner, but although the encouragement continued Clare's climax seemed infuriatingly elusive.

'It's no good!' Jack gasped, at last. 'I can't stop myself from coming now . . .'

His orgasm burst out of him explosively, filling the condom with spurt after spurt. Jack gasped as if in pain, and collapsed between her thighs. Soon she was drawing him to rest between her huge jugs.

'Ah, my poor baby, did I work you too hard?' she whispered, kissing him. 'I was too greedy. I wanted you too much. I'm sorry.'

'That's okay. It's me who should apologise. I'm sorry for leaving you high and dry, Clare.'

'I'm high, but not dry,' she smiled, taking his hand and placing it in her still-damp muff. 'Be a gentleman and finish me off.'

It didn't take long before she was thrashing about in the throes of a histrionic orgasm. Jack sighed inwardly with relief. It was gone two a.m. and he was looking forward to returning to the solitude of his room for a good night's sleep.

Clare wriggled close to him. 'That was wonderful! What a shame my silly niece didn't get to enjoy you. Tell me, did you suck her off?'

Jack felt embarrassed. 'I don't think I want to talk about it.'

'That's all right. She'll probably tell me all about it in the morning, anyway.'

'What?' Jack sat up with alarm. 'Look, you won't tell her I came in here afterwards, will you? I mean, I don't want to upset her.'

Clare laughed. 'Don't you worry, sweetheart! Melissa and I understand each other perfectly. She knows I'm a randy old dame, and I know she's a romantic young girl who thinks she's got to be in love before she can give her all. But I know which of us has the more fun!'

Aunt Clare's words did little to reassure Jack. It sounded like the pair of them would be comparing notes over breakfast. Or maybe they'd be having *him* for breakfast, instead! His mind boggled at the thought of a dual onslaught by the two women, each ravenous for it in her own way, and his sense of exhaustion deepened.

'Well, I suppose I'd better be getting back to my room,' he began, sitting up, but Clare put her arms round him and planted a wet kiss on his forehead.

'Not yet, please! Have some more of this delicious champagne. It tastes so much better after making love, don't you find?'

Jack allowed her to press another glass on him. While they drank she began chatting about her life. She'd lived in several different countries and had much to say about their varying moral codes. After a while her hands strayed to his crotch and she began to tease up an erection again.

'Er ... I think I ought to go,' he told her as, despite his fatigue, the familiar urge made a tentative comeback.

'What, just when things are getting interesting again?' She gave his scrotum a tickle. 'Besides, I want to come with you inside me. Now we've both climaxed once we can take things easy.'

'I'm rather tired...'

She got up and straddled him, smiling coyly. 'No problem. Just you lie there and let me do all the work. I'm pretty athletic for my age, don't you think? I do Hatha Yoga.'

There seemed little option but to do as she recommended. Clare's fingers delved into the cream and she spread a liberal dose over her private parts before impaling herself on his erect penis. She clutched at him eagerly as she entered, then proceeded to bounce enthusiastically up and down for a bit, her huge breasts hardly shifting position despite their massive size. Jack decided that he would rather play with a pair that jiggled about in a natural fashion than touch those man-made monsters.

'Is that good for you?' she gasped, doing an elaborate figure eight manoeuvre with her hips. 'It is for me!'

'Mm, very nice,' he answered, politely. But his physical response was sluggish.

'This is called "churning the cream",' she informed him. 'Our Yoga instructor told us it would improve our pelvic tone, but I find it improves my sex life too. Tom used to love it, bless his heart.'

Jack couldn't help wondering whether her husband had expired from over-stimulation. Had he, in fact, died on the job? The idea of living with this woman, night in and night out was daunting to say the least. The man must have been a world-class sexual athlete.

'I can feel myself warming up a treat,' she continued. Why she felt the need to give him a progress report was beyond Jack. 'As you get older it takes longer. That's why I use the cream. But I always get there in the end,' she gave him a wink, 'one way or the other.'

Jack could feel his prick struggling to keep awake, just like the rest of him. It didn't seem to bother Clare that he was less than enthusiastic. She was as fresh as a daisy, and looked as if she could keep it up all night. Suddenly she got off his flagging erection and came to sit on his chest. 'Give me a good licking, there's a dear. I love it when I've been at it for a while. It feels all cool and lovely.'

She positioned a pillow behind his head and thrust her mutt in his face. Wearily, Jack began to lick her creamy lips. The manufactured stuff tasted quite pleasant, like some spicy concoction. While he was doing it he could feel her reaching under the pillow and soon she was fixing something over his cock.

'W . . . what are you doing?' he gasped, freeing his mouth from her flaps for a moment.

'Never you mind. You'll find out soon enough,' she teased him.

Jack turned his head and glanced at the alarm clock on the bedside table. Nearly three o'clock! 'Look, Clare, I'm awfully sorry but I really don't think I can go on any more. It's been lovely, but . . .'

She got off him immediately and squatted beside him. 'Don't worry, I can see you're not as used to all-night sex as I am!' She put her fingers at the root of his penis

131

and pinched it firmly. Jack glanced down and saw that she'd placed a ring around his tool, with soft rubber teeth protruding. 'Oh my God!' he moaned.

Quick as a flash she was on his wilting erection again, this time pressing the penis ring close to her bulging clitoris.

'This won't take long now,' she assured him. Her frantic jumping around certainly had the desired effect, and this time her climax seemed interminable. Despite himself, Jack felt a feeble spurt come from his overworked penis, although he was too knackered to take much notice.

'That works every time,' she sighed, contentedly, snuggling up to him. 'What did we do without modern sex aids? I can remember when I was first married we didn't have anything like that . . .'

But Jack had drifted off.

He woke with a start some time later, wondered where he was, who he was with and what time it was. The first two came to him after a few seconds, and a deep distaste overtook him. As for the time, it was obviously still in the middle of the night. There was a hideous noise coming from somewhere – a kind of resonant gurgling splutter. Was it the central heating?

Then he remembered: Melissa had said her aunt snored. Horror gripped him once more as he tried to get out of the bed without waking her. She must have been exhausted after her exertions because he managed to pick up his clothes and tiptoe into the en suite bathroom, dress hastily and leave the room without her waking up.

Jack couldn't remember when he'd been so glad to get

into his own bed, even if it was only a hotel bed. He threw off his clothes, tumbled beneath the duvet and within seconds had fallen into a deep and, mercifully, dreamless sleep.

He was awoken by the sound of Good King Wenceslas at top volume. 'God, it's Christmas!' he thought, as the events of the previous night came flooding back with the daylight. He promptly dived beneath the duvet to complete his sleep-cycle, and when he finally awoke enough to peer at his watch he discovered that it was two in the afternoon and he'd missed the Christmas lunch.

Despite the fact that hunger was gnawing at his stomach, Jack felt relieved. The thought of facing Clare and Melissa again, at table or elsewhere, was decidedly unappealing. In retrospect he didn't know which he'd found most embarrassing, the coy niece or the rampant aunt. In theory, it should have been the Christmas Eve of a lifetime. In practice, it had been the Christmas Eve from Hell!

Around three, after showering and dressing, Jack ventured downstairs and quickly realised that most of the guests were still assembled in the restaurant. There were a few piss-heads at the bar, and in a small room off the foyer he spied a buffet table set with food. Trying to look casual, he entered the room and seized a plate from the pile at the end. The food was untouched, obviously intended for later, but he managed to snaffle a reasonable amount of salad, cheese and rolls, snatched a bottle of beer and sneaked off back to his room without being challenged.

There he resolved to stay, with only the television for company, for the rest of Christmas.

Around ten in the evening someone knocked at his door, but he lay low and eventually they went away. On Boxing Day morning, however, hunger drove him downstairs again and as he was enjoying a hearty breakfast in the restaurant Melissa and Clare appeared. Jack lowered his eyes to the table, but he needn't have worried. Much to his surprise, they started waving to two men on the other side of the room then made a beeline for their table. Jack breathed a sigh of relief.

Later, when he was taking a solitary stroll in the hotel grounds, Jack began to muse on his experience with aunt and niece. He concluded that one-night stands were risky encounters at the best of times, and that people would probably be better off using the Feelietron for casual sex. Things seemed to have changed since the days, over ten years ago, when he was playing the field. Today's women seemed more ... demanding.

Jack checked out on December 27th and went to stay with an old school friend for a few days. He felt depressed and disillusioned and Steve, twice divorced, was scarcely the man to restore his faith in marriage. Still, it was somewhere to go and there was a certain grim satisfaction in playing the crusty bachelor for a while.

New Year's Eve could have been a real low point, but Steve invited Jack along to a party. They took a taxi to the house in Notting Hill which was already humming with activity by the time they arrived.

Soon Jack was in the midst of the throng, squashed

right up to a rather tasty-looking female in a black sleeveless dress.

'Hi,' she smiled at him over her shoulder. 'I'm Petra. If you wiggle a bit and I fit my wiggling to yours, we might end up doing something like dancing.'

He laughed, beginning to gyrate to the music. She was small and slim, with short auburn hair and a strikingly made up face. And he liked the way her bum was thrashing against his groin.

'I'm Jack, by the way,' he murmured into the back of her head.

She turned and gave him a dazzling smile. 'Well, Jack, shall we go in search of more booze?'

Petra led the way, and at last they found themselves a relatively free corner of the kitchen where there was a wine box dispensing Liebfraumilch.

'I'll have it half and half with orange juice,' she declared. 'I'm dying of thirst.'

They ended up, like several other couples, sitting on the stairs. 'What kind of a year have you had?' Petra asked, her hazel eyes flashing green lights at him.

'Well, my wife's walked out on me, I've lost my job and I've nowhere to live. Otherwise, it's been a great year.'

Petra giggled. 'You poor thing. You can stay with me for a bit, if you like.'

'Oh no, I couldn't possibly!'

'Why not? I've been thinking of letting a room in my flat, and if you stayed for, say, a month I could find out whether I liked the idea of living with someone or not.'

'But we don't know each other.'

135

She grinned. 'I'm an impeccable judge of character. You don't smoke do you, so that's okay. And if you've just broken up with your wife you won't be looking for anything more than casual sex, will you? So that's okay too. See, we're perfectly matched.'

'Really?' Jack was thinking that Petra was just outrageous enough to be trustworthy. He liked her direct approach. And it would be a relief to have some breathing-space while he looked for a place of his own. 'Okay, you're on!' he agreed.

'Let's dance for a bit, then I'll take you home.'

They waited until the midnight ritual was over. Jack enjoyed sharing a long, luscious kiss with his new partner, but when he told Steve that he was staying with Petra for a while, his friend rolled his eyes.

'Complicated female that one, Jack. Better steer clear.'

'How do you mean?'

But Steve refused to elaborate. 'You'll find out!'

Petra lived in a spacious flat around the corner, off the Portobello Road. Jack liked its air of seedy decadence.

'This'll be your room,' she smiled, opening the door on a medium-sized room at the back of the house then putting a plug in a socket. 'Bit sparsely furnished, I'm afraid.'

'That looks fine.'

Jack turned to see her leaning against the wall in her black dress, surveying him thoughtfully. She looked like a woman waiting to be kissed. He duly obliged. Her mouth was soft and wet, her tongue ready to lock with his in a sensual caress. Soon Jack was tasting the sweet flesh of her neck as he pinned her, squirming, to the wall.

Petra's fingers delved into Jack's thick hair as she abandoned herself to his searching hands. He rolled her nipples with his thumbs through the thin black material, making her writhe and groan, then passed on down the smooth plane of her stomach to the protruding mons. She loosened her thighs, letting his fingers search out the crevice between her plump labia, still moaning softly.

They moved from the hall into her bedroom. Jack scarcely had time to examine the decor but he did notice, with surprise, that the whole room seemed to be painted black. There were black satin sheets on the bed, too. The girl sure had weird taste.

Petra stripped off his clothes without touching his flesh, then made him get into bed and watch while she undressed. Making quite a professional job of it, she slowly slid down her back zipper until the dress slid to the floor. Covering the cups of her basque with her hands she wiggled about for a while, letting Jack have a good look at what was on offer. He liked what he saw. Petra had a petite figure with small pert breasts and a narrow waist, but her legs, in the black stockings seemed long in proportion. She also had a nice firm arse.

'How much longer are you going to keep me waiting?' he complained. 'I've got a pole you could erect a tent on under here!'

'Good!' Petra reached behind and unzipped the strapless basque. The cups loosened, giving Jack a teasing glimpse of her pale freckled tits. She coyly undid her suspenders and rolled down her stockings, leaning forward so that her cleavage was enhanced.

'Very nice!' he murmured.

She turned her back on him and slowly shrugged her way out of the corset until she stood there in the nude, her neat bum swaying provocatively. Jack felt like making a grab at it, but managed to restrain himself. He could feel his hot flesh moving against the constricting sheets and longed to be able to give his tool its head.

At last Petra turned to face him, arms behind her head. Her muff was shaven smooth, and the sight of her bulging naked slit roused Jack's penis to its fullest extent. In the lamp-light her uplifted boobs appeared tawny gold, their small orange nipples already puckering with excitement.

'Come here!' Jack said, gutturally.

He flung back the sheet to let her in and, taking one look at his rampant prick, she spread her thighs over him, nudging his glans into her already streaming hole.

'It turns me on, undressing in front of a man,' she explained, superfluously.

While Petra rode him with uninhibited enjoyment, Jack reached out for her compact little boobs and squeezed their round firmness. His climax was imminent, and he tried to avert it by dividing the net profit on the sale of the house into two and pondering the injustice of it all, since he'd made the entire down payment and coughed up the mortgage every month. However, his musing soon became dangerously resentful, which didn't seem fair with such a delightful female going full pelt on his joystick, to their mutual satisfaction.

'Oh God!' he heard her cry, rubbing her naked nether lips with her finger. 'I'm right on the brink!'

'Me too!' Jack groaned. The wave finally engulfed him and he spewed his foam as the crest peaked. On the way down he felt the fierce undulations of Petra's quim and knew that she, too, was finally satiated.

They nestled in each others' arms for a while as their breathing slowed and their pulses settled. Then Jack felt an irresistible compulsion to feel the smoothness of her vulva. He reached down with tentative fingers, but she took his hand and guided him right to her still-throbbing button.

'I've ... er ... never encountered a shaven pussy before,' he admitted.

'Then feel your fill,' she giggled, opening her thighs a bit more.

Petra sighed contentedly as he probed and stroked her hairless quim. It wasn't long before he was working his way down her body with his mouth, kissing her nipples, her navel and, at last, her smooth, slitted mound. It felt wonderful, like mouthing a juicy peach. Jack licked and sucked away until her clitoris protruded stiffly and her crack was invitingly open. He stuck his tongue right in, sucking away on her outer lips, and soon she was thrusting herself against him and wriggling excitedly. Her vagina opened to his fingers and he proceeded, with a combination of cunnilingus and cunni*fingers*, to bring her to a second shattering orgasm.

'Wow, that was great!' she sighed as the convulsions faded. 'But now, would you be a pal and leave me to sleep? I'm bushed, and I prefer to sleep alone. I put the electric blanket on in your room.'

It would have been churlish to cause a scene, so Jack gave her a goodnight kiss and left her room. Even so, he was disappointed. After such an enjoyable encounter he would have liked to snuggle up in Petra's bed until morning.

When Jack awoke there was an eerie stillness, which puzzled him until he remembered it was New Year's Day and everyone would be hung over. He got up, put on his dressing-gown and went to the bathroom, then peeped into Petra's room. Her bed was neatly made. Going into the sitting-room and kitchen he found them also empty. But on the hall table was a note. It said, 'Gone visiting. Happy New Year. Petra.'

Jack felt deflated. She might at least have said how much she enjoyed last night – presuming she had. He remembered uneasily how she'd taken it for granted he would want a 'no strings' relationship. True, he did. But that didn't mean he wouldn't want to make love to her again, and as soon as possible. Still, perhaps she would be home in the evening.

It was strange being in Petra's flat without her. Jack felt guilty switching on the television, although he was sure she wouldn't object. He mooched about for half a day then went out in search of food, found a Pakistani grocer's open and brought back enough to cook himself a light meal plus some basic provisions. When he was halfway through it, Petra returned.

'Oh good, you've got some food in,' she said, casually. 'I'm going out tonight, so I didn't bother getting much.'

Without the elaborate eye make-up she looked small and frail, but still desirable.

Jack smiled. 'I enjoyed last night.'

'Yes, it was nice, wasn't it?' she replied, in the same casual tone. Jack felt his hopes sink. She didn't sound keen on repeating the experience.

'Look, we'll talk tomorrow about rent and stuff, okay? I must shower and change now. See you.'

Jack felt he'd got the message. He didn't know if he was still in with a chance of more sex or not but one thing was certain, there was to be little encouragement outside the bedroom. Despite the fact that she'd more or less forewarned him, he felt cheated. Even towards the end of his marriage to Suzanne there had been a certain amount of affection, and he was missing it.

Next morning Jack went to work from Petra's flat. It was an awkward journey by car but, until he got his home computer set up permanently, he would have to go into the office every day. By the time he got back in the evening Petra had already gone out. She seemed to have a very active social life.

For several days they kept missing each other. Then, mid-week, they met in the kitchen as Petra made herself a quick meal. After discussing finance, Jack said, 'Don't you ever spend a night in, Petra? It gets a bit lonesome here sometimes.'

'Look, I said you could share my flat, Jack, not my life. Okay?'

'Okay. But we did get rather friendly on New Year's eve, I seem to recall.'

She grinned. 'Well, I always like to see the New Year in with a bang!'

'It was great, wasn't it?' Jack put his arm around her, but she shrugged him off.

'Look, Jack, there's something you should know about me. I don't get involved with the men I sleep with, okay? And I rarely sleep with the same man twice running. So I don't want you having any false hopes, because it's not going to happen again.'

'I see.' Jack felt deflated. He was prepared to accept that it was nothing personal, yet it still hurt. Now he began to see what Steve had meant when he called Petra a 'complicated female'. Except that she would probably think of herself as being simple and straightforward!

After she'd gone out, a friend of Petra's phoned with an urgent message and Jack promised to make sure she got it when she came in. He was having a leak around midnight when he heard Petra return from wherever she'd been. By the time he emerged from the bathroom she had retreated to her bedroom. Undeterred, he knocked at the door. An incoherent cry came from within and, taking it to be an invitation to enter, he turned the handle.

The scene which met his eyes made him gasp. A blonde, naked female was lying face down on the bed with her arms tied behind her back and her ankles also bound. Petra was wearing a tight-fitting outfit in black leather with holes for her tits and crotch, and the sight of her pale flesh so provocatively visible at the erogenous zones gave Jack an instant hard-on.

Then he saw what she held in her right hand, and his blood chilled. Petra was wielding a short-handled whip, and the furious look on her face suggested that she had every intention of using it on him.

Chapter Eight

'Get out!' Petra snarled.

Jack considered quipping, 'Is this a private party, or can anyone join in?' but immediately thought better of it.

'Sorry,' he mumbled, retreating. He would leave the message by the coffee jar, where she was sure to see it in the morning.

So the bitch swings both ways, Jack mused as he lay in bed recovering from the shock. And into S&M, to boot! He wondered how much detail Steve knew about the 'complications' of Petra's love-life. He might have warned him a bit more specifically. Probably next time they met Steve would greet him with a knowing grin, the sod!

There was a sudden crack, followed by a whimper of pain, and Jack knew that the blonde masochist in the next room was being thrashed. He imagined those pale buttocks criss-crossed with red streaks and found himself back in the fantasy he'd shared with Debra. His penis, which had been flaccid and relaxed after his warm shower, was now hardening, and Jack's hand strayed to his groin. There came the noise of another whiplash, followed by a moan that hovered between pain and ecstasy, and Jack's erection grew. He began to move the loose skin over his shaft, feeling the familiar buzz of energy flood through his pubic area.

Soon Jack was imagining that Debra was being chastised by the redoubtable Petra, that it was her dark head which lay on her pillow, her buttocks that wriggled in perverse satisfaction at every stinging flick of the whip. He could see himself standing there with his hands on his hips, controlling the operation like some medieval lord.

'Fifty lashes, Petra, and don't spare the wench! She has done me a grievous wrong and must be severely punished.'

Afterwards he would claim his *droit de seigneur*, taking the bitch with abrupt force while she was still numb, enjoying her tears of humiliation as he rode her like a wild stallion that needed breaking in. At the same time he would reward Petra by licking her bald pussy, working his tongue well in between the smooth lips until he could reach her tasty pleasure bud. With careful timing he would make the two women climax simultaneously and then he would come himself, with a fierce, hot spurt into Debra's tightly convulsing quim. At the thought of it, Jack's busy fingers redoubled their efforts and brought him off in a satisfying gush that sprayed his stomach and left him wallowing in a warm and comforting glow.

Next morning there was no sign of either Petra or her submissive girlfriend. Jack was relieved. He didn't know quite what to say to her and welcomed the breathing space. Yet he began to feel that he would be better off elsewhere and resolved to search more urgently for a flat. Not that he minded in the least what Petra got up to, but it was clear that she was no longer interested in him, and he felt inhibited about bringing anyone else back to her flat. If he wanted to have any sex life of his own it would be better if he found himself a place as soon as possible.

Within a week he had found somewhere: a penthouse flat in a modern block in Norwood, that suited his needs perfectly. Once his furniture was out of store and he was surrounded by familiar things, he began to feel more secure. The jigsaw of his life had been re-shuffled, and the picture was coming out different from before, but somehow the pieces were fitting together.

There was just one gaping hole in Jack's life and it was proving hard to fill. For the past three years his sex life had been intimately bound up with his work and now both seemed sadly lacking. His new job was just a way of earning money, pleasant enough but without the challenges he'd had at Global, and he missed the extra dimension provided by the amazing Feelietron. So when he called in at the office one morning and Clive, the editor, asked him to do a piece on a new Laser-Sex Adventure Show in Crystal Palace, Jack jumped at the chance.

'Tell me more!' he grinned, as they both sat in Clive's cluttered office.

Clive lobbed a leaflet across his desk. 'Their blurb says it's a game for consenting adults over the age of eighteen. You get dressed up in suits and issued with a laser gun.

Then you have to hunt down your sexual partner for the night.'

Jack skimmed the brochure. It had photos of nubile women in pink and silver suits, skintight to reveal every curve. He had a hard-on just thinking about it.

'Looks good to me! When do I go?'

'Soon as you like. The place opens eight to midnight. No sex takes place on the premises, though. You have to make your own arrangements. I suppose it's like a dating agency, only more fun. What I need is a two-thousand word article for a double spread. Don't worry about pictures, we'll get those from the manager.'

Jack couldn't wait to do this particular bit of research. It might take more than one visit, so he decided to start that night. He finished the review he was working on and left early, giving himself time to shower and have a meal before he went.

Soon after eight, Jack was standing outside a black-fronted building which proclaimed Laser-Sex in luridly flashing lights. There was a doorman in a black and silver outfit, giving the place a club feel. Clive had warned Jack not to say that he was from the magazine so he entered like any other punter and paid the rather large entrance fee, saving the ticket for his expenses claim.

'The gents' robing room is through there,' the attractive girl at the desk said, giving him a delightful grin. 'You'll find a copy of the rules on the wall. Have fun!'

Jack went through the door and found himself in the company of half a dozen other males in various states of undress. Two of them were already in their suits, tight-fitting gold and black numbers. Jack selected one his size from the rack and began to search for the fastenings, which turned out to be Velcro strips.

Seeing him fumbling, the guy nearest him grinned. 'This is your first time?'

Jack nodded. 'How d'you get into this thing?'

They got chatting. It seemed that Bob had been coming at least once every week since the place opened a month ago.

'We're getting some smashing girls in here now,' he grinned. 'Word's getting round that if you want to pick someone up and have a great time doing it this is the place to be. I can guarantee you'll be coming back for more.'

'What do you have to do?'

'You just go in there with your laser gun and find your target! The girls all wear masks but these outfits really show off their figures. It may seem a bit crude, but when you go to a disco it's the way a girl moves her body that turns you on, isn't it? Well it's the same thing here.'

'So I choose the girl I fancy and aim the gun on her. Is that it?'

'Not exactly. You have to make three hits. The girls don't have guns, so if your target doesn't fancy you, or if she wants to play hard to get she can run and hide.'

'What if two men want the same girl?'

'Then you have to compete for her. Three hits by another man's gun and you're out of the running. It can get quite aggressive. But you know you stand a good chance of taking someone home at the end of the night.'

'Hm. What if she takes her mask off at the end and you don't fancy her?'

'No problem. You both have a veto once the game's over. It's a bit of fun, really.'

'Okay. I'm ready. Where are the weapons?'

They picked up their lasers by the swing doors and went through into a dark corridor, sporadically illuminated by flashing lights.

'You're on your own now, Jack!' Bob whispered, running ahead of him.

Jack followed circumspectly, trying to suss the lie of the land. Suddenly he found himself in a kind of grotto, with a small waterfall lit by flashing blue and green lights. Sitting by the pool was a 'mermaid' in a silvery suit that looked like fish-scales. She had long blonde hair and a full face mask daubed with fluorescent paint. When she saw Jack she leapt up, pretending to be frightened, and crouched behind a rock. Jack aimed his weapon at her but then decided it was too early to make his choice, and sauntered on down another corridor.

It soon opened into a chamber full of polystyrene stalactites. There were men and girls hiding behind them, and the occasional zip of laser fire could be heard. Jack settled down to watch for a while. He saw a woman with two red splotches on her silver suit cross the floor and get caught in some crossfire. As soon as she was marked by a third hit, a man came out of the shadows and claimed her. Laughing they ran off down a corridor together, hand in hand.

There seemed to be three girls left in the chamber and

only one other guy besides Jack. He sized up the prospects as best he could. One girl was a redhead with large, shapely jugs but a behind that was too flat for his taste. Another seemed rather too plump and her hair had been over-bleached. The third was small and trim, with short blonde hair and an attractive way of moving. So far she'd managed to escape being hit, whereas the other two had a red splodge each. Jack decided to make the blonde girl his target, so he concentrated on the area behind a rock where he knew she was crouching.

It would have been relatively easy just to go up and fire at her, but Jack had no way of knowing whether the other guy in the room would attack him too. The battle scene had gone quiet, except for the faint electronic music that was playing in the background. The fat girl made an occasional sortie, taunting them with a wiggle of her fleshy hips then retreating to her cover. Suddenly two more guys appeared. They sized up the situation and found their own vantage points within the fake landscape. The three girls made a brief appearance to let the new males know they were there, then all went quiet again.

Jack was now determined to have the fair-haired girl, no matter what the opposition. He could feel the blood pumping hotly through his pulses. He had the beginnings of a boner, and was relieved that the crotch of his one-piece garment had some elasticity to it. Fingering the trigger on his laser gun, he wondered how the hell he was going to get a shot at the girl's shapely chest or jutting ass if she stayed behind that damned rock all the time.

Then one of the new guys decided he could wait no longer and dashed out towards the girls' hideout with a warlike whoop. After that all hell broke loose. The fat girl emerged, shrieking, and went wobbling off down the nearest corridor, hotly pursued by one of the men. The redhead scrambled to another stalactite on her hands and knees but was hit as she went. Jack crept forward a few paces, but just as he was within shooting range of the blonde girl's rock, another guy pounced on her with glee and fired. Fortunately he missed, but Jack caught him on the thigh instead and a satisfying pool of red marked his silver and black suit. He turned with a growl and took aim at Jack, who dodged behind a stalactite, feeling the laser beam whizz past his ear. At least he now knew where he stood. He was going for the blonde girl, but he had a rival.

Their target proved to be cunning. While her two suitors were fighting amongst themselves she slipped off down the corridor and was spotted by Jack just before she disappeared round a bend. He set off in brisk pursuit, covering his back against the other guy's fire. Beams ricocheted off the walls of the tunnel as Jack followed the girl's elusive form into the next chamber.

The place was done out like a Pharaoh's tomb, complete with sarcophagi. Obviously no-one would make a sitting target of themselves by getting into a coffin, but there were plenty of other hiding places. Statues of Egyptian gods stood guard, interspersed with obelisks and miniature pyramids. It was anyone's guess which one the blonde was using for cover.

Jack crouched behind a mini-pyramid and watched his rival enter. The guy was going from point to point around the room, looking for the girl. It would have been easy for Jack to take a pot shot at him, but then he would have given his position away. For the time being he preferred to wait and watch. His patience was soon rewarded when the girl was flushed out from behind a statue of Anubis, the jackal-headed god. She gave a small scream and fled to the other side of the chamber, near where Jack was hiding. As the man advanced in pursuit, Jack took aim and fired. A red spot appeared on his rival's chest, and he immediately took cover behind an obelisk. One more shot and the guy would be dead . . .

But the girl was still unscathed. Jack felt he had to make his first claim on her, to make his mark on her virginal second-skin. He lay down on his stomach and started to wriggle his way along the floor until he could get an angle on her. She was kneeling on all fours now, her neat buttocks rearing up provocatively, her eyes peering into the semi-darkness ahead of her. Jack took aim and pressed the trigger. A red patch appeared on the girl's rump and she turned in dismay to see him taking aim again. Throwing caution to the winds she jumped up and ran across the open space into the next corridor, just managing to dodge the fire that came at her from both sides.

Once she had gone there was an awkward pause, with each combatant reluctant to expose himself. Then another woman entered the chamber, followed by two more men, and the battle hotted up. Jack slithered along on the floor, covered by shadow, and managed to get halfway along the corridor before anyone spotted him. He got quickly to his feet and sprinted the last few yards until he reached the next room, where the blonde-haired girl was still visible through the branches of a fake bush. Seizing his opportunity Jack fired at once, and was encouraged by the sight of a second red stain spreading over her right breast. She ducked down and scrambled behind the trunk of a tree. This was a woodland scene, and Jack soon found another tree to hide behind.

He waited with thumping heart, enjoying the vital surge of adrenaline through his veins and the hardening of his dick beneath the constricting costume. Just one more hit and he could claim his prize! But she was obviously going to be very wary from now on. Even so, Jack had the feeling that she wasn't averse to him going for her. It was almost as if she herself were calling the shots, willing him to conquer her. Now he came to think of it, she'd been far more circumspect with the other guy than she had with him, allowing him to get close enough to her to take proper aim. A smile crept over Jack's face as he thought of the satisfaction that lay ahead.

Confident that, this time, he could clinch it Jack decided to risk all and began to move from tree to bush, edging nearer to where the girl was hiding. When he was just a couple of leaps away, his rival suddenly appeared and took a shot at him. Jack felt the thud as the laser made its mark on his back, and cursed his careless stupidity. He whirled round with his weapon at the ready, but the man had already darted behind a tree. While this was happening the girl seized her chance and ran from the room, back the way they had come. Jack swore. If he wasn't careful she would slip into the arms of some other guy and he would have to start all over again with a new target.

Although every second meant that the blonde girl could be making good her escape, Jack was reluctant to expose himself to laser fire again. He'd lost one life already. So the two men settled into a stalemate, each awaiting his opportunity to make a move. It was only when two more females appeared, creating a diversion, that Jack had his chance. The other guy obviously decided to go for one of the new targets, an Asian girl who'd already suffered two hits, and so Jack was at last able to make his getaway. He sped down to the Egyptian room, which seemed empty, then on into the grotto where he was pleased to see Bob, crouching behind a stalactite.

'How's it going?' Bob grinned.

'I'm after a blonde girl with two hits on her. Did you see her come in here?'

'If she's the one I think you mean, she was in here already. But she left when I fired at the redhead who's behind that rock over there. I think she went back down that corridor.' He pointed in the direction of the Egyptian room.

'Thanks a lot.'

Jack hurriedly retraced his steps. The chamber still seemed empty, with only piped music to be heard. Jack was disappointed. What if some other guy had shot her and they'd already left? The thought of giving her up now was a real pain. He'd had so many tantalising glimpses of her firm buttocks and trim waist, of tightly honed thighs and cone-shaped boobs that he was hungry to see her in the flesh, to run his hands over those delightful contours and make his prey finally his own. To give her up to another hunter now, just as he was so near to claiming her, would be unbearable.

Yet he needed to know, first of all, if she was in the Egyptian room at all. As far as he could see the place was deserted, but there was one way to find out.

'Are you in here, my fair-haired beauty?' he whispered, loudly. There was a pause, then a faint giggle reached his ears. Surprisingly, it seemed to come from inside one of the painted tombs.

'Is that you?' he repeated.

'That's right!' came the now-unmistakable reply. Jack stealthily approached the sarcophagus, looking over his shoulder as he went. He flung back the lid and there, lying with arms crossed over her chest in typical Mummy pose, was the girl of his choice. He took careful aim and fired a shot at her crotch. She giggled and shook her pelvis at him as the red stain spread around her faintly defined vulva. Then she held up a hand in surrender and he pulled her out. She skipped nimbly from the coffin and, still holding his hand, began to lead him down the corridor towards the exit.

'Won't you take off your mask?' he asked her, but she shook her head. So he had to be content with the glitter of amusement that came from the small eye-holes. When they came to the changing-rooms he murmured, 'Meet you outside in five minutes' before vanishing through the men's door.

Jack scrambled out of his playsuit and back into his own clothes. A glance at his watch showed that the game had taken almost two hours, although the time had flown by. Other players were appearing now, well tanked-up in preparation, but Jack was glad he'd gone into it sober. He preferred to be clear-headed when making love.

Outside, in the dark street, the girl was talking to the doorman. She turned as he approached, and he saw that despite the slim youthfulness of her figure she was in her thirties. Her eyes were strangely mismatched, one blue and one brown, but apart from that one flaw she had a well-balanced face with full, sensual lips that were now parted expectantly.

'Hi, I'm Jack!' he grinned, holding out his hand.

Hers felt warm and relaxed. 'I'm Ginnie. Did you enjoy the game?'

They began to walk towards the car park at the side of the building. Jack considered revealing the purpose of his visit to Laser Sex, but decided against it.

'Not bad! Do you think it'll catch on?'

She nodded. 'Beats computer games any day, doesn't it?' She paused at a red Metro. 'Well, what now? Would you like to come back to my flat? I only live round the corner.'

Jack hesitated. He'd been hoping to take the woman home himself, to christen his new place as it were. But Ginnie mistook his hesitation for doubt.

'Look, there's no obligation to have sex with me, you

157

know. We could just have a chat for a bit. It's only half ten.'

'Fine.'

Jack got into her car and they drove down a street of large Edwardian villas. Ginnie sat with her short skirt showing several inches of thigh which, together with the way she laughed at his feeble jokes and brushed the back of her hand against his knee, convinced him that she would be as disappointed as he if they didn't end up in bed together.

Ginnie lived in a spacious top-floor flat with a computer work-station in one corner of the living-room.

'That's mine,' she told Jack, seeing his eye light on it with interest. 'I work for a firm of contractors, looking after their data bank. But I'm also a computer games junkie.'

They were soon deep in conversation about the latest games, but Jack only told her about his present job. Despite the way he'd been treated at Global he still respected the copyright protection clause he'd signed. Even when the conversation turned to the future of games technology he spoke in vague terms about the possibilities of VR.

'How about trying out the latest one I bought?' Ginnie suggested, picking a disk out of the pile on her desk.

It was a game that Jack had already reviewed, but he didn't mind humouring her for a bit, especially as it gave him a chance to get physically close. They sat side by side in front of the screen, taking turns on the joystick, each trying to outdo the other. Something of the excitement of the Laser adventure returned as Ginnie became engrossed in the maze-like chase that the game involved.

'Go on – get that black gnome!' she urged him. 'Great! Now try the snake ... gottim! That gives us access to that new cave.'

Jack was aware that she was wriggling about on her seat like an impatient schoolgirl, her cheeks flushed and her pulses racing. Her arousal was infectious. Jack clenched his thighs to ease the sudden surge of hot energy in his groin. His game character entered the cave, found the gold, fought the dragon – real basic stuff – and untied the maiden. Except he had a feeling maybe she'd have preferred to stay bound and gagged ...

'Brilliant!' Ginnie surprised him by throwing her arms around him and kissing him passionately. Then she withdrew, looking bashful. 'I get a bit carried away by these games,' she admitted. 'They sort of turn me on.'

Jack nodded. 'They can be pretty addictive.' She'd love the Feelietron ones he thought ruefully.

'You did brilliantly. I've been trying to get into that cave for days.'

'I have a confession to make. I've played it before.'

Ginnie giggled. 'That's not fair! You cheated me, Jack, making me think you'd sussed it right off.'

'I'm sorry. How can I make it up to you?'

She gave him a naughty smile. 'Come into my bedroom and find out!'

Jack raised his brows in mock surprise. 'The lady doesn't beat about the bush, does she?'

Rising, she took his hand. 'What's the point? We both know we want it. Anyway, you've played Sir Galahad twice tonight and won both times, so I think it's time you got your reward, don't you?'

Jack let Ginnie lead him into the next room, which contained a king-size bed and some Japanese erotic prints on the wall. Two silk kimonos hung behind the door.

'You like things Japanese?' he asked.

She smiled. 'My husband is Japanese.'

'Husband?'

'Yes. Don't worry, he never minds me bringing lovers home. In fact, he likes it.'

Jack still felt wary. 'You mean you've got some sort of open marriage?'

Ginnie pulled her T-shirt over her head. 'You could say that.'

She was wearing a pink see-through bra, that seemed to sit on top of her fleshy little tits rather than support them. The tawny nipples were squashed flat behind the transparent nylon. Jack had an urge to feel her boobs through the tantalising bra and moved forward. Ginnie unzipped her black ski pants but before she could roll them down Jack had taken her in his arms and was kissing her, his right hand enclosing her satiny left breast.

Ginnie kissed him back eagerly, with her sweet tongue-tip savouring his. He squeezed her tit and she moaned, pushing her hips against him. Jack felt his erection approaching its maximum and longed to get out of his constricting jeans.

'Mm, so good!' he heard her sigh, against his lips.

She reached behind her back and started to unhook her bra, but Jack stopped her.

'No, leave it on,' he begged. 'I love the feel of it. Do you have matching pants?'

Ginnie grinned, removing her trousers for him to see. The brown bush of pubic hair was squashed flat by the shiny nylon triangle. Moving to the bed, she lay down in a provocative pose while Jack stripped to his underpants. He could see her eyes on his throbbing bulge and noticed her little wiggle of excitement.

Jack moved in on her, resuming their kiss. He first kneaded the small, firm boobs in their slippery nylon pouches then slipped his right hand down to see how her mons felt, encased in the slick material. As he passed his palm over her he could feel tiny pinpricks where the hairs were just protruding through the weave. Further down, the damp from her pussy was seeping through. He sucked hungrily on her tongue, feeling her hand snaking down his erection to grasp his balls then gently play with them, keeping them separate in their sac as if they were a pair of Chinese dragon balls.

Suddenly Jack thought he heard the sound of a door being unlocked. He paused and raised his head.

Ginnie said, 'That's my husband. When I bring someone home he likes to watch. You don't mind, do you?'

'Since you've got me by the balls, would I be wise to refuse?'

She laughed, releasing him. 'Okay. If you really don't mind, Jack, it turns him on a treat. Me too.'

There was a knock at the bedroom door. Ginnie called,

'Come in, darling!' and a short, square-shouldered man in a navy suit entered. His brown eyes gleamed as he saw Jack, and he inclined his head slightly.

'Ken, this is Jack.'

'Very pleased to meet you.' He held out his hand. Feeling decidedly foolish, Jack shook it. He watched Ken kiss his wife lightly on the cheek then turn back to him.

'So, you won her in the game?'

Jack had to think for a moment. His erection had subsided a bit now, making him less embarrassed. Ah yes, the Laser game. He'd already forgotten.

'I *let* him win me, yes!' Ginnie giggled.

'Excuse me while I change out of my work clothes,' Ken said, turning his back on them and shrugging off his jacket. He went to the wardrobe and took out a hanger.

'How about a drink?' Ginnie suggested, leaping off the bed. 'Do you like saki, Jack?'

'I'd prefer whisky, if you have it.'

'Sure.'

Ginnie put on the blue kimono and left the two men together. Ken continued to undress while he chatted. 'My wife told you, I like to watch?'

'She did mention it, yes.'

'You don't mind?'

'I suppose not. It's not something I've taken part in before.'

'My wife is beautiful. I like to see other men enjoy her.' He added, inexplicably, 'We have no children.'

The Japanese was standing naked now, his thin penis hanging beneath sparse black hairs. Jack said nothing, not knowing what to say. Ken pulled the red kimono round him and sat down on the padded velvet chair opposite the wardrobe mirror. From there, Jack realised, the man had a double view: of the bed itself and of its reflection.

It was a relief when Ginnie returned with the drinks tray. Jack felt distanced from what they had been doing before her husband arrived. Now he felt he would just as soon go home after his whisky. He was apprehensive about performing in front of another man, and yet he had more or less agreed to it. Perhaps the alcohol would help loosen him up.

'Cheers!' Ken smiled, raising his saki cup. Jack responded, but couldn't help feeling that the situation was taking on a slightly unreal quality, rather like one of his own scenarios in fact. Had the previous twelve hours or so of computer and laser games begun to take their toll, blurring the edges between reality and fantasy in Jack's overworked brain? He downed the whisky in one go.

Ginnie sat herself next to Jack on the bed, one arm around his shoulder.

'You carry on,' Ken said, genially. 'Don't mind me. I was sorry to interrupt.'

She took Jack's glass from him and set it on the floor, then kissed him fully on the mouth, her hands on his shoulders. He was slow to respond at first, too conscious of the impassive brown eyes of the Japanese as he sat just a few yards away. But then the hot sweetness of her saliva began to work its magic and he kissed her back, caressing her bosom and feeling his penis twitch with the resurgence of his former lust.

Smoothly, and without taking her lips from his, Ginnie manoeuvred herself onto the bed and shifted them both up until they had almost regained their previous position. They lay length to length, thighs partially entwined, as their kiss grew deeper. Jack felt his pants being eased over his now erect prick, cool fingers touched his shaft and his balls felt taut to bursting. He fingered her hard little nipples beneath the nylon bra and she uttered a half-sigh, half-moan. Swiftly he groped between her thighs, felt the steamy wet labia, and his desire returned more urgently than before. He pulled down the scrap of shiny stuff that guarded her entrance and plunged his fingers into her streaming quim.

'Ah! Oh, you've found me!' she cooed, as his fingertips lighted on her swollen love-bud. Gently he massaged her most sensitive spot, his dick rearing aggressively as he held back from entering her too soon.

But his entrance couldn't come soon enough for Ginnie, it seemed. 'Now, take me now!' she moaned, gutturally. 'Here, put this on!'

She was groping beneath the pillow and soon pulled out a ribbed black condom. While Ginnie hastily removed her pants Jack put the rubber on, trying to ignore the fact that he was being watched by her voyeuristic husband. He looked down, proud of the shiny black tool that stood in readiness at the base of his stomach. It was both longer and thicker than the Japanese guy's.

Ginnie's eager hand reached out for his phallus, directed it between her open legs and enveloped it with her eager labia. Jack thrust straight in, giving an audible sigh as he met no resistance but slid smoothly into the cushioned interior. Behind him Jack was vaguely aware of sound and movement and soon, out of the corner of his eye, he saw Ken moving about the bed. He turned his head to look.

The man was prancing about like a referee at a Sumo wrestling match, grunting Japanese expletives while he watched his wife being shafted. As Jack prodded away Ken was dodging round the bed, trying to get a good view of the action and uttering what sounded like words of encouragement. By now Ginnie was bucking her hips and grinding her pelvis in a most stimulating manner, and Jack had got into a good rhythm. He began to enjoy the idea of providing entertainment for her kinky husband. Glancing round he could see that Ken was playing with his tool as he followed the action with wild, gleaming eyes, rubbing himself frantically while he urged his wife's lover on in fluent Japanese or broken English by turns.

'Go it, Jackie boy, prang my wife senseless!' Jack heard him say, followed by a torrent of incomprehensible syllables.

At last Jack felt a rush of energy sweep through him, like the adrenaline high of scoring a goal. He pumped out his fluid with a long moan and felt the walls of Ginnie's vagina clasp him tightly, squeezing out every last drop until he was quite empty. Ken had subsided into a series of long, searing moans that signalled the arrival of his climax too, and it wasn't long before the three of them were collapsed in a heap on the bed.

Exhaustion took over, and Jack lapsed into a doze. He was awoken by the feel of a hand stroking his buttocks. Opening his eyes, he saw that his head was near Ginnie's warm, soft breast and he took her teat in his mouth. She put both hands up to his face, stroking his cheeks, but he suddenly realised that the caressing of his other cheeks was still continuing. He recoiled in horror, pushing the Japanese away from his rear end, and leapt up from the bed.

'Er . . . I have to be going,' he mumbled, looking round for his clothes.

'Stay the night,' Ginnie pleaded. 'We could have lots more fun, the three of us.'

Ken lay sprawled at his wife's feet, his brown eyes distantly gleaming. 'Yes, Jack, do stay. We will give you a night to remember.'

'I think this has been quite memorable enough already, thanks,' Jack said firmly, pulling on his pants. 'I've a heavy day tomorrow, so I'd rather get home.'

The pair looked sulky as he continued to dress. But, as he was leaving, Ginnie smiled, 'Take our phone number, Jack. If you feel like coming to see us any time, just give us a ring.'

'Thanks, I might just do that.'

When Jack finally started on the ten minute walk back to his car, he felt a surge of relief, as if he'd just had a narrow escape. Sex with Ginnie had been fine. Even the presence of a voyeuristic cheerleader had been surprisingly good once he'd got used to it, increasing his excitement and hence his enjoyment. But the thought of including Mr. Inscrutable in the proceedings made him squirm. A threesome was fine when the other two were women, but he drew the line at making love with another man.

Chapter Nine

Jack wrote up the piece about Laser-Sex, but he felt no desire to repeat the experience. He concluded that the game had been sexy and exciting while it lasted, but there was no guarantee that satisfaction would follow. What if you really fancied your target woman but didn't manage to get in the regulation three hits? Or supposing she didn't want you once the game was over? If you were prepared to take it first and foremost as an adventure game, with sex as a possible bonus, fine. But if you were expecting an evening of Laser-Sex to end with an automatic bonking session you could be sadly misled. As far as the mating game went, you might just as well take your chances in the local singles bar.

Even so, the article was well received by his editor.

'I'd like you to do more of those undercover operations,' Clive told him, with a grin. 'They make a change from straight computer games. And the whole scene is getting raunchier. They're putting sex into everything these days, entertainment-wise. I've heard there's even an 'Adults Only' launderette in Soho where you can watch computer porn instead of your washing!'

'Sounds interesting!'

'Yes, but not quite our bag, I think. However, this may be. What do you reckon?'

He handed Jack a London evening paper with an advert circled in red:

VR Games Company requires volunteer testers. Generous payment for having a great time! The prudish and squeamish need not apply. If you want to know more phone us NOW, or contact us via Internet . . .

Jack felt his heartbeat quicken. Was this Global?

Clive seemed to have anticipated his reaction. 'No, Jack, it's not your old firm. I checked it out. The company's called Cyberco – I've not come across them before. Anyway, I liked the idea of sampling the latest VR games so I booked in under the name of Frank Wright for next weekend. Then I realised that, with your experience of VR work, it would be far better if you went along instead. Are you free?'

'Next weekend? Sure.'

'Great. You'll be our "Mr. Wright" then.'

I'd like to be *some*body's, Jack thought wryly.

'Just one thing. I think you should remain incognito while you're checking out these places, but a false name won't protect you if your face is recognised.'

'What, you want me to go in disguise?'

'That mightn't be a bad idea. A fake beard and glasses should do the trick. See what you can do.'

Although Jack was taken aback at first, he realised that if anyone at Cyberco did recognise him as having worked for Global, they might well suspect he was up to some industrial espionage. There had been reports in the media lately of 'mystery shoppers' and other spies being punished in nasty ways when discovered, and Jack was rather attached to his kneecaps.

The following Saturday morning 'Frank Wright' presented himself at the front desk of Cyberco Games International, Ltd. He had a dark beard and square-framed glasses, wore a beige raincoat and spoke with a slight Transatlantic accent. Jack had always had a secret leaning towards amateur theatricals.

The receptionist looked like a Barbie doll and sounded like a tape-loop.

'Okay, Mr. Wright, if you'd like to go through that door there the pre-briefing will start at ten. Coffee is being served now. The Gentleman's cloakroom is just down the corridor on your left.'

When Jack entered the room he found himself in the company of around fifteen other men, all drinking coffee and looking rather uptight. Soon after he was served from a trolley by a middle-aged woman, a female voice addressed them through the p.a.

'Gentlemen, if you'd like to take your seats now I shall be with you shortly.'

There were a few raised eyebrows as the men headed for the armchairs arranged in a wide semi-circle around a desk. Jack felt a frisson of anticipation as he sipped his drink. Beneath the atmosphere of nervous excitement he could detect a note of macho lasciviousness, like men waiting for a striptease to begin in a sleazy club. He wondered if any of those present knew exactly what they were in for.

At last the door opened and a woman walked in, brisk and confident, clipboard under her arm. Jack nearly dropped his coffee in his lap. He stared, incredulously, as she reached the desk then turned to face them, confirming what he hardly dared to believe.

'Hullo,' she smiled, her eyes briefly scanning the room. 'I'm the Consumer Research Officer here at Cyberia, and I shall be your co-ordinator for the weekend. My name is Debra Newcombe.'

So it really was her! Jack's mind was split in two as he tried to focus on what she was saying while speculating on what the hell she was doing there. Was Debra working full-time for this company? Then she must have quit Alistair soon after he'd left. How ironic! He recalled her hints about his talents being wasted at Global. If he'd played his cards right – i.e. screwed her – would he have ended up working for this outfit too?

Debra looked straight at him and he held his breath. Would she recognise him beneath the disguise? But her gaze passed on to the next man and Jack knew he was safe. It gave him a satisfying sense of power to know that Debra had no idea she had an enemy in the camp.

'What you are about to experience is something altogether new,' she was saying. 'We call it "Virtual Interfacing". When you use our equipment you'll enter a world of illusion so compelling that you'll be quite disorientated until you become acclimatised. I used that word deliberately because, in some ways, it's like visiting a foreign country. Your body will react to the stimuli, your brain will be confused and you may experience sensory over-load. But I can assure you there's nothing to worry about. Your bodily functions will be continually monitored and if there's the slightest cause for alarm I shall instantly disconnect you.'

Then Jack realised that Debra would be plugged into the network too and the germ of an idea made him grin wickedly. He didn't know if what he had in mind was possible until he had had a closer look at the technology. But if it *was* possible he could really have some fun – and at Debra's expense!

They were given the choice of sampling a 'sexually explicit' game or a 'fantasy horror' one, and Jack chose the former. He was curious to see whether Debra had brought any ideas or technical expertise with her from Global, although he presumed she wouldn't be foolish enough to violate the gagging clause in her contract and risk prosecution.

The men began filing through to the next room while Debra stood smiling at the door. She was wearing a blue silk blouse, beneath which the small pyramids of her breasts protruded erotically, and her tight-fitting black pants were moulded to the contours of her mons and buttocks. Jack noticed several of the men giving her the eye. His heartbeat quickened as he drew close and threw her a smile, but Debra's professional manner never wav-ered. He mentally thanked Clive for persuading him to attend incognito, and the hope that he might turn the situation to his advantage grew into an urge that was almost sexual in itself.

In the games room the players were again arranged in

a semi-circle with the control desk facing them in the centre. Quickly Jack took his place at a spare computer and surreptitiously examined the serial ports. In theory he should be able to make the communication two-way.

'Gentlemen, we shall begin with a test run,' Debra announced, when most of the positions were filled. Then she explained how to put on and control the VR gear, sounding much like an air stewardess going through the safety routine. Jack was interested to see that the Cyberian sensory apparatus differed in several respects from the version used by Global.

Beneath the mask, gauntlets and crotch-piece, Jack was throbbing with anticipation. It had been so long since he'd worn this type of gear. Like an addict only semi-cured of his habit, he felt the old cravings return. A heady elation seized him when he flicked a switch and found himself near a dazzling shore, with the impression of warm sunlight bathing his skin.

As the compelling image of a naked Venus rising from the foam appeared, Debra's voice spoke in his right ear. 'You should now all be seeing the Botticelli image of the Goddess Venus, standing in the sea. She should beckon you and you should have the sensation of walking on water towards her . . .'

The test run was certainly impressive. Jack could feel the shifting clamminess under his feet, smell the strong scent of seaweed and taste the salt on the wind. When the 'goddess' took his hand it felt warm and smooth. She led him ashore, and there was the gritty sensation of sand beneath his toes.

'Is everyone on the beach now?' Debra's voice enquired. 'If anyone is in difficulties, please raise your right hand ... Good! Now those who have chosen the "horror" option will find a new scenario unfolding. The rest of you will continue from here.'

Jack saw that the beach was occupied by many semi-naked women, all in provocative poses. Although he couldn't address the characters himself, due to the limitations of the Cyberian technology, Venus spoke to him clearly, in low seductive tones.

'You are on the shore of the Sea of Desire. Here all your deepest dreams can be fulfilled. Every woman that you see before you longs to lead you into the Elysian Fields of bliss.'

The woman nearest him had long dark tresses and coyly downcast blue eyes. The computer registered the object of Jack's gaze, let him zoom in on her, then Venus spoke.

'This is Daphne, who is ready and willing to subject herself entirely to your will. Anything you ask of her is yours. She will gladly obey your every whim and take delight in being your devoted slave.'

In response, Daphne began to fondle her large boobs while twisting and turning into every conceivable erotic posture, her swollen labia displaying the pink, succulent fruit within.

Jack wanted to survey more of the alternatives before he chose one to explore. His eyes turned in another direction and there was a big woman in a leather tunic, wielding a whip.

'This is Amazonia,' Venus said. 'She will take you to the dark threshold of your pain and beyond, letting you experience the keenest sensations of brutal pleasure before she is through.'

When Jack's eyes moved on, once again, to a woman dressed in a black rubber mini-dress and thigh-high black boots Venus responded at once. 'Here is Domina, who will treat you with the utmost disdain. If you wish for degradation, Domina will satisfy your most humiliating desires.'

After that Jack was introduced in turn to a buxom 'wet nurse', a woman who lay bound and gagged but with her orifices exposed, a transvestite, and a woman who was described as having 'no control over her bladder.' Well, they'd certainly catered for all tastes! Although the technical expertise was nowhere near Global's there was a certain naive appeal about the scenario which intrigued him. Had any of it been Debra's work?

In the end, Jack chose to go with Domina. Although he had no particular desire to be humiliated he was curious to see how they handled it. If there was time, he would also try out the Amazonia character, to see if they'd differentiated clearly between the two.

The woman bade him kneel before her in the sand. Then she put manacles around his wrists and fastened him, by a chain, to her belt. Jack could feel the cold steel quite clearly, and the slight pressure on his wrist bones was impressive.

'Come with me, worm!' Domina snarled. 'I have ways of dealing with snivelling pathetic types like you. Crawl on your knees, wimp!'

The sand was satisfyingly hot and scratchy on his knees. Jack felt himself being drawn up the beach behind his formidable mistress, who led him into the large hotel at the top. Still kneeling, this time on rough carpet (the fine distinction between sand and wool pile worked well) Jack was hauled into a room reserved for 'Sub-Humans'. Domina slammed the door behind them and unlocked the handcuffs.

'Now, slave, prostrate yourself before me!'

The carpet seemed to press itself against Jack's face and body as he stared into its crimson depths. Suddenly he felt the spiked heel of Domina's boot in the small of his back. She ground the stiletto into his flesh, and he actually yelped as his nerve-endings responded to the painful stimulus.

Domina came to stand before him and he looked up. Beneath the hem of her rubber skirt Jack could see the black, hairy vee of a naked pussy with the pink flaps just visible. Despite his recent painful shock, he felt his erection grow at the sight.

'You will do exactly as I say. Eat dirt, dog!'

To Jack's horror a bowl of disgusting-looking mud was placed before him. A prod from Domina's shoe was enough to encourage him to open his mouth. The taste and texture of the stuff was appalling! Jack couldn't help wondering who would actually enjoy such a disgusting experience.

The woman had gone to lie on a couch at the end of the room. Whenever he looked up she cracked her whip at him and repeated, 'Eat dirt, dog!' until the bowl was empty. Then she barked, 'Come here!'

Jack had the feeling of the carpet moving beneath his knees until he was lying face down before her. 'Now wash your mouth out with soap!' she commanded.

At once a bowl of water and a cake of soap appeared before him. Again, the taste was disgusting! It wasn't perfumed toilet soap but the coal tar variety, and he felt sick as his mouth appeared to fill with the strong-tasting bubbles. The guys at Cyberia had certainly mastered artificial stimulation of the taste buds, although the flavours tended to be rather crude.

'Now that your mouth is clean, I have a special job for you,' Domina announced. 'You must do exactly as I say, and to my complete satisfaction, or I shall punish you severely, worm! Rise to your knees and prepare to salivate at the sight of my juicy fruit.'

She lifted her skirt, opened her thighs and revealed her quim. Jack did indeed feel the saliva began to flow in his mouth, such was the power of suggestion. He also felt the blood flow to his penis, giving him a real stonker.

'Clean out my grooves with your tongue, cur!' the woman demanded. 'Do it on all fours, like a randy dog licking a bitch. And make a thorough job of it, or I'll force you to eat shit!'

Interested as Jack was in sampling Cyberia's taste-simulation expertise, he drew the line at that and resolved to perform the task to the best of his ability. They'd got female genitalia down pretty accurately: both the soft slippery texture of cunt flesh and the funky odour of pussy musk were well reproduced. Beneath the scent of woman, they had tried to include the smell of rubber, but the two did not quite blend satisfactorily. However, the tactile aspect was good. Jack could almost feel the labia flatten against his lips as he felt something moist and tasty touch the tip of his tongue.

'Lick me!' came the commanding voice from above. 'Use your lips and tongue to get all the sticky juice out of my crannies. Suck my love-button until it's hard and throbbing like a dynamo. Keep your mouth moving all around my parts as if your life depends on it, and try to justify your miserable existence, you pathetic apology for a human being!'

Jack enjoyed the cunnilingus sequence, but he found it hard to ignore the continual verbal abuse that rained down on him. When Domina whacked him about the ears for failing to bring her to a climax, the stinging blow delivered a charge to his system that revived his flagging penis into rampant life. However there seemed to be no opportunity for satisfaction in this scenario unless you were really into being dominated.

It occurred to Jack that he might be better off with Amazonia so he flicked a switch and found himself back on the beach, with the ever-present Venus at his side. When he looked towards the formidable female in the leather dress she came towards him, a scowl disfiguring her noble brow.

'Is this the foul creature who has betrayed his woman?' she inquired of the goddess. 'Hand him over to me and I shall give him the punishment he deserves!'

Once more Jack went up the beach, this time driven by the Amazon as she lashed his shoulders with her whip.

He could feel the keen edge of the leather cut into his flesh, and when she took him into the hotel dungeon and chained him to the wall he knew that he was in for more of the same.

'Vile traitor!' she snapped, flexing her huge biceps at him. 'Before today is out I shall make you beg for mercy. I am mistress of all the arts of pain, and shall introduce you to the taste of many a subtle torment before I am through with you.'

So saying, she selected a new whip, slender and flexible. Jack saw it snake out, fast and sneaky, catching him in the crotch, and a razor sharp pain bit him in the groin making him gasp. Amazonia laughed scornfully, fetching him another stinging nip. How can anyone get off on this? Jack wondered, at the same time mentally congratulating Cyberia for their skill in the science of inducing pain.

Just as Jack was coming to the conclusion that he couldn't stand much more of it, a message flashed before his eyes: *Concluding in fifteen seconds.* There was time for only a couple more lashes before the scene dissolved and he was left feeling numb around his crotch and with the usual disorientation, lasting for around ten seconds, at the end of a game.

Debra's voice invited them to remove their headsets. When all the testers were back in the land of the living, she apologised for having to break into their games.

'There will be an opportunity later for you to play your chosen game through to its conclusion,' she promised. 'But we should not forget that you are here for the purposes of feedback and assessment. Each of you will now receive a detailed preliminary questionnaire to supplement the data we already have about each one of you from our bio-monitoring. When you have finished you are free to go for lunch. We meet again at fourteen hundred hours.'

When Jack looked at the ten-page booklet he noticed a remarkable similarity with those produced by Global. Obviously Debra had had a hand in that, although she was not violating her contract since there was no copyright on the survey. He glanced up and met her eye. She smiled vaguely at him and he felt a slight current of attraction flow between them. Jack smiled to himself. It was amazing that she still had no idea who he was. Well, maybe he'd give her a few clues before the weekend was out!

Reflecting on his morning's experiences, Jack concluded that Cyberia certainly had the edge over Global in some respects, although overall their games lacked subtlety and sophistication. Jack had already come to some conclusions about the two companies. While his old firm reproduced erotic sensation and induced arousal more efficiently, this one was better at the simulation of pain.

Addressing himself to the tedious task of filling in boxes Jack sped through the questionnaire and finished before the others. He rose from his seat and placed the completed form in the box on Debra's desk, giving her a long searching look as he did so. Her face was impassive, well schooled. How different from the way he remembered her on that last occasion, her cool features disfigured by naked lust. For a moment he wanted to break his cover, to see that professional mask crumple with shocked recognition, but he knew that would spoil everything. What he had in mind was far, far better.

Lunch had been laid on for the volunteer testers in the top-floor restaurant, but first Jack needed some air. He walked along the road for a while, brooding over the plan he was slowly forming. Without taking a closer look at the equipment he didn't know if it was technically feasible and the only way he could do that was by getting into the games room alone. Would he get his chance? He would try after lunch, while the others were still eating.

Even if his plan were theoretically possible there were a few small practical obstacles . . . namely lack of equipment, time and expertise! Maybe he'd gone crazy. Debra did seem to have that effect on him. But Jack knew he had to try. As he was walking back towards the Cyberia building, he saw his car parked at the kerb and suddenly remembered something. Quickly he unlocked the door and was soon delving amongst the tissues, maps and sweet wrappers in the glove compartment.

'Got it!'

Jack withdrew the small plastic container with a cry of triumph. Inside the insulated package was a tiny chip, the one that Alistair had given him, months ago. On that day, Jack recalled, he'd gone straight home and had no time to put the chip with his other spares. After that, events had moved so fast that the MR chip had been forgotten and remained hidden in his car ever since. How very convenient!

Also in Jack's car were his miniature tool kit and a couple of spare cables. Jack pocketed them then hurried into the building and up to the restaurant, where a bunch of guys were already being served. He joined a table, made a few friendly noises then settled for being a more or less silent observer. The men were excited by what they had just experienced, keen to share their impressions.

'Did you choose the wet nurse too?' one was saying. 'Incredible knockers! And I liked the chocolate milk-shake flavour, that was a nice touch.'

'Talking of nice touches, did you go with that masseuse with the long red hair? I could feel her hands all over me, really feel them. And when she got to my naughty bits I couldn't hold out for long.'

'Hey, did you try the submissive with the big behind? Spanking her wobbly bottom was great!'

'No, I was in the horror scenario. They've got some tricks that make your hair stand on end and you get some really weird feelings. You should try it.'

Jack listened to it all with faint amusement. Half the time they were talking about their experiences as if they'd happened for real. A few of the men were in the computer business themselves and got into discussing the technology, but they soon formed a clique and Jack was not inclined to join them. He finished his meal quickly and looked around for Debra. He wanted to get back into that room before the others returned.

She was sitting at another table eating a salad, with four men clamouring for her attention. Jack knew that every time he spoke to her in person he was risking discovery and putting his scheme in jeopardy, but it couldn't be helped. He had to find out if his idea would work, and the only way to do that was to get a closer look at the equipment.

Jack rose and approached her, circumspectly. She gave him a friendly smile. 'Hullo, what can I do for you?'

'Sorry to interrupt, but I think I may have dropped my car keys in the games room.'

The barest flicker of annoyance creased Debra's brow. 'Then you'll have to wait until this afternoon's session, I'm afraid.'

'Is there no chance of getting in there beforehand?'

'I'm afraid not. The room is security locked. Sorry.'

She turned back to her meal, dismissing him. Leaving the dining-room, Jack returned to the ground floor and checked out the games room. Beside the door was a number pad for an electronic lock. Somehow he would have to witness Debra using it if he wanted to be able to use it himself. His hopes for the implementation of his plan began to recede.

Nevertheless, at five to two he was hovering with one or two others in the corridor when Debra appeared. She flashed them a smile and approached the door. Feeling like a credit fraudster trying to steal someone's PIN number, Jack watched closely as she tapped out the code. He mentally registered the pattern made by her quick fingers, hoping he'd got it right, then entered the room with the rest.

For the first few minutes Jack made a show of hunting

around his computer terminal for his keys while he made a closer examination of the hardware, but he also needed to get a look at Debra's computer. On the pretext of telling her that he'd found his keys, he sauntered up to her desk.

'I found these, Mizz Newcombe,' Jack grinned, waving the keys her, and she gave an answering smile. 'Just as I thought, they'd fallen out while I was playing the game. I got so involved in the virtual reality of it I didn't notice.' He began to examine her computer, feigning an air of casual curiosity. 'It's a powerful new technology you've got there, isn't it? And to think it all goes on inside this one small box. Amazing!'

'You're not in computers yourself then, Mr . . .?'

'Wright, Frank Wright. No, I'm a . . . teacher, actually. Thought I'd better find out what the kids of the future would be getting into. It's hard to keep one jump ahead of them these days.'

Satisfied with his brief appraisal of the technology, Jack cut short the conversation and returned to his terminal.

Debra began the afternoon session by thanking them for the care with which they'd filled in the questionnaires, then suggested that they might like to try a different game from the one they'd played that morning. Jack opted for the horror fantasy more from a sense of duty than pleasure. The more he learned about what their boys were capable of the more easily he would be able to turn it to his own advantage.

The new game was a somewhat infantile scenario involving alien invaders and relying rather too crudely on close encounters of the absurd kind. Some of the sensations were pretty good, though. The sucker-on-the-forehead trick was so convincing that he wondered if it had left a red mark, and the feeling of being crushed by gripping tentacles was almost real enough to be scary. For some minutes after he'd been released from the phantom embrace Jack could still feel it.

Soon, though, Jack switched back to the morning's game, which was far more to his liking. He decided it was time to sample the decadent delights of Daphne.

'Let me take you to my hotel room,' she cooed at him, her large breasts, oiled with tanning lotion, gleaming at him in the hot sunshine. Her hand was warm and fleshy, setting up a throb of anticipation in his groin. Maybe this time he would really get off on the virtual experience.

Daphne sprawled face down on the hotel bed, a veritable feast of flesh. Eagerly Jack clutched at her huge buttocks, enjoying the feel of soft, adipose tissue as it squidged beneath his fingers. She shifted position and he turned his attention to her huge tits, feeling the weight of them as he lifted each to his mouth and bit into the long nipple. Daphne didn't mind him biting her. In fact she seemed to enjoy it, making ecstatic little groans as he chewed more vigorously on her wet teats and nibbled his way around her mountainous melons.

Yet there was something missing . . . Ah yes, scent! The smell of suntan oil which had been pungent on the beach was inexplicably absent now. Jack mentally marked the programmer down for inattention to detail. His nose traced a path over her stomach, then checked out her lower region. There had been an attempt to reproduce the musky odour of female genitalia but again it was somewhat crude. They'd gone for the 'fishy' option and it was too close to their seaweed aroma to be really convincing.

Taste-wise, though, it was great. Not so much in terms of flavour, but in the realistic feel of a woman's parts against his mouth. Mouthing Daphne's quim was like munching his way through a plateful of oysters. Jack found the hard little pearl and grazed it with his teeth. Normally a woman hated you to be too rough with her clitoris, but Daphne revelled in it. The harder he gobbled at her the more voluptuously she writhed and the more his mouth filled with her juices. Jack knew it was his own saliva he was tasting, but the illusion worked well.

It was time to go fishing. Bunching his fingers, Jack thrust his hand into her hole and felt the slippery walls embrace him eagerly. He revelled in the dual sensation of his mouth and fingers wallowing in the steamy humidity of a woman's sex. Daphne had become one huge oral gratification machine, made for his pleasure alone. Jack could feel himself growing hard, responding equally to the sucking motions of her vagina and the sucking that he himself was giving her luscious labia. He thrust in and out of her with his fist and there were some good squelching noises, audible above the moans and cries that Daphne was emitting in her simulated progress towards orgasm.

At last Daphne reached the peak of her ecstasy, thrusting her hips back and forth and writhing against his wrist until Jack felt as if he were caught up in the innards of a well-oiled roller coaster. Inside the crotch piece his rampant cock was buzzing from root to tip with pent-up energy, sending a glow throughout his pelvis and beyond. The pressure built up and Jack began to long for release, but when it finally came it wasn't quite what he'd expected. Although his climax was fierce and intensely pleasurable, making the full circuit of his body and filling his veins with a golden warmth, for once he didn't ejaculate.

Jack had heard it was possible for a man to come without spilling his seed, but it had never happened to him before. When the delicious glow had subsided, scientific curiosity took over. Had the phenomenon been an effect of this particular piece of programming, or of this particular apparatus, or just some physiological quirk of his own? He wished he had a freer rein to make some controlled experiments.

Before they ended the day, the testers were given another, briefer, set of questions. In the 'Any other comments' section Jack mentioned what had happened to him. It had been a novel experience, all right, and highly pleasurable. For a while he became caught up in speculation about it, forgetting his plan to give Debra a novel experience of a different kind. Jack chided himself. Soon the first day would be over and he'd have to act swiftly. He couldn't afford to become distracted by other matters.

Jack knew exactly what he had to do now. Only half listening to Debra's 'thank you and see you tomorrow' speech, he planned his movements. A sudden thrill passed through him, almost sexual in its earthy physicality, like an aftershock from his orgasm. If this crazy idea worked he would get his own back on that scheming bitch in the most appropriate and satisfying way he could imagine. She'd asked them to clear the building quickly, so he would make straight for the Gents and lie low until they'd all gone. Then, like some busy nocturnal creature, he could get to work.

Chapter Ten

It was an eerie feeling, hiding in the building until everyone had gone. Jack lay low in the end cubicle of the Gents until the last echoes of voices and footsteps had died away. He was worried that there might be security men on patrol, or cleaners, but that was a risk he had to take. At six o'clock, after squatting on the loo seat for thirty minutes and giving himself pins and needles, Jack judged it safe to emerge.

The corridor stretched silent and empty. Although he was sure there was no need for caution, Jack tiptoed his way towards the door of the games room. He took a deep breath then tapped out the code he thought he'd seen Debra use. Nothing happened. He cursed softly, then tried the digit next to the one he was least sure of. To his relief, there was a slight click and the door sprang open. Jack made a mental note of the correct combination and entered the darkened room. He threw the power switch, then, finding the light too bright, restricted it to illuminating the area he'd be working in.

With his compact universal screwdriver it took Jack

only seconds to get into the computer he'd been using. The circuitry was familiar and there was room for an upgrade. Carefully he slotted the Mutual Reality chip into position then made the necessary adjustments to the wiring before replacing the casing.

That was the easy part, Jack reminded himself, as he switched the machine on. He was linked to the master computer now, but he still had to con his way in before he could start programming. As a teenager Jack had been an ace hacker, but it was many years since he'd needed those skills and nowadays the protection systems were more sophisticated.

The screen demanded that he key in his PAC, or personal access code. Jack's heart sank. He'd been hoping to break into the programme by some other route. There seemed no way of circumventing the security, and guessing someone's PAC could take all night. He knew what Debra's had been at Global: 'de-bra'. Her little joke. He wondered if she was using the same one . . . She wasn't.

Then Jack remembered a fellow-hacker telling him that most people used similar styles for their encryption. He racked his brains: how about 'bra-less'? That didn't work either. After trying several more ideas on the same theme he had a brainwave: 'de-brief'. To his amazement as soon as he'd typed it the computer supplied him with a menu of options.

Soon Jack was deep into the programme for the Beach scenario. It was relatively easy to change the beginning so that the player had to make a forced choice in favour of Amazonia. Re-programming the servo-mechanisms that finely tuned the hand-and-brain movements was more tricky. The MR chip required a constant feedback loop that was far more complex than what was already there.

Jack worked away in rapt absorption, intent on the task in hand, and when he finally took a break he found he'd been at it four hours. He badly needed a leak and his mouth was dry. He thought he remembered seeing a drinks machine outside the staff restaurant so, once he'd visited the Gents, he made his way up via the stairs. He was relieved to find that he could get not only a Coke but some crisps and chocolate as well. That should keep him going.

While he drank Jack realised how much he was enjoying himself. Not only was there the thrill of doing something illegal, with the slight risk of being found out, but he was also on a programming high. He hadn't been inside a games programme for months and there was an illicit enjoyment to be had from reading someone else's mind and perverting their work to his own ends.

Then there was the incredibly erotic prospect of seducing Debra through the game, of taking her by surprise and committing something like virtual rape. Of course, Jack knew she could always pull the plug and foil his plan, but knowing Debra, he felt sure she wouldn't. Curiosity would lure her into his scenario, deeper and deeper, until she was in so deep she couldn't get out of it but must dance to his tune right to the end. The very thought of it sent testosterone flooding through his veins, making his dick throb with pulsing energy. Whatever he'd ever wanted to do to that bitch was now within his grasp!

As long as he didn't let the chance slip through his fingers.

As Jack resumed his work on the programme he thrust to the back of his mind the niggling worry that, when it came to the crunch, the MR chip wouldn't function in an alien machine. He didn't know enough about the hardware to make many adjustments, so the thing would have to work more or less first time.

It was almost two in the morning before Jack felt ready for a test run. He set the programme running and put on the headset. There was his approximation to Debra, toiling up the beach. She didn't have to be that good since Jack was the only one who'd be seeing her, using her virtual body as a target for his pleasure, but he was pleased with the way he'd modelled her ass and small tits. Just for good fun, he'd made her features a good deal uglier than they were in real life.

After Jack had satisfied himself that the programme was working from his end, he went to put on the gear that hung at the side of the master console. Now he was Debra, plugging into the system routinely, unprepared for what she was about to receive. There would be little to alert her at first. The new technology would only kick into action once she got inside the hotel. Jack knew he would have to trick her into getting that far, but he had an idea of how to do it.

Now she was going down into the dungeon, and ... yes, there it was! A mild chafing of the wrist as Amazonia pulled her downstairs. The first clue that the MR chip was doing its work. Swiftly Jack returned to his computer and advanced the programme, then ran back to the main desk to check it out. It was awkward, trying to be in two places at once, but there was no other way to test it.

Absorbed in the proof of his success, Jack didn't realise how exhausted he was until he looked at his watch and saw it was five a.m. He had to go home. Staying in that place would drive him nuts. After shutting down both computers and doing his best to leave the room as he'd found it, Jack closed the door and made his way back to the Gents. He knew the outside doors would be locked, so he took a deep breath and just managed to scramble through a window into the bit of shrubbery beyond. Then he got into his car and drove slowly home through the deserted streets, his body a shattered shell but his brain still buzzing in overdrive.

It was nine-thirty when Jack awoke, head throbbing. He doused himself under the shower to perk up his brain, scrambled into clean clothes, grabbed a black coffee then drove to the Cyberia building as fast as he dared, arriving at ten-fifteen. Debra was in mid-spiel and threw him a disapproving glance as he entered the games room where all the others were assembled.

'Just wait, sister. You'll be sorry you crossed me!' he hissed, through his smiled apology.

Debra looked softer today, more vulnerable. She wore a pink dress of Thai silk with a mandarin collar, through which the sensors could easily make contact with her nerve-endings. I'll make her feel hot under that collar before the day's out, Jack thought with a flash of pure venom as he took his place. Seeing her standing there, so distant and composed, he longed to set the wheels of his revenge in motion and watch her squirm.

'Yesterday we asked for your first impressions of this new technology,' she was saying. 'But today we're hoping for a more detailed and specific response. As you know, we can glean quite a bit from the physiological feedback, but we'd like to know what's going on in your heads as well. And since we've not yet invented a computer that can read minds . . .' polite laughter rippled round the room ' . . . we have to rely on you to make notes. As you see we've provided each of you with a notepad and pen. We'd like you to use this whenever something occurs to you, however minor, about the game you're testing. Just press the 'pause' button and the game will stop. Click on 'resume' and you'll be back into it where you left off. I'd like you all to try that now, please.'

Jack got into his gear but this time he left the helmet unfastened so that, if he tilted his head back, he could see what was going on in the real, as well as the virtual, world. That was essential if he wanted confirmation that his efforts had worked. Quickly he logged on and accessed his new version of the game. Let the others dance to Debra's tune – he'd make her dance to one of his own!

Suddenly Jack's voice rang out above the hubbub of fourteen other computers going through their paces. 'Mizz Newcombe! I think there may be something wrong with this game. I wanted to go with the girl called

Daphne, but I can't! Maybe it's my computer.'

Debra frowned, and Jack suspected she already had him marked down as something of a troublemaker. He watched her link up to his terminal, telling the others to carry on while she sorted out Mr. Wright. Jack grinned. If anyone was going to be sorted it would be her, good and proper!

Jack knew she'd be entering the program at the point where the Goddess of Love was telling her that she must go with Amazonia and discover her true destiny. Debra would be aware that the player should have been given a choice of partner at that point in the scenario, so she'd be foxed. He watched her out of the corner of his eye as she shook her head incredulously. Jack couldn't see her face behind the visor, but the way she stabbed jerkily at the buttons and switches suggested she was in something of a panic. Turning his attention back to the game, he watched the virtual Debra try to escape as he caught her round the wrist. Jack was Amazonia, strong and relentless, determined to haul her off to the dungeon of the hotel and teach her a thing or two!

The real Debra took of her gear and crossed the room towards him. Jack's heart thumped rapidly, making his breath catch in his throat. Did she suspect, or was she just puzzled? Either way, it could mean the end of his little plan. He took off his own headgear as she approached.

'I'm sorry, Mr. Wright, it certainly seems as if there's been some kind of glitch.' Jack's sigh of relief was almost audible. At least she didn't suspect him of skulduggery.

'There must be something wrong with the wiring, but as it's Sunday there are no technicians on call. May I suggest that you move to the spare terminal over here?'

'No problem.'

Jack meant it. He could switch cables and use that computer just as well, starting the whole merry dance over again. The other players were by now totally immersed in their virtual worlds and had no idea what was going on beyond their own over-stimulated senses. So Jack knew he had an hour or so to play cat and mouse with his ex-colleague.

The second time Debra entered the scenario Amazonia already had her blindfolded and chained to the wall in the hotel dungeon. Jack made her select a knife from the impressive display on the wall-rack and slice off Debra's dress, from neck to hem. When it fell in tatters to the floor she writhed and strained against her bonds but, this time, Jack knew she was held captive by one of the most powerful forces known to man: curiosity.

He could see her now, clearly agitated behind all that paraphernalia, intent on discovering just what had happened to the programme and unable to rest until she had solved the mystery. Maybe, too, there was another force at work, a darker more primeval one that was interested less in the technicalities of programming than in exploring her own capacity for the sensual enjoyment of pain. Jack gave a covert smile as he observed her intent concentration on the game. The woman who, back at Global, had fantasies about having her bottom spanked was hooked on the prospect of keener punishment. Of that he was now convinced.

Debra was watching Amazonia's gloved hand pass amongst the various instruments at her disposal, wondering which she would choose. There was an interesting range of implements, far more varied than the original programmer had provided for this scenario. In his rôle as Amazonia, Jack surveyed the collection of scourges ranging from a tough leather bull whip to a thin cord used for whipping a Victorian child's top into humming action. There were rods of all types too, from pliable canes that had to be soaked to avoid splitting on impact to stout walking sticks. An array of bats and paddles, normally used in various sports, offered an alternative to the lashes and sticks, but Amazonia passed over them all.

Next she considered devices such as lengths of rubber hosing, leather belts, even the neck of an old guitar with the strings hanging loose to form an ingenious cat o'six tails. All were thoughtfully surveyed while Debra chafed against the rough surface of the wall, half longing for and half fearing the choice that Amazonia would eventually, inevitably, make. Common household implements such as wire wool and sandpaper, nail brushes and sink plungers, were given the same careful appraisal before she moved on to the opposite end of the tactile spectrum.

By contrast, here were all the gentle aids to sensual pleasure that man or nature could devise: a feather duster or a swan's-down powder puff; a freshly plucked rose or a velvet glove; a swathe of pure mink or a silk scarf... which would this sweet tormentress choose? For Jack had turned Amazonia into a subtle mistress of the art of touch, as adept at using the carrot as the stick.

First she would rouse Debra's dormant nerves, free

them from their confinement inside the clumsy second skin of the VR suit and let the sensors work their subtle magic. Amazonia picked up the delicate ball of swan's-down and trailed it, ever so lightly, across Debra's bare bosom. She moaned and shuddered, her skin tightening to goose-bumps. Crude though his representation of her was in his hastily executed programming, Jack knew something was happening to the woman for real, just over there at her isolated work station. He could see her shudder, knew she was caught up in the double-bind of fear and desire that his cunning had devised for her.

After the tentative touch of the swan's-down, Amazonia pinched the tight, yearning nipples between the finger and thumb of her leather glove, causing Debra to cry out at the sudden change. Then she was plunged into the contradictory sensations as one nipple was roughly tweaked, the other softly feathered. After a while Amazonia changed hands. Jack could see Debra beginning to writhe, her torso twisting and swaying as she gave herself up helplessly to the twin sensations. Good! He'd made an excellent start.

Suddenly Amazonia picked up the silk scarf and, holding it in her right hand, flicked it lightly over Debra's naked stomach and thighs. Jack watched her re-tune to the softer caress, relaxing a little as the silk passed up over her breasts then down over her belly again. This sensual circuit continued for a while, lulling Debra into false security as she gave herself up to the light slippery touch. Yet even as she was wielding the silk with her right hand, Amazonia was preparing another shock for her victim. Without any warning she pressed the wire wool to Debra's tits with her left hand, causing her to cry out as the steel fragments pricked her delicate skin. Roughly the pad of silver wire abraded her breasts, a parody of the swan's-down puff she had felt earlier. The real Debra arched backwards, as if to escape the cruel pinpricks, but she didn't – as Jack feared she might – unplug herself from the system.

Before the torture became unbearable, Amazonia changed tack again. This time she unchained her captive from the wall, forcing her to bend over a trestle to which her wrists and ankles were tied. Then she selected a birch broom from her armoury and proceeded to whack Debra on the bare buttocks with the bundled twigs. Soon the flesh was striped with red and Debra was writhing under each assault, revealing, beneath her bottom as she twisted and turned, the slick pink of her labia. Jack glanced over to where she stood and saw that she was now bent forward slightly, with her posterior protruding jauntily. As he watched she began to gasp, wiggling her backside as if she were receiving blows upon it from an invisible hand. He smiled, feeling his own behind tingle with sympathetic arousal.

He soon stopped smiling, however, when he reminded himself that she was the bitch who had lost him his job. He made Amazonia replace the besom with something more punishing, a short-handled whip. The first lash on Debra's already reddened cheeks made her start with pain and, as stroke on merciless stroke followed, he could see her flagging under the strain.

'Enough of this, craven hussy!' the flagellatress crowed, from her limited vocabulary of set phrases. 'Never let it be said that Amazonia does not temper pain with pleasure!'

Jack felt his fingers – *her* fingers – untie the straps. Amazonia led Debra over to a padded couch, where she lay face down while a salve was selected for her raw flesh. Tenderly the cool cream was smoothed over her lacerated skin, over the plump mounds of her behind and up her back to her shoulders, then down again to the sensitive flesh of her inner thighs. Jack sensed that the real Debra was relaxed and comfortable after the ordeal of her punishment, and he gave a secret grin. If she thought it was all over she had another think coming!

Amazonia's hands slid easily up and down the creamy thighs, just brushing the parted lips of Debra's sex. Jack's prick was throbbing hard now at the simulated feel of a female on heat. Amazonia inched a little closer to the dark cleft of her arse until she probed it briefly with one slick finger. Soon she began to explore both territories, gently working her way in between the still-red cheeks with her left forefinger while she dabbled gently between the pink labia with her right one. The cream was mingling with Debra's own natural secretions, forming a rich, odorous mixture. Soothed and lulled, her senses slowly coming to their warm and luxurious fulfilment, Debra lay immobile under the massage. Jack noticed how she had let her head come to rest on the desk as if she were taking a nap, her body slumped in her chair.

Suddenly, though, she leapt up as if she had sat on

a wasp. Taking advantage of her trusting compliance, Amazonia had picked up the guitar neck and thrashed her across the thighs with the steel strings. It was only one lash, but it left long red strips across her pale skin and made her wriggle and moan in anguished rage. Perhaps, too, Debra was angry with herself for letting her guard slip so completely.

'That'll teach you, slut!' Amazonia snarled.

Jack could feel the backs of his thighs stinging a little too, as a faint impression from Debra's sensors echoed back down the electronic link between them. After that it would be harder to trick Debra into relaxing. A different approach was necessary.

Stirrups were raised at the end of the couch and Debra's ankles were strapped in as she lay on her back, still blindfolded, her wrists tied to a rail above her head. Greedily, Amazonia attacked the naked body laid out for her pleasure, pinching all over the soft flesh with her leather-gloved fingers. At last she forced her hand into the wet alley of Debra's pussy, plunging the black gauntlet between the widely spread thighs again and again.

Jack saw how the real Debra was wriggling in her seat and he became excited too, his cock hot and stiff in its sensor-laden pouch. His hand was Amazonia's, first invading the soft vaginal tissue, then taking off the glove to feel the sting of impact as she slapped the quivering thighs hard where red weals were already forming. He saw Debra's head and shoulders rear back, her hips jerk upwards, but it was impossible to tell whether she was reacting to the pain or the pleasure.

Amazonia quickened the pace of her varied assault, bringing in an assortment of toys to aid her in her work. Some gentle stimulation of Debra's clitoris with a naked finger would be followed by the sudden slash of a leather thong across her breasts. Then, while she was groping deep inside the juice-filled cunt, she would bite without warning on a nipple or sandpaper a thigh. Soon the wave of Debra's arousal was moving inexorably towards its climax, no matter what she suffered. Jack watched her, fascinated to see how impossible it was to differentiate between the pangs of ecstasy and the throes of torment.

Observing both the real and the virtual Debra, feeling the chastened flesh respond with extreme passion to whatever he, in the persona of Amazonia, forced upon her, Jack was filled with raw emotion. It delighted him to see the bitch getting what she deserved. He revelled in the sneaky power he had over her in this strangely distanced yet compellingly intimate world.

Amazonia thrust a dildo into Debra's arse while her vagina was pulsating with a humming vibrator then, almost lovingly, began to tickle her boobs with a dried teasel. Jack could feel himself rising towards orgasm, propelled by the headlong rush that Debra was experiencing, and the tension at both ends of the computer link mounted to an unbearable pitch. Hot waves of cruel lust assailed him as he felt the woman squirm in her perverse ecstasy. She must be enjoying it, he reasoned, or she could simply opt out of the scenario.

Then, when Amazonia suddenly popped a couple of ice cubes inside Debra's overheated cunt, Jack felt her explode with sheer shock into a convulsing climax that tipped him over the edge too. Immersed in his own intense feelings, for several seconds Jack was totally oblivious of what was happening around him. But as the violence of his orgasm subsided, he realised that all hell appeared to have been let loose in the room. Dimly he perceived that the others were panicking. Below the frantic shouts there was a hissing sound, and an ominous smell of smoke.

Jack tore off his VR gear and at once a choking black cloud met his nostrils. Looking down he saw that it was coming from the back of his computer. Across the room, small flames were issuing from Debra's machine and she was slumped across her desk, with two men struggling to remove her helmet. The hissing came from the sprinkler system that had kicked into action, drenching everything and everyone in a fine rain.

'Christ!' he moaned. 'I must have blown a fuse!'

Pausing only to make sure Debra was still alive, Jack followed the crowd through the fire exit. Two of the men bringing up the rear were supporting Debra, staggering but still breathing, and someone ran off to phone the emergency services. For a moment Jack was assailed by guilt, but then self-preservation took over and he fled from the building with the rest, hurrying towards his car. He got in and drove away, anxious to put as many miles between himself and Cyberco as possible.

After driving non-stop for over an hour, Jack ended up on Clapham Common. Leaving his car he went for a brisk walk to clear his lungs and his head, stunned by the mayhem he had caused. Always presuming he really had been to blame. Although Jack knew there was probably a rational explanation, in terms of his faulty rewiring of the computers, he couldn't help speculating along other lines. What if the double orgasm at either end of the computer link had caused a power surge that the system couldn't handle?

Well, he'd certainly taken his revenge on Debra, he thought wryly. Yet the manner of it made him feel uneasy. Quite apart from the disastrous effect on the equipment, he was disturbed by the ease with which he had slipped into the rôle of tormentor. By giving over the power to Amazonia, his virtual persona, it had been so easy to renounce responsibility for what had ensued. What if some unscrupulous person were to subject his or her victim to VR torture against their will? Pain received through a sensor was still pain. The fact that Debra had been free to stop her ordeal at any point but had chosen to continue was small consolation to him. Perhaps, in some hideous future scenario, such an option might be denied to some wretched victim.

Full of such sobering thoughts, Jack returned to his car and drove home.

The local paper reported a small fire at the Cyberco offices but said no-one had been hurt and the damage was minimal. Jack was relieved but, in the weeks that followed, he felt a deep dissatisfaction with his life. His report for Clive expressed some of his disquiet about VR technology, yet he still missed the sexual high that he'd got from it. Casual sexual encounters no longer seemed to be the answer. The brief affairs he'd had since Suzanne had left only made him long for a real relationship again. Despite his wife's treachery, he was missing being married. Missing the day-to-day cosiness of their relationship, and the certainty of knowing that she was there if he wanted her. All this hunting and conquering could be very wearing and, ultimately, failed to satisfy him.

Just what was he supposed to be doing with his life, now that it had all fallen apart? Where was he going? The eternal questions buzzed in his mind like an irritating car alarm that wouldn't stop ringing.

Eventually Jack decided to enlist with a computer dating agency. That way he could at least hope to find someone with similar interests. He filled out a long form and went for an interview, at which an efficient-looking woman called Brenda quizzed him on his sexual preferences with alarming candour.

'You've said here you're "moderately" interested in CP,' she reminded him. 'Sometimes people say "moderately" when they really mean "extremely". Would you be one of those people, by any chance?'

Jack shrugged. 'I wouldn't say so, although I have been turned on by spanking a woman. You see, I used to work for a firm making sex-games . . .'

'Ah!'

'Now I'm no longer working for them I find I miss all the fantasy scenarios. Real-life sex is often a disappointment.'

'Maybe you're expecting too much, too soon, Jack. You must allow the relationship to grow over time, to establish mutual trust. Anyway, there's a couple of girls on our computer who seem to be looking for a guy like you. Would you like to see their details? We have videos, too.'

Jack asked to see the first computer choice. She turned out to be a long-haired brunette – not unlike Suzanne as he remembered her from the old days – with a face that would have been beautiful were it not for the slight crookedness of her over-wide mouth. She was tall, with an impressive figure, and Jack was pleasantly surprised by the mellow, confident tones of her voice.

'Hullo, my name's Barbara. I've never been to a dating agency before but I'm a busy working girl and don't really have to the time go out seeking new dates. My job as a computer programmer takes a lot of my time and energy, so I need a man I can relax with, someone who'll be there for me whenever I need him but who's not too demanding. I enjoy listening to all kinds of music and I appreciate the sensual side of life – good food, good wine, good sex – as well as good company. If you think our needs and interests are compatible, call me soon . . .'

'I think I'd like to start with her, if she's interested in me,' Jack said.

The next stage was to get his own video made. Jack was reasonably pleased with the way he presented himself and he was told that if 'Barbara' wished to go ahead with the pairing he would be given her phone number.

'Of course, we need to make a few checks in the meantime,' Brenda explained. 'Just as precaution, you understand. We have to make sure you haven't a police record for sexual offences or anything like that.'

'That's fine by me.'

'You should be hearing from me in about ten days' time.'

Meanwhile, Jack was working hard on a game of his own. His experience at the agency had given him an idea for an adult-oriented computer game. It would be one of a new generation of sex-adventure games sold by mail order under licence. They were becoming very popular, although Jack knew that once Global produced their Home Feelietron the bottom would drop out of that market. Of course, the first Feelietron sets would be very expensive, but inevitably the price would drop and then the computer games would seem boringly tame. All the more reason to get his idea out as soon as possible.

Please Please Me was based on a dating agency and gave the player a choice of three women. If you negotiated the first date successfully, saying and doing exactly the right things to please the female concerned, then you got to kiss her. If you continued to please her on the second date, you got to fondle her breasts, and so on. Failure at any stage meant you had to go back and try another selection. If you dated all three females without getting one of them into bed, you lost. Of course, all the women had secret fetishes and preferences that you had to discover, and you were kitted out with an appropriate range of dildoes, whips, ropes, masks, etc.

Jack became so caught up in his game that he'd almost forgotten about the real computer dating agency until, one evening, he had a call from Brenda.

'Hi, Jack, it's good news,' she began with her usual

professional enthusiasm. 'Barbara says she'd like to meet you. You can call her any evening after six.'

Brenda gave him the girl's number and rang off. Jack decided it was now or never, and dialled. He recognised the warm voice that answered, from her video.

'Er . . . my name's Jack, and I got your number from Compute-a-Date,' he told her, surprised by his own nervousness.

'Oh yes, I liked your video,' she answered, putting him at his ease. 'When would you like us to meet? I'm free this Saturday if that's any good.'

They fixed a time and place. A quiet drink would be best, she agreed, so they arranged to meet in The Vintner at seven. The wine bar would not be crowded at that hour and they could decide where to go on to later. Jack was relieved that the process of making the date had been so easy. Suddenly he felt like an excited teenager again, optimistic for the first time in ages. He recovered his lost pride in his appearance and bought some new clothes, then had his hair re-styled. It really felt as if he were making a new start, at last.

Chapter Eleven

Jack spent a long time on his appearance as their rendez-vous approached. After showering and splashing on his most expensive cologne he brushed back his newly trimmed hair into the style he thought made him look most youthful, put on a black cashmere polo neck under his new Armani suit and drove to Piccadilly, parking in a side-street near the wine bar.

It was amazing how jittery he still felt. Somehow the fact that they were already partially acquainted, if only through the magic of technology, made it harder for him. Jack ran through his imaginary conversational gambits: 'You said in your video . . .' But then he wondered if she would be somehow offended by being reminded of the way in which they'd been introduced. And, as the minutes ticked by, he began to fear that he might not recognise her.

He needn't have worried. Barbara was instantly recognisable as she entered the place, her elegant figure casually draped in a blue velvet poncho, beneath which black pants made the most of her long legs. She saw him, smiled unselfconsciously and waved.

'Hi, Jack! Hope I've not kept you waiting long. There was a delay on the Tube.'

Jack was relieved. Not only was she even more attractive than she'd appeared on video, but she seemed perfectly relaxed and pleased to be there drinking wine with him. As they chatted, Jack found himself warming to Barbara more and more. She had taken off her cloak and now he could see the fullness of her bosom beneath the striped velvet top she was wearing. He felt no urgent desire for her, just a pleasant warmth which he imagined would grow stronger as the evening wore on.

They agreed on an Italian meal at a nearby restaurant and the conversation continued to flow easily. Soon Jack had confessed that he was practically divorced and Barbara admitted that she'd had an unsuccessful marriage too. They began talking quite seriously about the difficulties of making monogamy work, and Barbara confessed she had become sexually bored by her husband.

The food and wine put them both in a mellow mood and when the meal was over neither Jack nor Barbara were inclined to move on. They lingered until eleven, then Barbara suggested they should order more coffee to liven them up for the journey home.

'Whereabouts do you live?' Jack asked her, his mind working overtime.

'Balham.'

'Really? That's not so far from me. Why don't you come back to my flat for coffee, then I'll drive you home.'

She looked rueful. 'I'm sorry Jack, but I can't tonight.

I've got my two young nephews coming to lunch tomorrow, and I have to get up early to prepare.'

Jack felt disappointed, but he told himself it was only natural that she should want to get to know him better before going to bed. Barbara was a serious date, not one-night stand material. Brenda had warned him about that. She prided herself on weeding out those who were just playing the field. Only those interested in committing themselves to a 'serious on-going relationship' were eligible. Jack reminded himself that was his goal too.

When they parted, Barbara gave him an encouraging kiss on the cheek, said how much she'd enjoyed the evening and promised to give Jack a ring during the week. Despite the fact that he had to return home alone, Jack felt warmly contented. He found he was relishing the simple straightforwardness of his evening with Barbara. How surprisingly good it was to be dating *normally*, without any technological props or bizarre sub-scripts. It was years since he'd done this – with Suzanne, in fact. He began to reminisce . . .

The Suzanne he'd first met had been an art student, long-haired and wide-eyed. As a teenager she'd only had one steady boyfriend and, since they were both inexperienced, the sex hadn't been wonderful. At college she'd become entangled with one of her married tutors. Although he'd been a more accomplished lover, they hadn't had much time together so still hadn't got the attention she deserved. When Jack came into her life she was recovering from that unsatisfactory affair, and the fact that Jack was both sexually experienced and unattached had been a huge bonus for her.

Previously inorgasmic, Suzanne reached new heights with Jack the very first time they made love. It was on their third date, after an evening at the pub, when she'd finally agreed to spend the night at his flat. Knowing how much she needed relaxing, Jack had first given her a sensual massage which had drifted imperceptibly into foreplay until she was begging him to come inside her. With great self-restraint he had held back, giving her cunnilingus instead, which resulted in the best climax she'd ever had. Gratefully she'd set about fellating him in exchange, until he was more than ready to take the plunge. Her cunt, already well lubricated, had gone into spasms of ecstasy almost immediately and, as he continued to tease further responses from her while keeping his rampant rod on a tight rein, she became a multi-orgasmic woman overnight.

In some ways they had never bettered that performance. Suzanne had become besotted with him and he was flattered by her love poems and little gifts. Sex wasn't all they'd shared, either. They both loved computer animation – Suzanne was doing a special course on it at college – and had dreams of collaborating on a game. Then Jack's career really took off and he had no time, while Suzanne had difficulty finding a job when she graduated.

Within six months of meeting they were married and, for several years, took their happiness for granted. Looking back, Jack thought he could date the subtle decline in their relationship from when he went to work for

Global. He'd worked very hard during his first months there, often returning late and too shagged out to make love. Suzanne appeared to bear it with good grace. He would often end up half-heartedly squeezing her tits for her while she used the vibrator.

Then, once the Feelietron was up and running at work, Jack found his sexual appetite returning. The effect on his home sex-life was stimulating at first. After a day of VR fantasy, he used to look forward to going home and having it away with his wife and she seemed delighted at his new interest. She seemed even more turned on when he described some of the scenarios to her while they were screwing.

But, at some point along the line, the situation became reversed. Jack found himself longing for the artificial stimulation of the Feelietron even in the middle of making love to his wife. He'd thought Suzanne wouldn't guess that while he fucked her he was dreaming of Dorabella. But at some subliminal level she must have known his mind wasn't entirely on the job in hand. After he'd come she would often reach for her vibrator, while denying that it 'mattered' that she'd not been fully satisfied.

Yet it had mattered to Jack. His efforts to bring her off had become more frantic. But using the vibrator on her before penetration hadn't resulted in any further climaxes once he was inside, and soon he was having trouble getting the old tackle up. Overwork became his constant excuse. Suzanne had done her best to seduce him on several occasions, but his erections soon lost their vitality when faced with that seemingly insatiable pussy.

Jack had let the situation drift on, with the Feelietron satisfying his own sex urges to such a degree that it was impossible for his wife to compete. He'd thought her resigned to it – what an arrogant fool he'd been! He could see now that it was unfair to presume she'd put up with second best for long.

Well, it seemed he was about to be given a second chance. He had high hopes after his first date with Barbara. She rang two days later and agreed to spend the following Saturday night with him.

'I've no guests for Sunday lunch this time,' she told him, with a coy giggle.

'Great! Bring your toothbrush!'

He remembered to ask how the nephew's visit had gone. Women liked you to show that kind of interest. As she warmly related the little horrors' adventures he could hear that she was pleased he'd asked.

Jack re-decorated the flat over the next few evenings, went out on Saturday and bought a new duvet cover and matching curtains. He showered and shaved with care, using his most expensive aftershave, pulled on a cashmere sweater and jeans, then put a bottle of champagne in the fridge. Barbara was a special woman and he intended to make their first night together a memorable occasion.

She arrived with a bottle of wine. Jack was a passable cook and had his most impressive offering simmering in the oven. From the flirty light in Barbara's brown eyes he guessed she'd been looking forward to this evening as much as he had and his heart lifted. The only problem was how to keep his lust at bay for a respectable period before bed. As he lifted the cape off Barbara's shoulders and the low-necked velour top revealed the depth of her cleavage, Jack felt his penis rear up, ready for action.

Barbara was even more delightful company now that he knew her better. Flirting with her across the table he was again reminded of the young Suzanne, who had also worn her dark hair long and loose. Although Barbara's eyes were brown, not green, she knew how to use them with good effect and had Jack practically creaming himself with her sultry, knowing looks. He began to fantasise about how she would be in bed. Somehow, Jack thought there would be no trouble getting her to give him a blow job. And she was sufficiently well-endowed for her to give him a tit-wank, if she was into it. His prick strained against his fly as he let his imagination wander.

'Mm, this is totally delicious!' she murmured, as a spoonful of chocolate mousse lingered between her full lips. 'How did you know I was a chocaholic?'

'I guessed you had a taste for the good things of life,' he smiled. 'Besides, you said so in your video – remember?'

'Oh, God! I'd completely forgotten that's how we met!' she laughed. 'It feels as if I've known you ages. Computer dating has certainly worked for us, hasn't it?'

'Look, why don't you put on some music while I make coffee? Then we can sit on the sofa.'

She chose a CD from his collection and, with the Tiffany lookalike lamp casting a soft glow over the scene, the stage seemed set for romance. Barbara was relaxed as she sat beside him, snuggling into his arm when he put it round her.

'Do you mind me asking how long it is since you did this?' she asked, quietly.

Her question stunned him into realising that none of his recent encounters had been this normal. 'Ages, I'm sorry to say.'

'I thought so. You must be out of practice, because you're pulling my hair something horrible!'

Jack lifted his hand in alarm. 'Oh. I'm so sorry, Barbara!'

'Don't worry, I've known worse.'

Jack put his arm around her again, drawing her close. He'd put a generous slug of brandy in her coffee, and after a while she relaxed completely. Kicking off her shoes she lay across his lap, like a sacrificial offering. His lips approached her long, dark hair and she sighed, stretching voluptuously. Jack took this to be an invitation and let his lips trail down her cheek to her lopsided mouth. Soon they were kissing with slow sensuality, letting their tongues alternately advance and retreat in each other's mouths.

His hands were exploring beneath her burgundy velvet top, toying with the cups of her well-filled bra, his thumbs searching for her nipples.

'Why don't I take it off?' Barbara suggested, after a few seconds. She sat up and pulled the top over her head, then undid her bra at the back so that the cups swung loose. She was about to remove it altogether when Jack interrupted.

'No let me!' he smiled, his fingers inching beneath the silky stiffness of the bra to find the equally silky skin beneath. Her nipples were already proud on the summits of breasts that were sagging a little under their own weight. Slowly he lifted the garment up so that the full glory of her pink-crested globes was revealed.

'You're gorgeous,' Jack commented, bending to take one demanding teat in his mouth. He took both hands to her breast and felt its fullness squash against his nose and chin as he suckled. At the same time a flowery-perfume filled his nostrils; it was like smelling a large and smooth-petalled rose.

Barbara was busy pulling Jack's shirt out from his waistband so that she could reach up and caress his naked skin. Her fingers gently raked down his spine. Lying in his lap, she must have been aware of the urgent bulging of his crotch beneath her own back. Jack put a hand on each of her tits, kneading their soft bulk. How good it would be to thrust his prick between those ample mounds!

Now she was undoing his trouser buttons, easing down the zip of his fly. He gave a sigh and shifted so that his tool could pop up, like a miniature Jack-in-the-box, unencumbered by the constrictions of clothing. His erection was full-blown, and received an appreciative sigh from Barbara, who soon shifted so that she was kneeling before him on the floor with her head in his lap. She gave it a tentative lick, sending a shudder through his loins.

'Come back here!' he grunted. 'I want to feel you too.'

Obediently she knelt beside him on the sofa, her boobs swinging within reach of his hands as her lips resumed their contact with his rearing dick. She flicked the top of her tongue up and down the shaft several times, taking him exquisitely near the edge as she occasionally wiped the flat of her tongue right over his glans.

'Look, if you carry on doing that, I'm going to come!' Jack warned her, with a smile. 'Maybe it's time to go into the bedroom and get more comfortable.'

Barbara readily agreed. He led the way into the newly decorated room, glad that the scented candle he'd lit earlier had extinguished the smell of paint.

'How delightful!' she smiled, unzipping her trousers and stepping out of them to reveal a pair of black velvet panties, trimmed with lace. Jack had never encountered women's underwear made of velvet before, and the sight excited him. To feel her prominent mound of Venus beneath that sensuous material would be a pleasure indeed.

She stood there, her long, dark hair falling over her chest, giving him a 'come-hither' smile. Jack hurriedly removed what was left of his clothing and walked towards her, still aroused. Suddenly he felt a strange apprehension come over him. He shrugged it off and took Barbara's warm shoulders into his arms. But even as he kissed her moist, expectant mouth he felt a slow relaxation of the tension in his cock and the puzzling uncertainty returned. This time it would not go away.

Jack told himself not to worry and put all his efforts into caressing Barbara's generously proportioned behind while his tongue performed a teasing dance with hers. Soon she was sitting on the edge of the bed, and her fingers were toying with his balls behind the now flaccid penis. He could feel her springy breasts against his stomach as they continued to kiss. Before long she was lying back and he was on top of her and his dream of stroking her velvet-clad mound was a reality. It felt as good as he'd hoped, especially when he sneaked a finger through one leg and found her wet and open to his touch. Slowly he rolled down her last protective covering and the musky smell of her desire intensified.

Jack crouched down and licked tentatively along her pink labia, finding the nub at the top already roused and eager. She moaned as he tongued it more forcibly, then he dipped a finger in the wet pool that lay hidden between the swollen lips. Her moans became little cries of encouragement, so he probed further, making her pelvis move with a yearning rhythm that provoked an answering stirring in his phallus. At last things were beginning to happen down there!

'Come up onto the bed,' Barbara urged him. 'I want to feel you near me. But don't stop what you're doing with your fingers, it's so good!'

So Jack lay by her side, idly fingering her melting pussy, while she lifted one teat to his mouth. He bit on it quite hard and she seemed to like it, squeezing her thighs together over his wrist. Her hand went to his balls again, weighing them in her palm, and as she fondled them her fingers kept teasing his shaft with feather-light touches so that he felt a rush of blood to his groin.

They kissed deeply once again, and Jack felt the urgency of her desire. By now he should have had a hard-on like a ruler, but his stubborn dick was still only at half-mast. What the hell was the matter with it?

Barbara was inching down his body, kissing his chest, his navel, rubbing her nose in his pubic hair. She began to suck his balls, taking the sac right into her mouth and licking it with her tongue while it was in there. At the same time her fingers went to work on his shaft, slipping the skin up and down with delicate strokes. It was all very pleasant, but the end result was sensual rather than sexual, and Jack was still nowhere near stiff enough to penetrate her. He began to feel seriously worried.

'I . . . I never had this problem before,' he whispered, as her efforts continually failed to get him higher than half mast.

'What problem?' she cooed. 'You're a little nervous, that's all. We'll have you up and running in no time. Want me to squeeze your thingy between my boobs? Most men seem to like that.'

Jack made a guttural noise of assent and she slithered down beneath him until her chest was under his dangler. Smilingly she placed it between her soft breasts and began to roll them with her palms so that they massaged his tool good and proper.

'Hot dog!' she gurgled, as there was a sudden stiffening. 'I think we have lift-off.'

Jack looked down at her flushed, excited face and at his own pink sausage, sandwiched between the pale flesh, and felt an unstoppable rush of energy coming. Before he could say a word he'd squirted straight into her face.

'Oh my God!'

Barbara let go of her breasts to wipe the spunk from

her eyes and spit out the drops that had strayed into her open mouth.

'I'm sorry!' he groaned, collapsing beside her. 'I guess I found that just a bit too . . . stimulating.'

Barbara giggled, still wiping her face with tissue. 'I didn't expect it quite that soon. Never mind, we've got the rest of the night ahead of us.'

Grateful that she'd taken it so well, Jack fully intended to pleasure her until he was stiff again, but as he began to kiss her neck he was overcome by drowsiness and drifted into sleep.

When he awoke it was morning, and he was curled up under the duvet alone. The smell of coffee came from his kitchen, and soon there was the familiar clack of his pop-up toaster.

'Hey, Barbara!' he called sleepily. 'Are you making breakfast?'

She looked round his bedroom door. Her hair was damp and tangled and she wore his towelling bath robe. 'Good morning! Coffee and toast?'

'You're the perfect guest,' he grinned. Then, remembering last night's escapade, he grinned ruefully. 'Even if I'm not the perfect lover!'

'Don't give it another thought! Black or white? One lump or two?'

Soon they were lying companionably beside each other in bed again, sipping coffee and crunching toast. Jack, feeling more lively, began to run his foot up Barbara's thigh beneath the bathrobe. His big toe reached her hairy mat and began to burrow its way in.

'That tickles!' she giggled.

'It's meant to. Don't you know that tickling is a sex substitute? Personally, I prefer the real thing.'

It didn't take them long to get into love-making again. This time Barbara lay, fully relaxed, on her stomach and let him caress her back and buttocks. His cock dangled against her skin, showing no signs of interest, but Jack found the long sweep of her back and the ample curves of her behind very erotic. He bent to kiss her bum cheeks, and found himself giving her a series of love-bites in the peachy succulence of her flesh. 'Oh, that feels *good*!' she sighed. 'You're a great lover, Jack. You really are.'

He wanted to believe she was sincere, but how could she say that when he hadn't even managed to penetrate her? Self-disgust threatened to overwhelm him for a moment, but then she rolled over and presented him with flattened nipples that were crying out to be tweaked into peaks of perfection. Hungrily he grasped her breasts and felt the blood pump into his dick at the same time. Although not yet fully primed, he was halfway there.

Barbara's hands slipped down between their bodies and, as he twirled her nipples between fingers and thumbs to harden them, she performed a similar service on his tool.

'You've got a nice thick one,' she remarked. 'Thickness is more important than length to a woman, you know. Something to hold onto when we squeeze with our vaginas, that's what we want.'

Normally this kind of talk would have got him aroused in no time, but Jack had an uneasy feeling that she was saying it just to get him up. There was this dreadful mistrust. It was ruining their love-making, gnawing away at his confidence, but he couldn't help it.

'Let me eat you!' he growled, swiftly descending to part her labia with his fingers and plunge his mouth into the juicy slit, like a thirsty man with a luscious fruit. She arched her back and moaned as he grazed her clit with his teeth and thrust the tip of his tongue as far as he could into her sweet hole, In and out he flicked until there was no telling his saliva from her cunt dribble. She became hot, began to swear at him, thrashed about with her arms, but he kept up his relentless tongue-dabbling while rubbing his nose against her protruding button. His hands reached up for her lolling breasts and he thumbed her nipples roughly, notching her up a gear until she was almost at her climax.

Then they got into the sixty-nine position and spent some time mutually licking and sucking at each other's parts. Jack felt his tentative erection grow more confident as she tongued her way up and down his shaft, and judging by her well-juiced pussy she was more than ready to take advantage of the situation. As soon as his cock got above the halfway mark she began sitting astride him, rubbing his sensitive glans gently against her equally sensitive clitoris.

'Ooh, that feels so good!' Barbara murmured, leaning forward so that her pendulous jugs were within his reach. Jack pulled on the large nipples, stretching them to their fullest extent, and she groaned, giving his dick a few quick rubs before placing it at the entrance to her hole, wetting its head with her love juices.

For a while she just wiggled his glans around in the soft gooeyness, without trying to push it further in. Jack felt a joyful surge of energy and the longing to thrust upwards became almost unbearable. At last he pushed his way through, entering the cushioned warmth with a sigh of pleasure. Barbara also moaned her delight and began squeezing him rhythmically as he bucked his hips. Then, with no warning, he suddenly squirted.

'Oh, bugger!' he exclaimed, as his prick began softening. He pulled out in disgust. 'That was a bloody flash in the pan, wasn't it?'

'Never mind, sweetie.' Barbara lay down, cuddling him.

'I'm so sorry.'

'Don't apologise!' she said, almost harshly. 'Never apologise when making love. It puts me off. But I was nearly there. Can't you do something about it?'

'Okay, I'll do my best.'

Jack bunched up his hand and thrust it into her gaping hole, making a squelching noise as he moved it about. She groaned and threw back her head again, the white mounds of her breasts taut with longing. He seized one teat while he finger-fucked her pussy and soon she was closing on him, squeezing against his knuckles until the first convulsions hit her, when she relaxed and let the sensations take over. Jack stroked her inner lips tenderly as the long orgasm continued. Then, when it had subsided, he returned to the top of the bed to take her in his arms.

'Oh Jack, that was great!' she smiled, sidling up to him.

'I wanted to do that last night,' he whispered. 'But I was too tired.'

They lay dozing for a few minutes, then Jack made more toast and coffee. Maybe, on this relaxed Sunday morning, they could finally make it properly. When they'd eaten their fill, he suggested they should share a whirlpool bath.

Jack felt all his worries melt away as he lounged in the soothing bath, letting the stream of bubbles massage every part of him with a gentle tickling. The exotic oil he had added to the water was relaxing too, and for a while Barbara lay floating on her back on top of him, so that he had free access to all parts of her with his soapy hands. His prick lay between the huge mounds of her buttocks as he played with her jugs, his hands travelling round and round their slick contours and every so often pinching the wet, rubbery nipples. Sometimes he gathered up as much of their mass into his hands as he could and gave them a good squeeze, nipping her on the nape of the neck at the same time. Barbara seemed to like that, and wriggled her bum against his cock to good effect: he felt it stiffening with lust.

Eventually his hands found their way down over her rotund stomach to her hairy mound. He reached for the soap and worked up a good lather then shampooed her pubic hair, letting his fingertips slip frequently into the open crack below. Barbara wriggled on top of him like a slippery eel, humming with sensual pleasure as he began to push urgently against her bum. At last she turned over and seized his knob, positioning herself so that she could guide it into her. The water slopped around in the spacious bath and Jack threw the switch to make the bubbles suddenly accelerate, tickling his balls a treat.

'Isn't this fantastic?' he grinned. 'I only had this put into the bath a few weeks ago, and this is the first time I've made love in it. I've been dreaming of this for ages!'

Jack's next thought was, 'I hope I won't be disappointed,' but even as the words came into his head he knew they would prove to be fatal. His erection subsided like a spent balloon and he cursed in frustration.

'Hey, Jack, don't! It doesn't matter,' Barbara crooned.

'It bloody does matter, and stop pretending it doesn't!'

They got out of the bath and she wrapped him in a huge, fluffy towel then led him back into the bedroom.

'Let me give you a massage,' she offered. 'That'll make you feel better.'

'You're being very understanding. You know why I think I'm having this trouble, Barbara?' She shook her head. 'Because you remind me of my ex-wife, that's why.'

'Oh, really?'

She frowned, and Jack could tell she didn't like the idea at all. He went on to explain, hastily. 'Only physically, that is. You're nothing like her at all, personality-wise. But you both have long dark hair and similar figures.'

'I see.'

Barbara still sounded miffed and Jack felt he'd made a mistake. He tried to correct it. 'Like I said, you're not at all like her as a person. For one thing, you're much more open-minded about sex. Suzanne had a lot of hang-ups that I tried to cure her of and only partly succeeded.'

'I'm not sure I want to know about all this, Jack. I think people's sexual privacy should be respected, don't you?'

'Yes, of course! But I felt I owed you some explanation.'

'Well, you don't, okay? Look, why don't we postpone the massage till another time. I really ought to get going.'

She left the bathroom door open, so he could see her putting on her deodorant and fiddling with her face. The sight of her large round bottom excited him, and his prick was soon standing to attention.

'Too late, old son!' Jack told it, wryly, as he swung his legs out of bed, put on the discarded bathrobe and made for the kitchen where he put the kettle on. Barbara said she didn't have time for more coffee.

He hardly dared ask if she wanted to see him again, but she pre-empted him.

'I'm busy next weekend,' she began, as he stood at the door, seeming to confirm his fears. 'Paying a return visit to my sister and her boys. But I'm free the weekend after next. I'll be in touch.'

She gave him a brief kiss on the lips, then departed. Jack felt depressed once she'd gone. What had begun so promisingly was showing signs of falling apart at the seams. He feared he'd made a tactical error in mentioning Barbara's resemblance to his wife. Or was it just that she was fed up with his semi-impotence and using it as an excuse?

Most disturbing of all, though, was having his trusty tool let him down. It wasn't as if Barbara was just a casual pick-up. He'd had high hopes of the relationship. Still had, if only he could overcome this temporary hitch. Now he had to wait two whole weeks before he could try again. Two weeks without sex seemed a long time, but maybe a rest was just what his overworked organ needed.

Perversely, his tool was now raring to go. Jack went back to bed and wanked furiously so that he squirted hot and long. Afterwards he pondered on Barbara's similarity to Suzanne. They both had long, dark hair and fullish figures, so probably that was the type he was most attracted to. Maybe he'd better choose a blonde next time. He'd had no trouble screwing Ginnie. Remembering her invitation, he was half tempted to give her a ring but then decided against it. She was great, but he couldn't cope with hubby again. Besides, you could never repeat an experience like that. Once it was over the feelings could never be fully resurrected, so there was no going back. And that probably applied to marriage, too. Jack gave a deep sigh.

Chapter Twelve

Two weeks passed and Jack hadn't heard from Barbara, although he'd tried to phone her a couple of times and left messages on her Ansaphone. He tried once more, and this time she was there.

'Hi. Barbara, it's Jack. I've been trying to reach you. Didn't you get my messages?'

There was an awkward pause. Jack felt his heart sink to his boots.

'Oh Jack, yes, I've been meaning to ring you.' He didn't like the sound of her voice, so distant and cool.

'I thought we'd agreed to meet again.'

'Did we? I'm awfully sorry. I've been busy.'

'How about next Saturday, then?'

Another long pause, then she said, 'Look, Jack, this is a bit awkward. Brenda rang me to ask how we were getting on and I said quite well, considering. She asked what that meant, so I explained that I thought you weren't really over your wife and I reminded you a bit too much of her. Anyway, Brenda said there was this other man interested and . . . well, I'm seeing him tonight.

231

I'd like to keep my options open a bit right now, if you don't mind.'

Jack tried to sound neutral, but his voice came out stiff and formal. 'Of course you're free to date other men as well as me, Barbara. And I hope you would give me the same freedom. But I did think we'd be giving it another go.'

'It's not . . . oh dear, this is embarrassing. It's just . . . well, I think you might be better off with someone who didn't look like your ex-wife. Only I don't want you to get any hang-ups, or anything.'

'Are you saying you don't want to see me again – at all?'

'Well, I suppose that is what I'm saying. I'm awfully sorry, Jack. I liked you a lot, but . . .'

'But I couldn't get it up . . . right?'

'No, Jack! It's not that . . .'

He slammed down the receiver. The two-faced bitch! Saying it didn't matter to his face, then as good as telling him on the phone that it did and she'd rather find someone else. What a cow! Still, at least he'd found out what she was like before he got too involved. After two weeks without her he wasn't that hot for her, anyway. And there were plenty more fish in the sea. And in the computer, come to that. Picking up the phone again, he dialled the number and asked to speak to Brenda.

'Ah yes, Mr. Bedford. I was expecting your call. I gather things didn't quite work out with Miss Tomkins.'

Was that her surname? Funny. He'd never found out.

'Yes. Nice girl but, in the end, not for me.'

'I have another client, Linda. She's currently available, and I also have it on record that she liked the look of you too. Would you like to see her video?'

'Er ... yes please,' Jack replied, a little hollowly. He'd had a sudden vision of himself working his way through all the women in the computer.

He called in at the bureau next day. Brenda presented him with a video of a blonde, busty female in a short skirt who flirted with the camera, crossing and uncrossing her long legs as she sat perched on a bar-stool. She spoke very quickly, in a squeaky voice.

'Hi, I'm Linda, and I'm looking for a man I can really relate to in an all-round way. I work as a hotel receptionist, so I'm not shy about meeting new people. When I'm not working, I like to relax by listening to my rock CDs. I have quite a collection! I also like going to the cinema. I enjoy cooking – just give me a ring, and I'll cook for you any time. After a sumptuous meal, what I like doing best is sipping liqueur by the fire, and have a man slowly seduce me. If this appeals to you, give me a call ...'

Linda was in when he phoned that evening. Her 'little-girl' voice squeaked with excitement when he introduced himself.

'Oh yes, Jack! You like computer games, right? And rock music, right?' she giggled. 'Me too! I thought, when I saw your video, *he* looks intrestin'! And you must have been intrested in me, right, or you wouldn't be phoning now, would you?' More giggles.

Jack rolled his eyes to the ceiling. Don't make hasty

judgements, he told himself. Give the girl a chance.

'Right. Well, how about meeting up then, Linda? Any chance of tomorrow night?'

'Funnily enough, Jack, I am free. There was this other guy I was dating, Pete, but we decided to call it quits. I mean all he wanted to talk about was football, football, football. Anyway, where shall we meet then, in a pub or something?'

Jack found out that she lived in Tooting, so he suggested a Greek restaurant in Streatham Hill that he'd been to a few times.

'Oh yes, that place in the high street, I know it! They do take-aways, don't they? I nearly went there once, only we changed our minds and had an Indian instead.'

'But you do like Greek food?'

'Oh yes, love it! When I went on this Club 18–25 holiday to Corfu I got really into stuffed vine leaves. And if we go to the Taverna Rustica you could come back to my flat afterwards, couldn't you? Save you having to drink and drive.'

It sounded too good to be true. Jack thought he'd better make sure he'd read her right.

'You mean, stay the night at your place?'

'Yeah, if you like. You're not into any really kinky sex or anything, are you?'

Jack pondered. Would she consider liking to be spanked 'really kinky'?

'I'm not sure what you mean, there are certain things I enjoy that some people might consider a bit weird.'

She gave a snort. '*Some* people think cock-sucking's

weird, don't they? No, I meant dressing up in women's clothes and stuff. I had this boyfriend once, right, who had a thing about shoes. He used to want me to wear high-heeled shoes and tread on him, right? Now I call that weird, don't you?'

'Yes, I see what you mean. No, I'm not like that, Linda. So shall we say eight o'clock, at the restaurant? I'll book a table.'

When Linda arrived she was plumper and shorter than she'd appeared on video, but she had the same chirpy manner and her bleached hair had been cut into a scalp-hugging style that accentuated her flirty blue eyes.

'Hullo, you must be Jack,' she grinned, as they met in the small bar of the restaurant. 'Same name as my brother, actually. Intrestin', isn't it? You're nothing like him to look at, right. Just as well, or I'd prob'ly have you down on the floor in a rugby scrum! We used to have terrible fights, me and Jack.'

Jack tried to picture the pair of them wrestling on the floor. It made a pleasant picture. Linda looked like she might be fun.

But could she talk! All through the meal she nattered away about anything that came into her head. Whenever she asked Jack a question she promptly tried to answer it herself.

'You're divorced, right. Any kids? No, you don't look the family man to me. Just as well, I always say. If you're going to split, do it before you have a family not after. Unless it's a long time after, like my parents. They've just divorced after thirty-five years.'

'That must seem strange to you.'

'Not really. 'Course it's upsettin', but the only thing they had in common was me and my brother. Once we'd left home there was nothin' to keep them together any more.'

After a while Jack began to switch off from Linda's incessant babble. Instead he focused on her pouty little mouth and bouncy breasts, that were shown off to advantage by the clingy blue dress she was wearing. The slow fire in his groin was making him impatient to get her alone, so when she suggested they skip dessert and move on to her place he agreed at once.

Linda lived in an untidy top-floor flat near Tooting Common. On the wall were framed pin-ups of rock stars and there were CDs strewn on the floor along with cushions, magazines and the odd coffee cup.

''Scuse the mess,' she grinned, picking her way through the debris. 'I worked all day today and I didn't have time to clear up. We have to work one Saturday in three. Not too bad, really. And three late nights a week. Makes it a bit difficult to get a social life together, which is why I went to Brenda's agency, right.'

'Have you been . . . in her computer long?'

She gave him a cheeky look. 'Oh yes, I've been through hundreds of men! Only kiddin', right. I'd say about six months. One boy I met, Tony, we went out together for three months, then he got back with his old girlfriend. Tea or coffee?'

Jack was impatient to get the preliminaries over with. He wanted to shut her up with a kiss, to handle that plump flesh and get into her juicy little cunt quick, before his burgeoning erection died down. But he had to be careful. Any attempt to move too fast and he could end up being blacklisted by Brenda.

'Choose a CD,' she invited. 'Anythin' you like.'

He put on a *Queen* compilation. She seemed to approve. Soon the coffee was forgotten as they kissed and cuddled on her battered old leather sofa. Linda had very sexy lips and she knew how to use them, mouthing him voluptuously in a soft, relaxed way that sent tingles down his spine. She employed her tongue to good effect too, searching every cranny of his mouth with its flexible tip. Jack began to wonder how it would feel to have her fellate him, and his erection hardened most satisfactorily.

'You're a great kisser, Linda,' he told her, when they paused for air.

'I've had plenty of practice. But I do have other talents, too.'

Her eyes sparkled wickedly at him, and Jack began to think he was onto a good thing. She stood up and held out her hand, to pull him to his feet.

'Shall we go into the bedroom?'

The bedroom was as disorderly as the rest of the flat, but with only the bedside lamp on it didn't look too bad. Linda moved to a cassette player in the corner and selected a tape, but before she switched it on she told Jack to lie down on the bed.

'I've got a surprise for you.'

'Really?'

She unzipped her dress and slipped out of it. Underneath she wore an extraordinary bikini-type garment in dazzling purple and red, with sequinned motifs and tassels.

'Is that your *underwear*?'

Linda laughed. 'No, silly! Just lie there and watch. You'll soon see.'

She switched on the music and at once the raucous sounds of middle eastern music filled the room. Linda raised her hands in a sinuous gesture and posed in the centre of a mat. Jack saw that she had what looked like an eye tattooed around her navel. He tried not to laugh as she began wriggling her belly and the eye winked at him.

'You're a belly dancer!' he exclaimed. 'Amazing!'

'I've been going to these classes, right,' she explained, as she undulated away in time to the insistent drumbeat. 'They're run by an Arab lady, so they're quite ethnic. Last year I did the beginners' class and this year I'm in the advanced class. It's not as easy as it looks, right. There's a lot to learn.'

'I'm sure there is.'

At first it seemed so incongruous that Jack couldn't find it sexy, but after a while the sight of all that pulsating flesh got him more aroused. She was turning round now and waggling her fat little bottom at him. There were bells sewn onto her costume that jingled cheerfully, and when he saw her put her hands behind her back and unfasten her top he became really excited.

'Of course,' Linda explained, still with her back to him, wiggling away, 'In a proper belly dance you'd never take your top off. That would be considered most obscene by an Arab, right. But I like to do a striptease when I'm dancin' in my own bedroom. It's more fun.'

'I've no objections,' Jack grinned, his prick swelling as she slowly revolved to face him.

Linda's boobs were small and pert, the pale nipples already peaking as she brushed the sequinned bra across them. Now she was flexing her flesh like a body-builder, making her tits jerk up and down in a most erotic fashion and all the while the eye of her navel was making its comical winking. The thrusting of her pelvis was firing Jack's lust quite intensely now and he groaned as his erection was strained further.

'It's no good, Linda,' he gasped. 'I'm going to have to take my trousers off.'

She just smiled, beginning her slow revolution again. She was working her small butt quite frantically now and her hands were down inside her pants, pulling them lower and lower. Soon the naked globes of her buttocks appeared, pink and plump, as the embroidered panties slipped down her thighs.

'God, Linda, if you wanted to turn me on you've definitely succeeded!' Jack groaned.

She looked back at him over her shoulder with smiling eyes. 'Good!'

Neatly Linda side-stepped her remaining garment as the music redoubled its pace. Now she was shaking all over, like a jelly in an earthquake, and she began turning back to face him. His first view of her nude body was sideways on, with her uplifted breasts flexing, her hips and belly circulating and her pelvis thrusting. Jack tried to imagine how that would feel if he were inside her and a serious leakage occurred from his impatient prick.

'I can't take much more of this, Linda!' he warned her.

She smiled, knowingly, and began to inch towards him. Soon she was standing above him, everything on the move, a pulsating heap of flesh that he could no longer resist. He reached up and grabbed her hips, pulling her close, then buried his face in her still-shaking midriff. It was overheated and slightly sweaty, arousing him still further.

'Mm!' she murmured, her fingers in his hair. 'It turns me on too, right.'

Eagerly he lowered his head to her musky slit, where the fluids were already running. Linda gasped as his thrusting tongue played first with her small button then with her tight hole, while his hands clasped at her clenched buttocks.

'Let me do all the work,' she pleaded, after a while. 'I can make myself come with your tongue. You don't have to do a thing, right, except play with my breasts.'

Jack reached up and soon had two squidgy handfuls of flesh to squeeze while Linda rolled and thrust her hips against his mouth to her evident satisfaction. She was clearly expert at manipulating that part of her body to a climax and, in a few seconds, she succumbed to violent waves of pleasure that made her gasp and swear.

'Fuck me!' she exploded, making Jack wonder whether she wanted him to take her literally. 'That was fuckin' fantastic!'

Almost immediately Linda sank to her knees and began to suck him off. He didn't need much stimulation either, which was rather a pity because he was relishing her tonguing technique. When he began to gush she pulled away and the spurts fell on her tits and stomach.

'Lick me!' she suggested afterwards.

Once he'd recovered from his shattering climax, Jack began to lick his salty spunk off her. She loved it, and was soon fingering her own clit excitedly. When he took one of her teats into his mouth and bit on it, softly, she came in a series of wild convulsions that had her bucking and swearing even more wildly than before.

They sank, exhausted, into each other's arms.

'Wow, you're quite a girl!' Jack told her, as she snuggled up to him. 'Do all your boyfriends get this treatment?'

'Only if I feel like it. You were lucky tonight. I was feelin' really randy, right.'

It wasn't long before she was feeling randy again. Her fingers strayed beneath the sheets to his wilted tool and she began to finger it lightly.

'I want your lovely hardness inside me,' she whispered. 'I want to bump and grind, with you fillin' me up this time. And I think you want that too, don't you?'

'Mm!' he groaned.

Soon her lips were on him, sucking the limp flesh and squeezing his balls. But the longed-for erection didn't happen. The more Linda licked and sucked and squeezed, the less interested his deflated penis seemed in the proceedings, till at last she was obliged to give up.

'Never mind, I've got somethin' here that can do the job almost as well, right,' she told him, opening a bedside drawer.

Linda drew out a huge, bulbous dildo with French tickler attached. 'This cost me a packet but it works a treat. You don't mind, do you? Only I'm dyin' for my cunt to be filled, and I can't wait.'

Jack took the thing in his hand. There were a couple of switches discreetly hidden in the end. Linda lay back with her legs spread and her hands fondling her tits. Even in the dim light of the bedside lamp Jack could see how wet she was, with the engorged tip of her clitoris protruding from between her lips. He put his finger into her slimy slit and felt the warm goo, but he was too tired to do more than she'd asked and merely poked the knob end of the dildo between her legs, flicking the switch as he did so.

'Press the other switch,' she groaned, her hips beginning to move in rhythmic motion.

When Jack did so, the vibrator hummed into weird life. The thing whirred and bored its way into her hole of its own accord, like some heat-seeking missile, while the soft rubbery tendrils fitting snugly round her rampant lovebutton. It pumped in and out, making slurping, sucking noises, and at the same time seemed to be inflating and rotating, so that it must have filled every inch of her eager quim.

'Oh what a screw!' she sighed. 'If this little darlin' was attached to a man I'd marry him right now! Oh! Aah! Tweak my nipples, Jack, I'm almost there!'

Although he did as she'd asked, Jack felt humiliated. It was his dick that should be in there, pumping away, not that obscene thing. He pulled on her nipples quite hard, so that she gave a little cry of pain, but she was beyond caring and soon the vibrator took her over the edge, thrashing and screaming and swearing as the hot convulsions rocketed through her.

'Satisfied?' Jack asked her, ironically. But he didn't feel good, even though she put her arms around him and planted kisses all over his neck before they both fell asleep.

Jack woke early, with his usual morning erection, while Linda was still asleep. Remembering with some shame what had happened the night before, he reached for the packet of three by the bed and rolled a condom onto his penis, hoping to take advantage of the situation. Gently he nuzzled his glans in between her chubby thighs and soon found the crevice he was seeking. Linda groaned a little in her sleep, but didn't waken. Jack pushed a little more, feeling the resistance weaken as he plunged his knob into the tight hole. He pushed harder, inched further in, feeling the thrill of achievement as his solid prick did what it was made to do at last. Suddenly Linda awoke, with a cry of pain.

'Hey, take that fuckin' dildo out, you dick-head!'

'It's not a dildo, it's my penis,' he whispered, with modest pride.

'Well, it's in the wrong hole and you're hurtin' me like hell. Get it out!'

Oh God, thought Jack, as he realised he was trying to

bugger her. Not that he wouldn't have tried that, if she'd wanted it, but she was now telling him, in no uncertain terms, that she didn't. By the time he'd made his hasty withdrawal, his erection was just a tantalising memory.

'I'm sorry,' he mumbled, into her hair. 'I thought I was giving you what you wanted. I was trying to make up for last night.'

'You were stretchin' my arsehole somethin' chronic,' she moaned. 'It didn't half hurt! Now go and make yourself useful, for fuck's sake. Get us a cup of tea.'

As Jack made his way home mid-morning, he felt really low. Something told him that Linda wouldn't want to see him again, so that was two failures he'd notched up at the computer dating bureau. Soon that Brenda would begin to wonder just what was wrong with him. He was beginning to wonder himself.

Feeling thoroughly miserable, he was sitting at home that evening when he suddenly remembered his pleasurable encounter with Sexy Sadie. He could really do with some of her particular brand of satisfaction tonight. Finding her number in his wallet he picked up the phone.

To his frustration, he had to leave a message on her Ansaphone. After that he sat on tenterhooks, pretending to watch TV but all the while waiting for the phone to ring, like a junkie waiting for his next fix to arrive. Then, at last, came the longed-for sound. Jack leapt to the phone and was reassured to hear her familiar low voice saying, 'Sadie here. How can I help you?'

'Er . . . you came to see me once before,' Jack began, suddenly embarrassed.

She took over with her usual efficiency. 'And you'd like me to visit again tonight?'

'Yes, please.'

'Same as last time, or something a bit different?'

Jack had already given this some consideration. 'Er . . . did you say you could do a Nanny and naughty boy?'

'No problem. Just give me your address and I'll be there in ten minutes.'

This time, Sadie wore a nurse's outfit with a very short skirt, black stockings and, concealing her splendid chest, a starched white apron. In answer to his greeting she merely gave a stern frown and strode in through the door. She stood in the hall holding out her hand, until Jack realised what she wanted and hastily fumbled in his pocket for the cash. Then she put it into her purse and replaced it in the large bag she was carrying.

'I hear you have a naughty little boy living here. One who needs a firm hand.'

'Oh . . . yes, that's right.' Jack felt excitement ripple through him as he remembered his last spanking. 'It's my little Willy. He's not been behaving at all well lately.'

'Let's go into his bedroom and take a look at him then, shall we?'

Jack led the way into his bedroom and she closed the door behind them. 'Now then, what seems to be the trouble? How, exactly, is your Willy misbehaving himself?'

'Well . . . he seems to be very obstinate. I want him to stand up for himself, like other boys, but he refuses.'

'Oh dear! Still, you've hired the right person. I'm very

good at teaching naughty children to do as they're told. Now where is he?'

Jack pointed to his fly. 'Just in here, Nanny.'

'Get him out, then.'

Obediently, Jack undid his zip and brought his limp dick out for inspection.

'Yes, he is a naughty little thing, isn't he. Never mind. We're going to teach him a lesson he won't forget in a hurry. But first, I'm going to take my apron off, because I don't want to get it dirty.'

She untied the apron at the waist and lifted if off over her head, revealing her massive boobs. 'Nice, aren't they?' Sadie flashed him a brief smile. 'Sometimes I let little boys like Willy snuggle up to them, but only when they've been very good and learn to stand up for themselves.'

'Are you going to punish him, then?' Jack asked. The thought of plunging his dick into that deep, fleshy ravine was giving him the beginnings of an erection.

'Of course. That's the only way to treat naughty boys. Take off his trousers and make him bend over my knee. We'll soon show him what happens to little Willies who won't grow up to be big boys.'

Jack stepped out of his trousers and took off his pants. His rod was fairly firm, but still pointing downwards. To his surprise, he found he was trembling with excitement. Sadie sat down on the bed and patted her huge thighs.

'Bend over my lap, Willy. I'm going to smack your wicked little bottom, hard!'

Jack knelt on the floor so that Sadie's huge knockers

were at his eye level. He was aching to touch them but knew he must wait. Nanny was in charge, and he couldn't risk breaking the rules in case she took umbrage. He bent down over her thighs, and when she leaned forward the full weight of her mammaries fell onto his back. He was so aroused by this novel sensation that his penis shot up at once.

Sadie leaned right over him to take off her flat nurse's shoe, pressing her chest harder against his back and making his erection grow further. Then she began walloping him with the sole on his naked buttocks.

'Bad, bad, bad boy!' she chanted, with every stroke. Jack felt his cheeks begin to tingle and then to sting. Soon his behind was hurting quite a lot, but Sadie kept up the relentless battery. Then, after a dozen blows, she suddenly stopped and lifted him off her lap.

'Now then, let's see if Willy has learnt his lesson.'

Jack stood up and his pecker sprang to attention. A beaming smile spread across Sadie's face. 'Good boy! That's much better! See what a little discipline will do? Come here, Willy dear, and let me see how strong you are.'

She clasped him with a strong hand, and Jack felt rock solid. It was the best stiffy he'd had in ages, and tingling desire was spreading from his groin all through his body, making every nerve-end cry out for satisfaction. Even the soreness of his bum was now reduced to the level of a warm, pleasurable glow.

Sadie settled herself comfortably on the bed with her head against the wall, her back against the pillows and her legs stretched out in front of her. The navy mini-skirt was riding up, revealing black suspenders and a hint of black frilly knickers at the top of her fat thighs. Jack couldn't help staring at her enormous knockers, with their stiff upturned nipples. Would he get a chance to get his hands on them soon?

'Now then, come and sit on Nanny's lap, there's a good boy.'

Jack did so at once, and was soon sitting as instructed between Sadie's straddled legs with his head between her outside mammaries. His prick was standing up for itself beautifully now, the pinkish-purple glans beginning to sweat a little spunk. Sadie reached down and took it firmly in hand, saying, 'As you've been *such* a good boy, Willy, I'll let you have a suck on Nanny's lovely sweetie.'

She lifted her left tit with her free hand and offered him her nipple. Turning his face he licked at it eagerly, grasping the heavyweight boob with both hands. The nipple almost filled his mouth and the soft flesh pressed against his nose so that he was almost suffocated, but he didn't care. This was bliss!

Sadie began to work his dick with expert fingers, applying just the right amount of pressure and speed to keep him deliciously on the edge of orgasm. All the time she cooed at him in a nursery voice, 'There's a good boy! What a well-behaved Willy! Nice and hard for Nanny now!'

With increasing fervour, Jack sucked hard on the brown teat, lost in some infantile Land of the Giant Mammaries. He squeezed her nipple between his finger and thumb, the tip of his tongue licking back and forth over its tip, and half expected milk to spurt out. Instead, it began to leak from his glans.

'Ooh, we're getting to be quite a wet little boy!' Sadie commented. 'Never mind. We'll wipe it all up soon, won't we? And maybe we'll rub some nice soothing cream into his sore little botty for him, too.'

The thought of this was too much for Jack, who opened his mouth in a silent cry of ecstasy – silent because he was stuffed with Sadie's nipple – as he felt the flood gates open and a wash of pure sensation seemed to pour all over him. Faintly he could hear Sadie still murmuring, 'There's a good boy! Come for Nanny!'

When the great gush was ended he flopped back onto the generous cushion of her breasts. She let him lie for a few seconds, then took a tissue from the box by the bed and mopped him up with nurse-like efficiency. He watched through hazy eyes as she took a black sweater from her bag and pulled it over her head.

'There you are then, dear. All over. If you need me again, you have my number.'

She turned to go, pausing at the door to blow him a kiss. 'Night night, Willy! Sweet Dreams!'

Jack lay exhausted on the sofa for some time. She was good, he had to give her that, playing her rôle to the end. Well worth the money. His behind still stung, but it was more of a sore tingling and quite bearable. Nothing that a good soak in a warm bath wouldn't soothe. And the sense of total satisfaction that his climax had given him made the whole thing worth it. Physically, he was quite content.

Mentally, though, he was somewhat disturbed. It came

to him later, as he lay in his bath, that his most satisfactory sexual experiences during the past few months had been by means of Virtual Reality or flagellation at the hands of a whore. All his attempts at real-life sex with ordinary women had been more or less disastrous. Just what the hell was the matter with him?

Chapter Thirteen

The puzzle pursued Jack through the days that followed. Just was *was* wrong with him sexually? Had his broken marriage left him somehow scared of women, was that it? Or was it something more deep-rooted?

As before, Jack threw himself into his work to try and escape the vexing questions. He didn't bother contacting Linda again, fearing a repetition of his humiliating failure in bed. Yet he knew he couldn't go on like that forever. One day he would have to address his little problem and the underlying reasons for it. One day.

The computer game was going well. Jack had perfected the graphics so that each of the girls on the dating agency's books was individually attractive. He was having trouble differentiating their voices, though. He wanted Sharon (short, busty, bubbly blonde) to have a cute, girlish voice. Delia, on the other hand (tall, hefty, with cropped dark hair) required deep, almost butch tones, while Veronica (a sultry, kittenish redhead) needed to purr seductively. The speaker on his own computer was nowhere near as advanced as the latest models, so his attempts at sound engineering were inevitably crude. If the games company took his game on they would tweak the sound up to the highest standards, of course, but he was still waiting to hear whether they were definitely interested.

He was also waiting to hear about his divorce. There had been a flurry of letters from Suzanne's solicitor when the house sale went through, but nothing since. She hadn't given him her new address and it was frustrating not being able to contact her. Jack realised she didn't even know that he'd lost his job. He'd written to let her solicitor know his new address, so Suzanne could get in touch. It hurt him that she didn't seem to want to. After all, they had been together long enough to still care about each other a little, surely?

That he still cared about her was evident to Jack. Not that there was any point in dwelling on it. Whenever the pain threatened to overcome him he buried it and went back to his keyboard.

One evening he had a call from Brenda, at the dating agency. He'd forgotten that he was still on her computer files.

'I gather you're not still seeing Linda,' she said, in a solicitous tone. 'Are you interested in dating someone new? I have a young lady who liked your video and wants to meet you.'

For a few seconds Jack was tempted. Then he thought, What's the use? There was no guarantee that a new affair would work out any better than the last two.

'Thanks, but I think I'll give it a rest for the moment.'

TOUCH ME, FEEL ME

There was a pause. Then Brenda said, 'Don't take this the wrong way, Jack, but are you all right?'

Sudden paranoia overtook him. 'Has Linda said anything? Or Barbara?' He realised how bad that must sound and grew even more nervous. 'I mean, things didn't exactly work out with them, but I don't want you to get the wrong impression about me.'

'Don't worry, Jack, we all go through rough patches in our sex lives. Half the people who come to me do so out of desperation . . .'

They *had* been talking! Oh God!

'Look, I've just broken up with my wife, okay? I probably went into this too soon.'

'Have you had any counselling, Jack?'

'Counselling?'

'Yes. There's usually some psychological debris to clear up after a separation, and rushing into new relationships before the scars of the old one have healed can make things worse.'

'That's why I'm giving it a rest.'

'So you want me to withdraw your details and video, do you? At least for the time being.'

'I . . . I think so, yes. But thanks for . . .'

'Look, Jack, I'm going to give you a phone number. Got a pen handy? It's for a counsellor. His name's Gary and I can thoroughly recommend him. He's helped lots of my clients. You don't have to ring him, of course, but if you just take the number down it'll be there if you feel you need it. Okay?'

She was only trying to be helpful, Jack told himself as

resentment welled up in him. He took down the number and thanked her, but the thought that either Barbara or Linda – or both! – might have told Brenda about his potency problem was eating away at him. He imagined Brenda sitting there like some randy old spider in the middle of the web she'd spun, gathering juicy titbits of gossip about her clients' sexual habits. Then he realised that was unfair and he should stop being so suspicious.

A few days later, the computer games company rang inviting him to talk to them about his game. He took a morning off and visited the Docklands headquarters of Arcadia. It was weird going back to that part of London. Jack had to pass the street where Global was situated and resisted the urge to drive down it, but he still felt a frisson down his spine. Who was sitting in his seat now, creating scenarios, trying them out on the Feelietron? Whoever that man – or woman? – was, Jack envied them. Everything had been so simple when technology had control of his sex life.

Phil Greenaway, of Arcadia, was a pleasant young man with a neat appearance and intelligent eyes. They got down to business straight away in his ultra hi-tech office.

'So, you were with Global VR, were you?' he said, glancing at Jack's CV. 'Good experience with both scenarios and characterisation, I see. Well, you're better off sticking to computer games. That's where the future lies now. Virtual Reality is all very interesting but the best skill and expertise is in the computer industry.'

Jack wanted to disagree, but realised he couldn't argue his case without mentioning the Feelietron and breaking the confidentiality agreement. Still, he felt slightly uncomfortable knowing that once the world was introduced to Feelie Sex they wouldn't be thinking in terms of computer games any more.

Phil slotted the disk Jack had brought with him into the computer and they spent a couple of hours going through his programme. It was very instructive. Phil could see at once how to improve on the sound, as well as several other aspects which Jack hadn't thought about.

'Jack, I think your game would be ideal for a new gimmick we've invented,' Phil said at last. He handed him a kind of black plastic condom into which electrodes were implanted. 'We call this a Joystrap because it's part joystick and part jockstrap.'

'You mean you wear this thing to play the game?'

Phil grinned. 'For years people have been saying computer games are for wankers. Now we can prove it!'

Jack realised at once that this was a kind of halfway technology between conventional computer games and Virtual Reality. As such, it could fill a gap in the market until VR became affordable. He was impressed.

'Would you like to try it?' Phil smiled. 'We have a game called Snorkel that you might enjoy.'

Phil led the way into a booth where a screen showed a man with a snorkel chasing a nude woman under water. Jack stripped off his trousers and underpants then strapped on the 3D goggles and electronic condom. At first, his prick dangled uselessly inside.

'Does it work if you don't have a hard-on?'

Phil nodded. 'Try it and see.'

Jack gripped the Joystrap and at once the scene changed to the snorkeller's eye view. A buxom female was swimming just in front, twisting and turning seductively in the water.

'The idea is to score as many girls as you can, using your snorkel,' Phil explained.

Jack found that he could change speed and direction easily by manipulating the Joystrap, but it felt strange at first. The leather pouch of the Feelietron had been roomy, but this seemed to mould itself to his dick like a thick and rather elaborate condom. It was a bit like a novelty number he'd once tried, covered in knobs and ridges.

Before him, in the water, reared his 'snorkel', a long black tube with a red end into which a ball was fitted giving it a rounded tip. There were realistic bubbling and heavy breathing noises, but none of the other sensory input that he was used to. The graphics were good, however. Jack liked the realistic way the girl's heavy boobs shifted around in the water and the sinuous curves of her waist and hips as she swivelled around. There were some nice touches, too. At one point a large fish tried to nibble at her nipples and was brushed away. Another attempted to nose its way between her legs and was given a sharp slap. Seaweed often drifted across her anatomy giving a tantalising 'seven veils' effect, yet still she remained out of reach. No matter how hard Jack pulled on his plasticised penis he couldn't quite catch up with her.

Still, his real penis was showing signs of life. Whether it was the continual friction or the erotic visual display that was turning him on – probably a combination of both – he could feel himself hardening. And as his erection grew, so did his speed. The gear must have been designed so that the electrodes responded to the pressure against them and worked faster. Neat!

As Jack saw himself gaining on the sexy mermaid, he suddenly found he had a rival. A giant octopus had wrapped its tentacles around the girl's body and had fastened its suckers over her mouth, breasts and genitals. It was difficult to tell what her reactions were. At first Jack presumed she was struggling to free herself but after a while it looked as if her frenzy was more sexual than fear-driven. If he wanted some of the action, however, he would have to confront the beast.

Pulling his joystrap to the left, Jack veered round and tried to use his snorkel like a harpoon, to poke the octopus in the eye. Just as he thought he had a clear shot at it the creature snatched his snorkel with a spare tentacle. The thing snapped it in two and the screen went blank for a second before GAME OVER flashed.

'Bad luck!' Clive laughed. 'You're supposed to poke the girl, not the octopus, by jabbing between the tentacles. If you can get your snorkel into her snatch before he gets one of his suckers in there, you've won a round and a new girl appears.'

When Jack took off the goggles he found an unexpected side-effect: he was temporarily blinded. 'Hell, the old wives were right. It really does make you blind!'

Clive laughed. 'Only for a few seconds.'

Jack declined a second go, but declared himself well pleased with the technology. It was nothing like the Feelietron, of course, and erotically speaking it was no more exciting than wanking over a nudie mag. But it definitely had potential. If Please Please Me came out as one of the first to use the new Joystrap it would really catch on.

On the way home, Jack felt as if a new chapter in his life was about to open. For the first time since leaving Global his career seemed to be back on course. If only he could say the same for his personal life. He recalled what Brenda had said to him on the phone. Maybe he could do with some advice after all. It was just that it was so embarrassing to have to confess to some stranger that he had trouble getting it up. Not that he wouldn't be used to hearing such things, of course, being a counsellor.

Jack agonised over whether to ring the number for several days. In the end it was becoming too much of a distraction so, deciding it was better to lift up the phone and get it over with, Jack dialled. A pleasant female voice answered.

'Hullo, Gary Martin's secretary. Can I help you?'

'Er ... well, I'm not sure.'

'Are you a client of Gary's?'

'Not yet, but he was recommended. I'm ... er ... not sure if he can help me or not, actually.'

'Well why don't I make you an appointment? The first consultation is always free. Gary likes to make sure that he and his clients are compatible. I have a cancellation tomorrow at six o'clock. Will that be convenient?'

Jack gulped. He hadn't expected anything to happen quite so soon. But he was reassured by being offered a trial session. There could be no harm in going to that, at least.

After he'd made the appointment, Jack found himself wondering about Gary Martin. Was he a doctor? A psychiatrist? A sex therapist? He had nothing but Brenda's recommendation to go on. Next day, as the time of his appointment approached, he grew quite nervous and sweaty at the thought of baring his soul to the man. Was he going to be faced with a load of awkward questions?

The address was not far away, in a road of once-elegant Victorian houses that had mostly been turned into flats and offices. Jack glanced around furtively as he approached the steps leading to the front door. Did everyone around know what went on in that innocuous-seeming building? Then his eye fell on the four brass plates at the door, and he realised that he could just as well be visiting a dentist, a solicitor or a Miss E. King, so he relaxed as he went into the communal hallway, up the staircase and found a door marked 'Gary Martin, F.S.P.C.'

He entered a pleasant reception area where a woman sat at a desk in front of a computer monitor, surrounded by potted palms and ferns. Her dark-blonde hair was in a neat French plait, and she smiled at him in a friendly fashion, her brown eyes warm.

'Hullo, you must be Jack. I'm Hazel. We tend to be on first-name terms here, as it helps maintain confidentially. Gary will see you in a moment, if you'd like to take a seat.'

Jack sat next to a table bearing a selection of magazines and Hazel returned to her work. The magazine on the top of the pile intrigued him and he picked it up. It was obviously a desktop publication, but the contents were like nothing he'd ever seen before. Page after page of women and men in straps or chains illustrated stories and articles with titles like, 'Restrain me, please!', 'Chained Melody' and 'Your Word is My Bond'.

He glanced at the next magazine. It was called 'CP Fantasy' and this time Jack found the contents quite arousing. The first story was called 'Six of the Best' and the picture showed a Victorian school marm administering the cane to a young man who was kneeling on all fours. It vividly recalled Jack's last encounter with the redoubtable Sadie and his prick reared in his pants as he remembered that seat-warming episode. He flicked through the rest of the magazine and found more similar pictures. There were stories with equally suggestive titles, all on the same theme, and articles on where to find good quality canes, a history of the Scottish Tawse and on famous thrashings in literature.

Still furtively roused, Jack found more copies of both publications, together with a good many others. One was aimed at cross-dressers, another at foot-fetishists, another at rubber freaks. It was obvious that Gary Martin had set out to please all tastes, however obscure and perverted they might be. Jack was reading a story called 'Horsey, Horsey!' when the inner door suddenly opened and a man's head peered out.

'Jack's here, Gary,' he heard Hazel say, and looked up to see a man with thinning light brown hair and grey eyes smiling at him. Gary was in his mid-forties and casually dressed in a cashmere sweater and cords. Jack decided at once that he was all right.

'I see you've found our collection of literature,' the counsellor smiled, coming towards him with a welcoming hand. 'We try to cater for everyone, although there's no telling what the human mind can invent for its own amusement. But wouldn't life be dull if we all used sex for procreative purposes only?'

He stood back to let Jack enter his room. There were no sinister couches or off-putting medical charts. It was a light and airy room looking out onto a quiet garden, with easy chairs and a desk with a computer set unobtrusively in one corner. There were more potted plants, soft guitar music playing and even a white cat dozing before a gas fire. Jack felt instantly at ease.

Gary walked to a cabinet and opened the door. 'Would you like a drink?'

Jack was startled, but accepted a whisky gratefully. Then the two men drew up armchairs to the fire and sat with the cat purring on the floor between them. Gary took a gulp of his whisky then gave Jack a wry, but friendly, smile.

'Okay, tell me about your first sexual experience.'

Jack was nonplussed. 'But don't you want to know why I'm here?'

'I know why you're here, to talk about sex. So tell me about the earliest experience you can recall which you'd label as sexual.'

'What, you mean my first kiss, that sort of thing?'

'For some of us it's a kiss, for others a grope. Or even a horse-ride. When were *you* first aware of being sexually aroused?'

Jack thought. His first girlfriend? No, earlier than that. Much earlier. Seeing his Dad's early morning erection, perhaps. Or his mother's breasts. No, he knew when it was! He could remember her clearly now. That baby-sitter, what was here name? Sara. That was it. Everything was coming back to him. But did he really have to talk about *that*?

'Have you remembered?' Gary prompted, gently.

'Yes. It was before I went to school when I was around four.' Jack cleared his throat. 'I had a regular baby-sitter called Sara. She was a student, I think. Lived in a bedsit down the road. That was the point, really. Being in a bedsit she had no proper bathroom, so she used to take a bath in our house whenever she looked after me.'

'And what happened to you while she was in the bath?'

'I used to go in with her. I can remember touching her breasts, and her laughing. I'd get a hard-on, and she'd laugh at that too, calling me a "little man". She'd wash me with her soapy hands and it would feel good.'

'Did anything more happen with Sara?'

'I used to make her cross, and then she'd ... she'd put me across her knee and spank me. Once ...' Jack hesitated, embarrassed to recall the incident. 'We were in the bath, and I played a trick on her. I said there was a funny spot on my tummy, and when she bent down to take a closer look I peed in her eye.'

'So then she had to punish you, yes?'

'Yes. She hauled me out of the bath and put a towel on her lap. Then she made me bend over her knees and slapped my wet bottom. It stung all the more because we were both so wet. I'd had an erection in the bath, and I was still stiff. I think I might have had my first orgasm then, I don't know.'

'And you still enjoy being spanked, do you?'

Jack took a last swig of his drink. 'I only found out recently.'

'I've heard many similar stories to yours, Jack. Sometimes the source of the fetish is easily found, like yours. Sometimes it's more obscure, takes longer to ferret out. But the important thing is that you should feel good about yourself and not be ashamed of your individual preferences.'

'But other people don't always see it that way, do they?'

'Sadly, no. Usually because they've got hang-ups of their own which they're too timid to confront. So, to move on, can you recall anything from your early days at school? We usually get some sort of informal sex education from other children, even if it's only in the form of dirty jokes.'

Jack racked his brains. If anything like that had occurred it would either have been at break, in the asphalt playground, or outside school altogether. Suddenly he recalled a little girl, catching up with him in the corridor. He couldn't remember her name, but he could see her grimy face with its wicked blue eyes, and the untidy ponytail tied with a red ribbon. He could hear her voice, too, aware of its own naughtiness, as it whispered in his ear, 'I'll show you mine, if you'll show me yours. Behind the sheds, at playtime.'

Driven by curiosity, he'd agreed to the rendezvous.

'There was this little girl,' he began. 'We met behind a shed in the playground and showed each other our genitals.'

'Can you say how you reacted at the time?'

'Well, I do remember being quite puzzled. There was just this slit in her skin, between her thighs. I found it very odd. Probably because I'd already seen my mother and the baby-sitter naked, and they'd had hair there.'

A flashback to Petra's shaven mons suddenly made it all fall into place. No wonder he'd been excited by the idea of a hairless quim!

'What about her? How did she react to the sight of your penis?'

She . . . she said it was smaller than her big brother's. That didn't bother me, I'd already seen my Dad's. And I presumed that it would grow along with the rest of me. No, I was more confused by her anatomy.'

'Confused?'

'Yes. First because she was hairless there and second because of the split. I suppose Sara's had been hidden by her pubes when I was in the bath with her. Anyway, I remember asking my Dad about it when he came home from work. He seemed to know the answer to everything in those days.'

'Can you recall the conversation?'

Jack frowned with the effort of remembering. 'I think I said, "Are girls just like boys, only without a willy?" or something similar.'

'How did he react to that?

'He laughed and then launched into a biology lecture. It was a bit over the top, with far more information than I was able to take in at the time. But I did get the basic message, which was that boys and girls are born different. He said something which stuck with me: boys have all their important bits on the outside, while girls have them inside.'

Gary rose from his chair and paced about a little, going with some thought-process of his own. Then he came to rest, leaning on the back of his chair.

'That's rather significant, isn't it? A remark like that can trigger a whole series of responses to the words "outside" and "inside". They can never have quite the same ordinary meaning again. "Inside" comes to mean the women's world of home and family, nurturing and safe but also restricting, imprisoning. Think of the colloquial phrase "he's been inside!" But then there's the concept of the "great outdoors", with all that implies about freedom and adventure, a man's world. However we try to get away from these sexual stereotypes they're still there, subtly imbedded in our language.'

Jack had heard something like this from Suzanne, who had gone through a feminist phase but, fortunately, had emerged relatively balanced in her views. He began to wonder about Gary, though.

His mistrust must have showed on his face because the counsellor laughed, saying, 'Don't worry, I'm not going to preach the feminist gospel at you! But we do need to be aware of how our attitudes are shaped. Can you recall any further incidents of that kind?'

'I'm not sure.' Jack paused for thought. 'Lots of things used to puzzle me. Mostly dark female secrets. How was it that girls could occasionally have babies before marriage? And what exactly were "sanitary pads?" Were they like the writing pads my Dad used? Or my Mum's shoulder pads?'

Gary was smiling. 'How we agonise over such details when we're young! But what about female anatomy and the sex act itself?'

'Oh, after that chat with my father I flattered myself I knew all about how women were made. By the time I reached junior school I knew they had a womb (I thought of it as a "room") where babies grew, and a channel leading to it in which sperm swam up and, nine months later, babies came down. I suppose I was pretty well clued up for a ten-year-old.'

Gary nodded. 'Reproduction details are usually fairly easy to take in. It's the finer points of the sexual act that are never discussed.'

'That's right. I knew nothing about the clitoris, for instance, until a girlfriend explained.'

'Tell me about it. How old were you?'

'I was fifteen, and she was seventeen.' A smile spread over Jack's face at the recollection. 'Her name was Liz. She'd had three boyfriends before me and she used to read her Dad's girlie magazines, so she knew a lot more than most of the other girls.'

'Was she your first girlfriend?'

'The first serious one, yes. I'd kissed a few girls before her, at parties and so on. Then there were girls I knocked about with in the company of my mates. I'd taken one of them to the pictures, but nothing came of it. We sat in the back row and I tried to put my arm round her, because that's what I thought you were supposed to do. But she told me to keep my filthy hands to myself, so that was the end of that.'

'But with Liz, things went a bit further?'

Jack grinned. 'Quite a lot further, although not "all the way" as we used to say in those days.'

'So you got into heavy petting?'

'I suppose so. It was the baby-sitting thing again. Every Saturday night she used to baby-sit for her married sister, and I used to go round there. My parents assumed that the friend I was visiting was male.'

'It sounds an ideal situation for early sexual experimentation.'

Jack found nostalgia starting to roll over him in pleasant waves.

'It was. The very first time I turned up she took me upstairs to the spare room. The baby was asleep in the room next door. I got very excited when she took her top off. She was quite well-developed, and when she took her bra off and let me fondle her tits I came in my pants straight away.'

'Were you embarrassed?'

'I tried not to let on what had happened. After that it seemed a bit easier. I wasn't so tense, and when she took off her knickers and let me have a good look at her private parts I felt as if my sex education was at last being completed.'

'Did she let you touch her, too?'

'Not at first, but she parted her lips with her fingers and showed me all the details. "This is my hole," she said, putting her finger right into it. "But this is the part I like having rubbed, this bit up here." And she showed me her clitoris. Then she proceeded to masturbate in front of me while I stroked her breasts. I had no idea what would happen so when she began gasping and thrashing about I grew quite frightened. I thought she was having a fit, or something.'

'Did she explain?'

'Yes. It was the first time I'd heard the expression "coming".'

'And did you associate it with your own self-pleasuring?'

'Sort of. Except that she seemed to make a lot more noise and fuss about it!'

'What happened next?'

'Then it was my turn. She made me take off my trousers and pants, which I did very carefully so she wouldn't notice they were wet with semen. I had another erection by then, and she said I was "nice and big" which pleased me. I knew she'd seen at least three other penises, so I thought she knew what she was talking about.'

'Did she touch you?'

'Yes. She said it was my turn now, and made me lie down on the bed. I had no idea what she was going to do, and I felt a bit scared as well as extremely excited. She fiddled around with her fingers, rather inexpertly, for a bit. But then she did something extraordinary. She took the whole of my prick into her mouth. I had no idea about fellatio. Although I'd heard the expression "blow-job" I thought it meant just blowing on a penis!'

'So she gave you a blow-job, then?' Gary prompted.

'Not completely. I wanted my prick to stay in that warm, wet mouth but she took it out and began handling it again. Then she rubbed my glans on her nipples and I came almost immediately.'

Gary sat forward with his elbows propping his chin, staring into the fire. 'Was that the usual pattern of your behaviour with Liz, or did it develop from there.'

Jack considered. 'It developed a bit. Although I used to feel her up, I never quite managed to bring her off, manually. She used to finish it herself. I never used my mouth. That didn't seem to occur to her.'

'But no penetration.'

'Oh no! We were both far too scared of her getting pregnant. We had no form of contraception. I would have died rather than ask for a packet of three in the chemist's and I didn't know of any machines in those days.'

'I see. Did this mutual masturbation ever take place simultaneously?'

Jack frowned. 'I don't think so. No, it was always her first, then me. Maybe once or twice we did it ourselves. Yes, I'm pretty sure that happened. We sat facing each other, sitting cross-legged on the bed, both of us wanking away. I think it was to see who could come first. Otherwise, it was always done separately. Strange, really, now I come to think of it.'

'Not really. You were both playing safe. Masturbating

in front of a partner is a form of exhibitionism and doing it *for* your partner enables you to remain in control. Mutual sex involves a blurring of boundaries, the giving up of oneself to the other. It's a sign of maturity to be comfortable doing that.'

For the first time in the session, Jack felt a twinge of guilt. Had he been able to do that with Suzanne, to really surrender to her and not be thinking, selfishly, of his own needs? But there was no time to explore that thought. Gary was looking at his watch, rising from his chair.

'Good. Look, Jack, I want to leave it there today, okay? You'll probably find that more memories come flooding back to you in the time before you see me again. If they seem important, jot them down.'

He rose and offered his hand. Jack gripped it and smiled. He felt both relieved and elated. 'I didn't realise this would be so easy. I feel better already.'

Jack made another appointment for a week's time. He'd been impressed by Gary's expertise. How on earth did that man manage to access hidden memories so easily? Hypnotism? Suggestion? Or was it that he simply gave his clients space for their subconscious to provide the answers? Whatever his technique, it certainly worked.

When Jack left he felt as if a muddy pool had been stirred and all kinds of interesting creatures had been prised from their hiding-places. Despite the murkiness, he felt cleansed. Perhaps those experiences which seemed so fraught and worrying at the time had, after all, been 'just part of growing up' as the adults around him had been fond of saying.

Over the next few days Jack felt at a loose end, with little to occupy him at home. Good ideas for new computer games remained stubbornly elusive, even though he scoured the magazines to discover the latest trends and tried to think of ways to improve on the current examples.

More and more he found his thoughts turning to Suzanne. How successfully was she re-building her life with her new lover? Were they still planning to marry, buy a house together? Have children? The thought of her doing all those things that had once been their joint dreams filled him with anger and hatred. Did she ever think of him? His frustration at knowing nothing grew. Picking up his pen he decided to write her a note via her solicitor, asking her to get in touch and fill him in on whatever was happening in her life. Whatever was going on, and however much pain it might cause him to learn the truth, Jack felt he had to know. Perhaps if she managed to convince him that Rupert was the best man for her to share the rest of her life with, he would finally come to accept it. Or at least accept that there was no hope for him.

Because, deep down, Jack knew he still had hope. A fragile thing it was, but there all the same. His various adventures with other women had only made him realise how much he had lost through his own lack of awareness. If he ever got into a stable relationship again he vowed he would monitor its progress, every step of the way.

First, though, there was the past to deal with.

Chapter Fourteen

Jack was disappointed when another week went by and he hadn't heard from Suzanne. He felt so low one evening that he was tempted to call Sadie, but the urge wasn't as strong as it had been. He thought maybe his confessions to Gary were making him reassess his sexuality, and he needed a period of abstinence to sort himself out. Furthermore, he only masturbated once that week, and it was a purely mechanical business with no fantasising involved. I'm losing my libido altogether, he thought gloomily.

Jack arrived promptly for his appointment and was shown straight in. This time no drink was offered and Jack realised it had been an ice-breaker, for the first occasion only. Well, now he was relaxed enough not to need it. Gary sat in the same chair by the fire and motioned Jack into the other one. This time the cat was on the wide window-ledge, catching the last of the spring sunshine, and there was no music playing. Only a faint purring broke the silence.

'Had a good week?' Gary opened, conversationally, as they took their seats.

'Not particularly,' Jack grimaced. 'A bit worrying, actually. I seem to be losing my sex drive altogether.'

Gary was unperturbed. 'It happens. Think of your sexual drive as being like an internal combustion engine. You can't expect to be driving along while you're peering under the bonnet.'

Jack laughed. 'But I'm not even tinkering with it. Not much, anyway.'

Gary went into what Jack had come to recognise as his 'reflective' mode. 'It's amazing what we expect of our poor penises, isn't it. They've got to be up and running as soon as we switch on, or we start to panic. Sometimes the battery runs down, or the engine's cold. We have to wait until we're recharged, or the climate warms up.'

'Okay, I take your point. Look, can I talk about what's been happening to me more recently? I've been thinking a lot about my wife lately. We're separated, coming up for a divorce.'

'It's a big leap from your first sexual experience, Jack. I'd rather work up to the present, if you don't mind. Filling in the details of someone's sexual history is important, because each new encounter is related to the previous ones in some way. It's a complicated picture, but I find it does help if we take it stage by stage. Last time you told me about a relationship when you were fifteen, involving mutual masturbation. Where did you go from there?'

Jack felt disappointed. He'd wanted to free himself from his endless circular thoughts about Suzanne, to have someone else throw light on it for him. But he realised that Gary was right: no part of his life existed in a vacuum. Casting his mind back to those turbulent teenage years, he remembered that he'd had a series of short-lived girlfriends after Liz.

'I got curious about women after that,' he began. 'I wanted to see their naked bodies, to find out how they were similar and how they were different.'

'Did you look at men's magazines?'

'Sometimes. Especially the ones with revealing poses. But I began hanging around the youth club and the girls' school gate, learning how to chat them up. I got quite good at it, too.'

'You had lots of dates?'

'I was still at school and didn't get much pocket money, so I couldn't take girls out very often. I'd meet them over the park and go into the shelter for a grope. The main thing Liz had taught me was that girls liked it as much as boys, so I had no hesitation about trying to get into their knickers and, mostly, they let me. I'd stick one hand down their pants and the other up their bra and we'd be away!'

'Did any of them touch your genitals?'

'Not many. I was always scared of being caught with my dick out. It was easier with a girl, you'd just take your hands away quickly if anyone came and she'd arrange her clothes and that was it. But I sometimes came while I was feeling them up and, if I didn't, I'd go home and bring myself off in my bedroom.'

'So you didn't get the privacy to explore much further at that stage, then?'

'Not until I was about eighteen. Then I got an older girlfriend and everything became much more intense. Her name was Ann. She'd left school and had a flat in town. She'd had a steady boyfriend before me who was twenty-four and she wasn't a virgin. I couldn't believe my luck when she told me she was on the pill.'

Jack paused to savour the memory. It would be hard to put it all into words, but he'd try.

'I went round there one Saturday afternoon and she'd left the door on the latch for me while she had a bath. So there I was looking down at her naked body, all pink and luscious. I suppose there must have been echoes of Sara, the baby-sitter, there.'

'Ah, yes.'

'Well, I got into the bath and we started to wash each other. She kept praising my erection and said she could hardly wait to feel it inside her, so I knew that this was it. I was going to "do it" for the first time.'

'What did you feel at that point?'

'Nervous, excited. All the usual things. A bit afraid that I wouldn't match up to her previous boyfriend. But I was too keen to get in there to worry much about that.'

'Did she help you?'

'Yes, quite a bit. We got out of the bath and she started kissing me and fondling my prick, then we draped the bath towels over us and went to her bed. We lay down, kissing and cuddling, and she said I had to make sure she was wet. Like a fool, I said, "Of course you're wet. You've just been in the bath. Do you want me to dry you?" Then she laughed and called me silly, but quite sweetly. She said "wet down there"! and put my finger into her quim, which was only a bit moist. I asked if it was wet enough and she said no, but it soon would be if I stroked it a bit.'

Gary said, 'And by now you were quite practised at that, I presume.'

'Yes, but I'd never actually brought a girl to orgasm that way. They'd always finished themselves off. And with Ann she was more keen to have me screw her. She helped guide me in and, after that, I suppose instinct took over. It didn't last long. A few thrusts and that was it. But since I had no idea that it *could* last longer, I felt really proud of myself.'

'Did she seem satisfied?'

'Not really. I soon understood that a bit more was expected of me when she said something like, "Well that was a five-second wonder, wasn't it?" She started to play with herself, making me realise that girls weren't as easily satisfied as I was. Still, I'd done it. That was the main thing.'

'How did your affair with Ann develop?'

'It only lasted three weeks after that. We made love a few more times, but I don't think I was experienced enough for her. She expected me to know what to do, but I needed instruction. Mind you, I struck lucky next time.'

Jack smiled as he thought of gorgeous, randy Evelyn.

'Before we go on to that, I want you to think about what you'd learned about sex by this stage.'

It was hard for Jack to think himself back into the mind of his eighteen-year-old self, so much had happened since then.

'Well, I reckon I knew my way around female anatomy

quite well by the time I left school. I knew they had orgasms as well as men and that they liked being fucked, but I hadn't quite put the two together yet. Fucking still seemed a bit strange to me. It was over too soon, just as I was getting into it. But I certainly liked the feelings I got when I was in there.'

Gary rose and paced about the room as he did his thinking. 'It seems, from what you tell me, that you'd explored the physical side of sex quite a lot, but the emotional hardly at all. Is that fair?'

Jack nodded. 'I guess so. Sex was just something you did, like football. I think maybe some of the girls had a crush on me, I don't know. They seemed to keep their feelings to themselves, although I had my share of Valentine cards and stuff like that.'

'So your dealings with the opposite sex didn't make you feel emotionally vulnerable at all?'

'Not really. Like I said, for me it was an athletic exercise, that's all. Once I got involved with Evelyn, though, everything was different.'

'Evelyn?'

'Yes. I suppose you could say she was my first true love. The only trouble was, she was a married woman.'

'Another older woman?'

'Yes, she was thirty-two. Her husband was a long-distance lorry driver so he was away from home a lot. I don't know if he knew his wife had affairs, but she'd had several lovers before me. Looking back, I think she still saw other guys even during the time I was with her.'

Jack felt a warm rush fill his veins, like alcohol, as a

picture of Evelyn filled his mind. She was lying on the bed, waiting for him, her red-gold hair spread over the pillow, her brown eyes dark with desire. He could see her trim, lightly tanned body (she used the solarium in the local gym all winter) with its firm, uptilted breasts and slim waist, the fuzz of golden hair over her bulging mons, the slim and powerful thighs. He could hear her soft voice exhorting him to hurry up, see her hand stray to her breast or her slit, feel the urgency of his longing. Already he had a hard-on, just thinking about her.

'Did that bother you?' Jack was hauled out of his reverie. He looked at Gary blankly. 'Did it bother you that she was probably seeing other men?'

'Not at the time. I knew I couldn't see her every night, because of her husband. And if there were others I never found out about them.'

'How often did you get to see her?'

'It varied. Sometimes Bill would be away a week and then I'd see her almost every night. Then he might not go away again for a month, so I couldn't see her at all. Except that, once or twice, she came to my place during the day. But that was risky because I lived near the pub where Bill drank.'

'Okay, so what happened when you did see her?'

'Pure bliss! She was amazing. That woman lived, breathed and dreamed sex. She taught me so much. The very first time we got together she blew my mind. We met in the computer shop I was working in. I was on day-release from college. Anyway, she came into the shop to find out about buying re-cycled paper for Bill's printer

He was self-employed and she used a computer to do his accounts and correspondence.'

'Did you chat her up, or did she come onto you?'

'Oh, Evelyn definitely made all the running. I was quite shy in those days, and she was that much older. But we shared the same sense of humour and I soon had her giggling away. She had wonderful flirty eyes. Anyway, when it came to the crunch she said her car was in the garage and she couldn't carry all the paper home so could we deliver? It wasn't our policy, but I said I'd run them over to her in my lunch hour. I think I knew then what was going to happen. I was incredibly excited.'

'Did she seduce you there and then?'

'Not exactly. She asked me in and said she was just having lunch herself so would I care to join her. We sat in her kitchen eating sandwiches and drinking beer, and she soon found out I was single and unattached. We obviously fancied each other something rotten.'

'But you knew she was married?'

'I knew her husband was away a lot and she hinted that she got lonely in the evenings. She said Bill would be away for another four days – he was on the continent – so I knew we were safe. I realised this was a perfect chance for me to further my sex education. So when she invited me round that evening I didn't hesitate.'

Jack felt an ache in his groin as he remembered that night. Every detail was etched indelibly on his memory. They say you always remember your first time, but for him all previous occasions were eclipsed by his first time with Evelyn. He could still see her seductive smile as she opened the door to him, a smile of anticipation, of hunger for pleasure long imagined and soon to be obtained.

She'd been wearing a loose pink silk top with a V-neck, that showed off her beautiful breasts, and a long black skirt slit to her thigh, revealing tantalising glimpses of flocked black stocking and, when she moved, the occasional flash of black satin suspender, trimmed with a pink bow. She knew how to turn a man on, all right!

'Evie had a meal waiting for me, with wine. It was Friday, so I didn't have to worry as it was my Saturday off that week. Little did I know, as I walked through that door, that I wouldn't be walking out of it until the early hours of Monday morning!'

Even Gary's noncommittal eyes widened in surprise at that!

'It didn't take her long to get down to business. I don't think we made it to the sweet . . . No, I distinctly remember us sitting up in her bed after the first session, eating chocolate mousse.'

'How did you get there – into bed, I mean?'

Jack laughed. 'I'm getting ahead of myself, aren't I? We chatted for a bit over the meal, then she got up and put her arms round me and gave me a big kiss. She'd been driving me wild with her come-to-bed eyes and I couldn't wait to touch her. I put my hands under her top and found she wasn't wearing a bra. Her tits weren't huge, but they were very firm because she worked out in the gym. Not so that she was all muscular, just well-toned. She had a fantastic body.'

'And no doubt she knew how to use it?'

'You bet! And she was keen to show me. She took off her top so I could get a good look at her boobs as well as feel them. I think she knew how excited she was making me and she was enjoying every second of it. Then she suggested we move into the bedroom. My dick was near to bursting by now and she did a very sensible thing.'

'What was that?'

'Well, we both stripped off and then she gave me a blow job, straight away. She was brilliant at it, kept taking me to the brink then pulling back until, when I finally came, it was an incredible explosion. I remember feeling a bit disappointed, because I didn't know what she was up to. I said, 'Don't you want me to come inside you?' She laughed and said, 'Yes, but not the *minute* you come inside me!' She knew that if she brought me off first I could take things more leisurely after that, more as she liked it.'

'And how did she like it?'

'Every which way under the sun! I suppose on that first weekend we took it fairly straight. I was delirious with desire most of the time. I'd never believed sex could be that good. The first thing she showed me was how to tongue her to a climax, which didn't take long. By the time she was thrashing around I was hard again and in I went. It was like diving into liquid honey. She told me not to move and just caressed me with her inner muscles for a while, keeping my erection going without making me come. It felt incredible! Then we began moving very slowly and I found I could keep going for ages like that. I think Evelyn kept coming, though, because every so often I'd feel this squeezing along my shaft. Sometimes we'd stop altogether and she'd caress my bum and finger my crack, or gently play with my balls. The idea that screwing could last and last, that you didn't have to come after a few quick thrusts, was a revelation to me.'

'Sounds like a good lesson to learn!'

'That's not all I learnt that weekend. We used lots of different positions, too. I liked it when she sat on top and eased herself very slowly up and down, rubbing my glans with her labia. I also liked it when she bent down, legs apart, and grabbed her ankles so I could come in from behind, standing up.'

'Have you any idea how many times you made love that weekend?'

'As far as I can remember it was more or less one continuous session. We had very little sleep. And we ate from her fridge when we were hungry. I had a huge bowl of cornflakes at three in the morning! It was just one long orgy, from start to finish.'

'And how did you feel afterwards, when it was over?'

'I crawled back home in the early hours of Monday feeling like I'd been reborn. I was besotted with Evelyn, of course. Couldn't stop thinking about her. I was completely useless at work next day. Everyone noticed. 'Too much bed, not enough sleep' was the general opinion. If only they'd known!'

'Did you think you were in love with her?'

'I was quite sure I was. As soon as I finished work I went to the florist and sent her some roses. I think her husband was due home that night, so heaven knows what he thought. But I was discreet, I didn't send a message. I thought about it, but words couldn't express what I felt. All I wanted was to see her again, as soon as possible, and that's when the torture began.'

'Torture?'

'Yes, of not knowing when I'd see her again. I was terribly afraid that one passionate weekend was all she'd wanted out of me and that would be it. Every evening I agonised by the phone, and once I even dialled, but when a man's voice answered I said it was a wrong number and hung up. I imagined all sorts of things. That she screwed other men just so she could describe all the details to her husband. Or that she had a different lover each time. Or she was just getting revenge on her husband for his infidelity. I tortured myself with such thoughts. And at night I masturbated furiously, re-living our lovemaking over and over again.'

'But she did contact you again?'

'Eventually, after about three weeks. I was in despair by then. I'd gone through the whole thing of writing her letters and poems and tearing them up. I'd driven past her house dozens of times, hoping to see her. I was like a lovesick adolescent.'

'Did she have any idea how you felt?'

'She might have guessed, but I didn't tell her. I was too ashamed of my weakness. But when she did phone, out of the blue, and asked me to go round one evening I was in seventh heaven.'

Jack paused to savour the memory of his joy. She'd come to the door in a black velour dressing-gown, he remembered, looking absolutely stunning with her red-gold hair over her shoulders and her tanned cleavage in full view.

'This time I wanted to tell her I loved her. I couldn't bear to think she didn't love me, or didn't want me as much as I wanted her. So when she said she'd been thinking about me I launched into my little speech, telling her how I felt.'

'How did she react?'

'She smiled, rather sweetly, and told me I mustn't confuse love and sex. I felt bewildered. If what I had for her were 'only' sexual feelings, then I wanted to go on feeling like that forever. I didn't care about love, sex was enough. We went straight upstairs and she gave me a kiss that made my toes curl. She made me lie on my stomach then she took some oil and and gave me a massage. After that she took off her gown and lay on me, wriggling around with her breasts against my back and her hairy mons against my buttocks. It was incredibly arousing and my erection started to be quite painful, digging into the bed, so she let me turn over and started massaging my chest.'

Jack realised he had buried all those details and never thought of them till now. When he'd started seeing Suzanne he had tried his best to put Evelyn out of his mind. It had seemed unfair to be making comparisons when the two women were so far apart in experience. Now, though, he delighted in reminiscing.

'She was kneeling behind my head, massaging my chest and stomach, so her tits were hanging down above my face. We began playing a game where she dangled her nipples just above my mouth and I had to try to catch them with my lips. I couldn't stand it for long – I had to grab hold of them. She told me I'd lost, so I had to do a forfeit. When she said I'd have to be tied up so she could have her wicked way with me, I felt excited and afraid at the same time.'

'So she got you into bondage. Did you enjoy it?'

'I loved everything she did, everything. On that occasion she just tied my hands behind my back with the belt of her dressing-gown. Then she knelt over me, facing my feet, and told me to lick her while she licked me. She climaxed first, I think, but she went on fellating me. When I came she moved up so I spurted over her tits and then she made me lick them clean.'

Gary glanced at his watch. 'Look, Jack, I don't want to rush you but I do want us to summarise as we go along. From what you're telling me, you had most of your sexual instruction from Evelyn and you experienced your first powerful feelings of love, or infatuation, with her too. Is that right?'

Jack nodded. 'The feelings grew more powerful as time went on. I suffered terribly from frustration and jealousy. I began to spy on her and her husband. I hated the idea of her sleeping with him.'

'So the relationship began to go downhill, did it?'

'Not for quite a while. I was so afraid of spoiling things that I kept quiet about my feelings. While I was with her everything was wonderful, but as soon as I got home I fell into a depression. I was totally obsessed with her.'

'How long did this go on for?'

'About a year. Then I started making demands on her. I asked her to come on holiday with me, to visit me at weekends, anything that would give us more time together. But what I really wanted was for her to leave her husband. She said there was no chance of that, but I didn't believe her. They had no kids. Surely she'd rather be with me? I kept on nagging at her, I couldn't help it. Then she told me she wouldn't see me again.'

'Was that the end of the affair?'

'No, it dragged on a bit. I kept phoning, writing letters. In the end she agreed to meet me in the park. She said she was sorry, but although she was fond of me she didn't love me. I asked her if she loved her husband and she said it was none of my business. I just couldn't understand what made her tick.'

'Did you make love again?'

'Only once. I was keeping watch on her house at weekends and I saw Bill, her husband, drive off so I knocked at the door. I was amazed to see she'd been crying. She let me comfort her and one thing led to another, but when I tried to find out what had been going on she shut up like a clam. Then she told me it was over between us, and I wasn't to contact her again.'

'Did you accept it?'

'Of course not. I kept following her, trying to phone and stuff. But the next time her husband went away she went with him. They must have been having a holiday because they were gone two weeks. It was during those two weeks that I met Suzanne.'

'Suzanne?'

'Sorry. My wife. The one I'm divorcing at the moment.'

'I see. That's very interesting. We have a lot to talk about here, Jack, but it will have to wait until next week. If any thoughts occur to you between now and then, you will write them down, won't you?'

Jack left in a strange state, a mixture of exhaustion and elation. Re-living his affair with Evelyn had reminded him how good real-life sex could be, but also how painful the aftermath often was. Now he was going through another aftermath. It was not quite so keenly felt, since the element of obsessional desire was absent, but with Suzanne what he missed were all the everyday things, the routine togetherness that he had once taken for granted. It was a deeper pain, more chronic than acute, but no easier to bear.

When he got home, there was a message on his Ansaphone. Jack was sure it must be from his wife, half believing he'd contacted her in some telepathic way by thinking about her so intensely, but it wasn't. The cool tones of Phil Greenaway informed him that Arcadia would definitely like to buy his game, and could he come to see them and discuss terms and conditions. Delighted, Jack rang him back at once and arranged to see him next day. At least something in his life was going right.

After his meal, Jack had a sudden urge to poke around in his memorabilia. Talking about Evelyn and thinking about Suzanne had made him nostalgic. He pulled out photo albums, love letters, cards, and began going through them. The few relics he had of Evelyn were in a chocolate box. A faded Polaroid of her in her front room wearing a flouncy dress gave him a shock. Instead of the gorgeously desirable sex object he remembered, a rather ordinary-looking housewife stared at the camera with an awkward smile, ankles crossed, hands in her lap. Was that the woman he would once have died for? Was that his mistress, his eternal love, his goddess? He hadn't looked at that photo for nearly ten years and now he saw it through jaundiced eyes.

There were letters too, letters he'd written but never sent. Nothing from her except one jokey rude Valentine. And a lock of her pubic hair, tied with cotton. He'd snipped that off while she slept. It was brittle and wiry, unpleasant to touch. Jack tossed it into his waste bin, then decided to throw the rest in after it. There seemed no point in trying to keep alive a flame long dead.

Jack turned to the photos of him and Suzanne on their various holidays. By contrast she looked radiant, standing on sunny beaches or windy hills in a selection of summer frocks, her dark hair blowing free. What nice legs she had! And that endearingly wry smile she always put on for the camera, as if to say 'I'm no beauty, so why are you photographing me?'

When had it all started to go wrong? That was the question that plagued him now, and had been troubling him for some time. Next week, with Gary, he would have to dredge it all up and he was dreading it. Talking about his teenage romances, and even about Evelyn, had been relatively easy. Those affairs were closed books to him now, read and enjoyed, but finished. His relationship with

Suzanne was not yet finished. Not until the divorce. Again he wondered why he'd heard nothing from her or her solicitor.

The phone rang but not even its shrill tone could startle him entirely out of his reflective mood. He picked it up absently and was startled to hear a familiar voice.

'Hullo, Jack, it's Suzanne. How are you?'

Jack's earlier superstitious belief that she must have picked up on him thinking about her returned. 'Suzanne! I was just . . .'

He couldn't bring himself to say he'd been looking at their holiday snaps.

'. . . I was just thinking about you, wondering where you were and what was happening. Did you get my letter?'

'No, I've been away on family business. My Aunt Jessie died. Remember her? I've had to come up to Wales to sort things out.'

Jack pictured the formidable old lady that they'd once visited on a holiday in Pembrokeshire. 'Oh, I see. I'm sorry, I didn't know.'

'Look, we can't catch up with each others' news on the phone. There are things I need to talk to you about. Can we meet sometime next week? How about Wednesday?'

The day after he'd seen Gary. Probably a good time. 'Okay.'

'I gather that you're living in Norwood now. Shall we have dinner somewhere near you? Find us a restaurant and book us a table for eight, then I'll call and take you there. My treat. See you soon, then.'

'Yes, Wednesday night. I . . . I look forward to it.'

God, what had made him say that, Jack wondered as he replaced the receiver. Did a condemned man look forward to his execution? Well, maybe in a way he did. At least he knew the suspense would be over soon, that the cruel hopes tormenting him would die with him. Of course she would want to discuss the finer details of the divorce. She might even produce the papers, for them to sign away their joint life over coffee and after dinner mints. Better make it 'After Eight' mints, since they were saying goodbye to eight years of marriage. Jack made an exasperated noise and shoved all the photos back into the cupboard, slamming the door.

Chapter Fifteen

Jack felt absurdly excited at the thought of seeing Suzanne again. It was nearly six months since that last extraordinary sex scene and he wasn't proud of the memory. Of course he'd been infuriated by the sight of his wife being screwed by that dick-head, but he'd treated her roughly afterwards and kidded himself that she'd enjoyed it. Maybe she had, but humiliating her in that way had left a nasty taste. Still, she'd certainly got her own back after the desk incident, so maybe they were quits.

Would it have made any difference if he'd been sweetly reasonable with her, or even wept and wailed? Probably not. It was all a huge mess and Jack supposed he should be glad that she was prepared to even speak to him again, let alone share a dinner table with him. As he speculated on her motives his earlier fears returned. Was she about to announce that she was pregnant by Rupert? That was the one thing that would really screw him up.

Before Jack kept his date with his wife, though, he had his third meeting with Gary. He was feeling apprehensive about that, too. So far, Gary hadn't really said very much.

Jack hadn't known what to expect from counselling, but it seemed that Gary saw his role more as listener than adviser. Would he come up with anything new next time?

Hazel smiled warmly at Jack when he arrived and asked if he'd mind waiting a while. While Jack thumbed through some of the magazines he found himself glancing at her pleasant face and well-rounded bust, wondering about her. Was she just an employee, or did she and Gary have a more intimate relationship? He considered his own relationship with the counsellor. It was strange to have such one-sided dealings with another man. Gary knew all kinds of personal details about him but he knew nothing at all about Gary. He might be gay, for all Jack knew.

The door opened and a very pretty girl was ushered out. Jack couldn't help wondering what sexual problems she could possibly have. Gary beckoned him in, and when Jack sat in his customary chair he found the seat was still warm. The thought of such an attractive woman sitting in that same chair, just moments before, and revealing secrets of her sex life was a real turn on. Jack wondered if counsellors ever got turned on by what they heard in the modern equivalent to the confessional.

Gary glanced through the notes on his lap, as he usually did at the beginning.

'Well, Jack, have you had any interesting thoughts since I last saw you?'

'Quite a few. Actually, something unexpected happened. My wife phoned and we're meeting tomorrow night. I don't know exactly what she wants to talk about, probably our divorce, but I'm bloody nervous. I was hoping that today's session might throw some light on why she and I got ourselves into the mess we seem to be in.'

'It may well do, but I can't promise anything. These things take time, Jack. If you'll permit me another metaphor, it's a bit like mining for precious metals. You dig away, sometimes for months, and then one day you might see a faint gleam of what you're looking for. A lot more digging and you have your vein of gold. Then you can enjoy the wealth that follows – a sense of ease and well-being. A new optimism in the future.'

'I think I still have a vein of optimism where my wife's concerned. I hope I'm not crazy.'

'Did you ever discuss having counselling, marriage guidance?'

'No, things seemed to move too fast for that. They certainly moved too fast for me. One day I came home to find her *in flagrante delicto* with her lover. The next thing I knew she was telling me she'd moved in with him.'

Gary nodded, setting his notebook on the floor and picking up the cat, which was mewing for attention. He sat stroking the creature while Jack talked.

'Anyway, I supposed I'd better go back to how we met. It was very soon after my affair with Evelyn – too soon, probably. With Evelyn it had been sex, sex, sex, with no pretence at anything else. But with Suzanne it was different. We had a lot in common, so I suppose you could say it was a meeting of minds. We talked for hours before we ever touched. She was an art student and on the rebound from a love affair too. We commiserated about having had a married lover – all those snatched moments of bliss that only left you wanting more, the jealousy, the lonely nights.'

'You comforted each other?'

'Yes. We spent long hours just talking. But the talk became more intimate as time wore on. I soon discovered that she'd found sex unsatisfying. She put it down to the stress of screwing a married man, then I found out that her first boyfriend had been inexperienced so she hadn't really been turned on by him either. Once I knew that, my ambition was to show her how great sex could be. After all the ways I'd learnt to pleasure Evelyn, I was confident I could do it. So I invited her round to my flat one night with seduction in mind.'

Jack smiled to himself as he remembered that night. It had worked like a dream, but then she'd afterwards confessed that she'd been equally determined to seduce *him*! They'd met at a pub, had an earnest conversation about art, then gone back to his place so he could show her his books on pop art and computer graphics. She'd sat on the floor looking through them and he had started fondling her long, dark hair and placing small kisses on the nape of her neck. It hadn't taken long for her attention to wander.

'She didn't take much persuading!' he laughed. 'That night I discovered how incredibly satisfying it is to initiate someone else into the delights of sex. She'd been used to quickie sex but I spent ages on foreplay.'

'It sounds as if you played the same initiatory role that Evelyn had played with you.'

'I suppose that's right. I was certainly using my knowledge about what turned woman on. I massaged her slowly first, paying lots of attention to her boobs, then I licked her clit and, eventually, she came. It was the first time she'd climaxed that way. She really loved it and when I finally got inside her she came again, straight away, then several times more.'

'How did you feel?'

'Great. A sense of achievement, pride. And she was starry-eyed after that. She fell in love with me, kept sending me little gifts and phoning me up. I'd never had a woman make the running before and I suppose I found it very flattering.'

'So she was infatuated, just as you'd been with Evelyn, and probably for the same reason.'

Jack had never thought of it quite that way before but, now Gary mentioned it, he could see it was true. Up to a point.

'The difference was, I was quite happy to accept her love, while Evelyn didn't want mine.'

'You didn't love Suzanne, then?'

'Not at the beginning. I enjoyed the sex and I found her an interesting woman, but I suppose a part of me was still getting over Evelyn. Deep down, I think I still believed I was in love with her.'

'So there was an imbalance at the start of your relationship with Suzanne.'

It hadn't seemed like that at the time. But now Jack could see that maybe Suzanne had railroaded him into marriage. They'd been seeing so much of each other during those first six months that it seemed the natural thing to live together. And, since her parents had disapproved of them being live-in lovers, marriage had been the only option if he wanted too stay with her.

'I . . . I don't know. I'm all confused about it.'

'Okay, let's try to shed some light on it, Jack. You had great sex, mainly because of Suzanne's new-found orgasmic ability, and you had other interests in common. You were spending a lot of time together, so Suzanne suggested you should get married. But a part of you still felt you were in love with Evelyn. Is that a fair summary?'

Jack nodded. 'Maybe it wasn't so much love I felt for Evelyn, as a kind of loyalty. A feeling that I really shouldn't love anyone else. It was quite negative, really.'

A sudden, shameful memory hit him. He didn't even want to think, let alone speak, about it. But that was what he was there for, so he blurted it out.

'I can even remember thinking about Evelyn while I was making love to Suzanne! It seems terrible, with Suzanne being so in love with me, but I couldn't help it. God, I'd buried that one deep!'

'Okay, Jack, this is important. It sounds as if you were becoming hooked on fantasy in your sex life. Does that make sense?'

'Considering I went on to make my living in sex fantasy games, yes it does!'

'Right. So you formed a pattern of thinking about Evelyn while you were making love to Suzanne. Can you remember if this happened every time?'

'I think it was mostly during the first six months, before we were married. Once we were wed I suppose I felt entitled to think of myself as loving her.'

Jack felt an excited tension in the air, as if they were really getting somewhere at last. Gary leant forward in his chair, frowning. 'That's a strange way of putting it. It suggests you still didn't feel as if you really loved Suzanne, even though you'd married her.'

'I was pressured, that I can say. Not so much by Suzanne as by her parents. They were nice people and I got on well with them, but they made it pretty plain they hoped my intentions were honourable. And I was twenty-six. I could think of no good reason why I shouldn't be married. Most of my friends were. I liked the idea of having sex on tap, so to speak, and I enjoyed her company. I guess I loved her as much as I could love anybody at that time. She wasn't keen to have kids straight away, so that wasn't a problem. It all seemed kind of inevitable, looking back.'

'And once you were married, did you miss your freedom?'

'Not really. I started working for Global and it was very exciting. Even before I worked on the fantasy games I was really into the computing side of it. I went on several training courses and seminars. I wanted to get on in the company and when the new technology arrived I was well prepared for it.'

'How did Suzanne react to your enthusiasm for work?'

'At first she thought it was great. She wanted me to get on as much as I did. Once she graduated from art college, though, she found it difficult to get work. She did some work at home, small commissions, and we talked of collaborating on a computer game but that never happened. We were happy though, both of us.'

'When did things start to slide?'

'I suppose it was when I started working with the new technology I mentioned. It was an advanced form of Virtual Reality and you could say it took over my life. I found myself thinking about it even when I was making love to Suzanne.'

'A habit you'd previously broken? I mean, had you stopped thinking about Evelyn?'

'Yes. But Suzanne seemed to become more demanding. I was often exhausted when I came home from work. Satisfying her was becoming a chore.'

'And what about your own sexual satisfaction?'

'I suppose that happened at work. I can't say too much about the technology, Gary, but when it gets onto the market it'll revolutionise everyone's sex life. Girlie mags, porn videos, vibrators – they'll all be outdated overnight, I can promise you.'

'Really? Sounds fascinating. But I wonder if anyone's considered the social consequences.'

Jack shrugged. 'If a lot of people can make a lot of money at something, since when have social consequences been in the equation?'

'That's a very cynical view.'

'It's a cynical world out there.'

Gary took the fiercely purring cat off his lap and put him down on the floor.

'All right. But let's get back to you and Suzanne. What have you discovered this afternoon?'

'I'm having to confront the question of whether I really loved her and I find that painful. I'm starting to wonder if I know what love is.'

'None of us really know what love is, Jack. Most of us are content to let it remain a mystery. But we can examine the way we behave towards others and our feelings about them. Never mind the labels. They just get in the way. What matters is whether being with that person makes us feel good or bad.'

It sounded like a cue for the end of the session. Jack was disappointed as Gary picked up his notebook and began to scrawl down a few things. He'd felt he was really getting somewhere, but he needed more time.

Gary looked up, smiling. 'We'll leave it there, Jack. Same time next week? Meanwhile, good luck when you meet Suzanne.'

'Yeah, I'll need it!' Jack grinned, making for the door.

Everything about this situation was so damn *weird*, Jack thought as he drove home. To be scared of facing your own wife was ridiculous but that was how he felt. Was it because he should have faced her years ago but had always avoided it?

Before Suzanne was due to arrive Jack tidied up the flat obsessively, spent ages on his appearance, rehearsed speeches, imagined scenarios. He knew it was ridiculous but he couldn't help it. Always, before, he had been the one in control. Now she was calling the shots, and it was damaging to his already fragile self-esteem. He was afraid of the woman, damn it! Afraid of the power she had over him, of her new found sexual independence. This

was a new Suzanne and, along with his feeling of being
threatened by her, Jack also felt irresistibly drawn to her.
He thought he'd known the old Suzanne, but the new
version was a mystery to him.

She even looked different. When she came to his door
with short hair and wearing a smartly tailored jacket over
well-cut pants, Jack hardly recognised her. She'd lost a
few pounds, too. The new hairstyle suited her, throwing
her large green eyes into startling relief. They surveyed
him coolly and Jack felt a wave of hopeless lust sweep
through him.

'Hullo, Jack. It's good to see you.'

She gave him a light kiss on the cheek, filling his
nostrils with some new and sophisticated perfume. Conscious of the absurdity of the situation, Jack wanted to
crush her in his arms and kiss her firmly on the mouth
but he felt paralysed.

'Hullo, Suzanne. You're looking good.'

The ritual of greeting over, Jack invited her in. She
made some complimentary noises about his flat, refused
his offer of a drink then suggested they make a move.
Jack was surprised when he found himself being ushered
into a sporty little two-seater car.

'My pride and joy,' she confessed, with a wry smile.
'I've always wanted one of these.'

But all Jack could think of was her and Rupert living
life in the fast lane, together.

'It suits your new image,' he told her, as they roared
away. 'Independent girl-about-town. Is that what you're
aiming for?'

'Perhaps.' She flashed him a sidelong smile that had his pulse accelerating with the engine.

They entered the restaurant, which Jack had chosen because he ate there quite regularly and was known by the waiters. They had secured him a quiet corner table, as he'd requested, but he felt self-conscious as he led the way towards it, aware that this was the first time he'd dined there with a woman. Sitting opposite his wife he was reminded of happier days and, from the melancholy shadow that suddenly passed over her face, he guessed she was remembering, too.

They were scarcely into the first course when Suzanne dropped her first bombshell of the evening.

'You know I've just come back from Wales? I'm hoping to live there, at least for a while. It's so lovely and peaceful and I'm tired of city life. But it partly depends on you.'

'On *me*. Why?'

'Well Aunt Jessie left her house to both of us. Of course, she expected us to still be together. Anyway, half its value is legally yours. I'm prepared to put it on the market straight away if that's what you want, but I'd like to stay there until it's sold, if that's okay.'

Jack was angry. Was the bitch asking his permission to live there with her lover?

'What about Rupert?' he asked sullenly. 'Would he be moving there too?'

She shook her head. 'I need some time away from him, actually. Everything's been moving too fast for me. I must have a breathing space.'

So everything wasn't quite so hunky-dory between

them, after all. Jack felt a surge of optimism. Then he cautioned himself. Even if Suzanne left the guy there was no guarantee she'd come back to him.

'Well, if you're going to be there alone, I don't see any harm. As for selling the place, that's up to you. I mean, she was your aunt, I hardly knew her. The idea of being left something in her will is a bit bizarre, really.'

'She must have had faith in us as a couple. Poor Aunt Jessie. She never did learn to move with the times.'

Jack turned his attention to the meal, unwilling to face the mixed emotions that were welling up in him. He had an absurd longing to go to that secluded old cottage with Suzanne, to spend a whole week making passionate love to her, healing the wounds they had inflicted on each other. But it was pure fantasy, like so much of his life had been.

Even so, it was a shock to discover that he still desired her as much as he did. Maybe if Suzanne had remained as she was he wouldn't have fancied her. But there was a new air of confidence about her that was very appealing. He envied that smug bastard Rupert. Why should he have the best of her now when it was he, Jack Bedford, who had initiated her into the delights of sex?

'Tell me what you're doing these days, Jack,' Suzanne smiled, making an obvious effort to get back onto safe ground. 'Are you still with Global?'

'No, I left before Christmas. Now I'm reviewing games for *Joystick* magazine. It pays the rent. But I've just had a game of my own accepted by Arcadia.'

He tried to sound casual but couldn't stop a note of excited pride entering his voice.

Suzanne's face lit up, and she beamed delightedly. 'Really? That's wonderful, Jack! Congratulations?'

'It's a start, anyway.'

'Tell me about it.'

Jack described the game, rather warily since he wasn't sure Suzanne would approve. It came as a surprise to him that he still wanted her approval. She seemed genuinely interested as she questioned him about the details. Jack speculated that if they could have worked on a game together, as they'd planned to at the start of their marriage, they might never have split. Still, it was too late now.

Suzanne took his hand and squeezed it. 'It sounds brilliant – and great fun!'

'It's not like working at Global, but in some ways I prefer it,' Jack admitted. 'Having complete control over the whole concept is great.'

'You haven't told me what happened at Global,' she reminded him. 'Why did you leave?'

He gave a rueful grin. 'Skulduggery. But it was supposed to be "sexual harassment".'

'What?' Suzanne's well-defined brows rose incredulously.

'It's what I was accused of, although the boot was on the other foot. And, my, did she know how to put the boot in!'

Again, Jack felt obliged to offer a censored version of what had happened. He was none too sure that Suzanne believed his side of the story, but she chose not to comment on it.

Instead, she remarked, 'Well, in view of recent events

you're probably well out of the VR scene.'

Jack was puzzled. 'Events? What events?'

'Surely you've heard? About the banning of VR sex games in the States?'

Jack felt his jaw drop. 'God, no! I've not heard anything. Tell me more.'

'It's been on the news. They're thinking of introducing similar legislation here. I'm surprised you don't know about it.'

'I've been so busy lately. But, come to think of it, Phil at Arcadia did hint at something like that. Did you say they've actually *banned* the kind of games I was working on at Global?'

'Yes. They test-marketed them over six months and found that a high proportion of men became impotent.'

'*What*?'

'Exactly. When I heard that, I naturally put two and two together regarding our own sex life.'

Suzanne's eyes were looking straight into his, their expression one of wry regret. Jack was stunned. Could it be that all their problems had been due to the seductive power of the Feelietron?

'I think you'll find that Global will be out of business before long,' she continued. 'Unless they diversify. VR might remain a possibility for adventure games, although they're still looking into the effects of those. You got out at the right time, Jack. But it's left our marriage in a bit of a mess, hasn't it?'

'Our marriage'. Jack took heart at the phrase. It suggested they still had one, and that maybe the mess could be sorted. 'Are you saying if I hadn't got hooked on Feelie sex we might still be together?'

'It's a possibility, don't you think?'

'But what about Rupert?'

Suzanne's eyes slid away from his. 'I think he was a mistake. Quite honestly, Jack, I'd probably have gone for anyone who offered me sexual satisfaction. I know it makes me seem fickle, or something, but our love-making had degenerated into going through the motions. You just weren't *there* for me, Jack.'

'I know, and I bitterly regret it, Suze. I've missed you terribly, every since.'

Jack sighed. There, he'd said it! He searched her face for signs of reciprocal feeling. The green eyes locked in sympathy with his and her mouth curved into a regretful smile.

'We should have tackled the problem sooner. The trouble was, I don't think either of us fully realised what the problem was. It was only when I heard about the American experience of VR that I began to understand. Apparently, the men began by fantasising while making love but, when they didn't get the instant gratification they got with VR, they came to prefer Virtual Sex to the real thing.'

Jack shrugged. 'I suppose it should have been foreseeable.'

'Maybe.'

The waiter intervened to ask if they wanted a sweet.

'Not for me, thanks,' Jack smiled. 'How about you, Suze?'

She shook her head. 'No thanks. I ... er ... think I'd rather get going.'

Jack's heart sank. Was she, having delivered her load of bombshells, just going to let him pick up the pieces? She insisted on paying the bill and led the way out of the restaurant to her parked car.

'I'll run you home, Jack.'

And then? Jack tried not to let his hopes rise as they sped through the streets. He'd be devastated if she gave him another peck on the cheek then left. But was he expecting too much? Had he been reading more than was intended into those regretful, sympathetic glances?

They got to Jack's street and Suzanne parked at the kerb. For a few seconds, neither of them spoke. Then, when the silence threatened to become an embarrassment, Jack said:

'About your Aunt Jessie's house ...'

'Sod the house!'

He turned to see her smiling at him, a faint appeal in her eyes. 'I was only going to say do what you like with it. I don't need the money right now, and ...'

'I don't want to talk about the house, Jack. You and I are more important. I made a stupid mistake, and I've been kicking myself ever since. What I want to know is, will I ever get the chance to put it right?'

Jack let the floodgates restraining his emotions open a crack. 'Are you trying to tell me that you don't want a divorce, after all?'

'Not if you don't. I'd like to give our marriage a second chance, Jack. Things went horribly wrong between us, but ... Stop me, please, if I'm speaking out of turn. I mean, you might have someone else by now, and . . .'

'There's no-one else.'

The silence that followed was deafening. Jack turned to his wife with a half-smile.

'Can you forgive me?' she whispered.

His kiss crushed against her lips with painful intensity. She gasped beneath the impact, but was soon embracing him, her breasts thrust hard against his chest. Jack felt all his pent-up lust flow into his prick and the knots of tension in his jaw and temple dissipated as Suzanne ran eager fingers through his hair. Slowly he eased himself into the feel of her, warm and soft to his touch. God, how he wanted her! Like at the beginning, when he'd made her come and come. He wanted to wipe out all the pain with one perfect, healing session of love.

'Jack, please take me to bed!' she whispered, her voice thick with desire.

They scrambled out of the car and went, hand in hand, into the lift. Jack unbuttoned her silk blouse until the lacy cups of her bra were accessible, then began to nuzzle at her cleavage. She was breathing hard and hot now, her knees weakening so that Jack had to support her with his arm as she slumped against the back of the lift. His erection was reaching the threshold of pain, so he was relieved when they lurched to a halt. Scooping his wife into his arms he strode to his door, fumbled for the key then at last was safely inside. Still carrying Suzanne, he made straight for the bedroom and threw her down onto his bed then struggled out of his clothes while she did likewise.

'God, what you've put me through!' he grunted,

launching himself onto her naked body at last.

They tussled for supremacy awhile, but Jack won. He pinned her arms down and speared into her without any preliminaries. He was reclaiming his wife, damn it, and this was no time for sexual niceties. Not that she was complaining. Her pussy was wet and willing, clamping his tool enthusiastically as he bored his way in.

Jack grabbed hold of her rearing tits and kneaded them, thumbing the nipples to rigid peaks, while she dug her nails into his buttocks, urging him on. He could feel her wriggling and manoeuvring beneath him, trying to get her engorged clitoris in contact with his shaft. He slipped a hand down between them and gave her a rub, making her moan with renewed pleasure. She was pinching his bum harder as he increased the friction. Her vagina was clasping rhythmically at his prick every time he drew back, squeezing his glans with her labia so that her swollen bud could experience every last tickle of sensation.

At last he felt her convulse, the whole of her cunt rippling its way up and down his shaft and triggering his own explosive climax in the process.

'God, Suze, I love you, you witch!' he gasped, biting at her neck.

She arched her back, still in the throes of her extended orgasm, and gave a long, guttural moan. Then they lay, utterly spent, for what seemed like ages.

At last Jack murmured, softly, 'That'll teach you, bitch!'

'Bastard!' she replied, with equal tenderness.

'Tell me that fuckwit you ran off with never made you come like that.'

'He was a total bore,' she giggled. 'He thought he was God's gift to women, but he went through the same routine every time. Talk about screwing by numbers! His motto was, "if it works the first time, don't change it." Nothing between the ears, you see.'

'They do say the brain is the most erotic organ in the body!'

'Exactly.' Suzanne smiled, snuggling down. 'God, how I've missed what we used to have! Not just the sex, but the conversations, the laughs, everything.'

Jack felt a weary guilt creep over him.

'But you missed all that long before you met Rupert, didn't you?' he said, sadly. 'I put everything into my work and there was nothing left over for you. What a bloody fool!'

'As long as it doesn't happen again.'

'It won't!' he said, fiercely, turning her her face to his so he could seal his promise with a kiss.

She pressed her breasts against his chest and reached down to fondle his balls. Jack felt the blood course down to his penis again. As it rose between them he remembered, with a wry smile, that not so long ago he'd begun to fear that he could never against sustain an erection. More bloody foolery! He just needed the right woman, that was all. *His* woman!

Suzanne's gentle fingers were rising up his shaft now, their tips brushing his glans with just the faintest tickle. Jack dealt equally with her nipples, coaxing them back into budding life. They kissed, tongues probing in leisurely fashion between softly cushioned lips. Now that their first urgency was sated it was time to explore each other again, to re-visit all those long-neglected places that had once brought them such deep and satisfying pleasure. This time, though, the pleasure was like that of returning after a long and troublesome journey.

Jack felt his wife clamber on top, lowering her still-wet opening onto his hardening erection, letting its engorged tip nuzzle gently against her loose lips and nose its way slowly into the cushioned channel beyond. At last she took in the full length of him, sinking down onto his thighs with a sigh, letting herself be filled with his hot flesh.

'Oh, this is so damned *comfortable*!' she laughed, as he reached up to fondle her heavy breasts. 'This is what I've been missing, the feel that we can do and say anything to each other, anything at all.'

'What do you want me to do?' Jack asked, suddenly aware of the infinite possibilities of pleasure between them.

'Everything!'

'Then get onto all fours and show me your big, beautiful arse!'

Obediently she shifted position and he spread her fat cheeks, seeing her tight bumhole contract as he looked at it. He gave her buttock an experimental slap and she contracted her cunt. Poking one finger into her arse he entered her other hole with his rampant tool thrusting furiously, pinching at her behind with his free hand.

'I'm going to punish you, bitch! For running off with that bastard.'

'Yes!' she moaned. 'I've been so bad, darling. I'm a wicked, wicked woman and you must make me pay for it.'

Remembering how she'd seemed to squirm ecstatically last time he'd 'punished' her, Jack redoubled his efforts and soon she was coming wildly, almost unseating him with her bucking hips, bringing him off a treat. They collapsed as the pulsations faded and lay exhausted while Jack whispered crude endearments in her ear.

'You've always been the best fucking lay, Suze. I was a bloody fool to risk losing you. You've got the bounciest breasts and the biggest buttocks and the creamiest cunt of any woman I've met.'

She turned to him with a satisfied smile, the passionate depths of her eyes full of new secrets, hidden promise.

'And I'll bet you met quite a few while we were apart, didn't you?'

'A few,' he conceded, with a grin.

'Bastard!' Suzanne gave him a playful slap on the behind, then turned over and lay with one arm behind her head, lifting the contour of her bosom so that it stood up firm and proud. Jack gave her nipple a soft tweak.

'All right, ' she dared him. 'Tell me all about them . . .'

A month later, Jack and Suzanne were heading for their new home in Wales. Jack had decided that he could work there as well as anywhere and, besides, Suzanne had offered to help with his new computer game. Called 'Sex War' it was for two players and charted the decline and fall of a marriage or, if the players were really skilful and co-operative, eventually reconciled them. It was what

Jack had always dreamed of, working with Suzanne on a game, and he had high hopes of this one. Especially as they'd planned it during a weekend of imaginative and exciting sex that had the artificial pleasures of the Feelie-tron beaten hands down.